D0408844

Ralph Compton:
The Dangerous Land

RALPH COMPTON:
THE DANGEROUS LAND

MARCUS GALLOWAY

THORNDIKE PRESS

A part of Gale, Cengage Learning

GALE
CENGAGE Learning·

Farmington Hills, Mich • San Francisco • New York • Waterville, Maine
Meriden, Conn • Mason, Ohio • Chicago

GALE
CENGAGE Learning®

Copyright © 2014 by the Estate of Ralph Compton and Penguin Group (USA) LLC.
Thorndike Press, a part of Gale, Cengage Learning.

Thorndike Press® Large Print Western.
The text of this Large Print edition is unabridged.
Other aspects of the book may vary from the original edition.
Set in 16 pt. Plantin.

LIBRARY OF CONGRESS CATALOGING-IN-PUBLICATION DATA

Galloway, Marcus.
    Ralph Compton : the dangerous land : a Ralph Compton novel / by Marcus Galloway. — Large print edition.
        pages ; cm. — (Thorndike Press large print western)
        ISBN 978-1-4104-7609-8 (hardcover) — ISBN 1-4104-7609-X (hardcover)
        1. Large type books. I. Title.
PS3607.A4196R325 2015
813'.6—dc23   2014043966

Published in 2015 by arrangement with NAL Signet, a member of Penguin Group (USA) LLC, a Penguin Random House Company

Printed in Mexico
1 2 3 4 5 6 7 19 18 17 16 15

THE IMMORTAL COWBOY

This is respectfully dedicated to the "American Cowboy." His was the saga sparked by the turmoil that followed the Civil War, and the passing of more than a century has by no means diminished the flame.

True, the old days and the old ways are but treasured memories, and the old trails have grown dim with the ravages of time, but the spirit of the cowboy lives on.

In my travels — to Texas, Oklahoma, Kansas, Nebraska, Colorado, Wyoming, New Mexico, and Arizona — I always find something that reminds me of the Old West. While I am walking these plains and mountains for the first time, there is this feeling that a part of me is eternal, that I have known these old trails before. I believe it is the undying spirit of the frontier calling me, through the mind's eye, to step back into time. What is the appeal of the Old West of the American frontier?

It has been epitomized by some as the dark and bloody period in American history. Its heroes — Crockett, Bowie, Hickok, Earp — have been reviled and criticized. Yet the Old West lives on, larger than life.

It has become a symbol of freedom, when there was always another mountain to climb and another river to cross; when a dispute between two men was settled not with expensive lawyers, but with fists, knives, or guns. Barbaric? Maybe. But some things never change. When the cowboy rode into the pages of American history, he left behind a legacy that lives within the hearts of us all.

— Ralph Compton

CHAPTER 1

Colorado, 1886

In his life, Paul Meakes had been plenty of things. When he was inclined to boast, he would mention his time spent as half a lawman working as a deputy for a marshal in Kansas. Those had been an exciting couple of months but hadn't amounted to much apart from riding on a few posses without ever being offered steady employment. He'd had a few lucky strikes as a miner while panning in the rivers of Wyoming and California, but plenty of men had stories like those. During his younger days, he'd been a trapper on the Nebraska plains skinning buffalo and dragging their hides from one trading post to another in search of the best price.

Paul didn't have much use for boasting anymore. Some years ago, he'd worked a few cattle ranches and picked up odd jobs in mining camps on his way into the southeastern portion of Colorado. Once there, he'd met a lovely little woman named Joanna and opened a little general store that stocked bits and pieces the locals weren't likely to find anywhere else. He kept one of the best-stocked selections of books in the county and was known throughout his town for the oddities displayed in his front window. Residents of Keystone Pass knew where to go for blankets, oats, shoes, or tools. When they wanted something to read, a newspaper from any of a number of bigger towns, or fashions left behind by merchants on their way to New York or San Francisco, they went to Meakes Mercantile.

Before long, Paul's little store had acquired something of a reputation throughout Colorado. Those in favor of his place regarded it as a haven for fine goods and intellectual delights. Those who weren't feeling so generous called the shop a dumping ground for yellow-back novels and wares from every snake oil salesman who'd dared showed his face east of the Rockies. Either way, Paul made a decent living. He was a far cry from being rich, but he managed to keep his head above water when it came time to feeding his little family.

Joanna was a beautiful woman. Short and a bit stout in stature, she had stolen Paul's heart the instant he saw her smile. When he worked up the nerve to ask her to a dance, hold her in his arms, smell her soft blond curls, marriage was a foregone conclusion. She was a caring wife and patient mother.

Was.

Paul thought of her often, so his brief respite while arranging the books for sale in his store was nothing new. Neither was the pinch at the corner of his eyes or the grief that stabbed at his heart when he thought of her in terms of *was* or *used to be.* She'd passed fourteen months ago. Fourteen months during which he'd felt the passage of every single moment. The whole town missed her. Joanna was the sort of woman who took it upon herself to remember folks by name and ask about their young ones whenever they passed in the street. Paul, on the other hand, was more likely to nod to familiar faces in a friendly way without being overly enthusiastic about it. Without Joanna at his side, he was only left with silent nods from partial strangers.

For the most part, that suited Paul just fine. He'd spent most of his life roaming from one spot to another, one job to another, surrounded by a fair number of other people or none at all. When he was alone, he enjoyed the silence. When he was part of a community, he knew it was only a matter of time before he'd break away to become part of another. More than likely, folks remembered him fondly but not very often. Since he remembered them the same way, Paul was content to let things remain that way.

Whenever his spirits needed lifting, he only had to look at the faces of his two children. Abigail and David were both the spitting images of their mother, even though he'd been told the nine-year-old boy bore a mighty large resemblance to his father. If he wanted to be reminded of himself, Paul would look into a mirror, so he chose to only see them for what they were and as fond reminders of his sweet Joanna.

Standing with a pile of books cradled in his arms, Paul hadn't realized he'd been lost in his thoughts until it was pointed out to him by the young woman looking through a small stack of dresses that had arrived all the way from New Mexico earlier that week. She was in her early teens and a bit tall for her age. Long, light brown hair was braided and draped over one shoulder to display a yellow ribbon tied at the end. Rolling her eyes, she rooted through the clothing with exaggerated vigor and let out a pronounced sigh.

"What's wrong now, Daddy?" she asked.

Paul shrugged and got back to stocking the bookshelf. "Why does anything have to be wrong?"

"You're staring at me."

"Because you're beautiful."

Abigail started to roll her eyes again but blinked and showed her father a smile instead. It was a halfhearted gesture, but it served its purpose well enough. "Thank you for saying so."

After placing the last book upon its shelf, Paul walked over to the table displaying the store's most recently acquired articles of clothing and rubbed his daughter's shoulder. She was almost as tall as him even though she tended to stoop a bit to hide her height. "I'm not just saying so. It's the truth."

"You're the only one who thinks so."

"I doubt that very much."

"Yes, well . . . thank you all the same."

Walking to the back of the store where a few crates had been opened, Paul said, "I imagine you could corral any boy you wanted."

Another sigh from the girl was followed by a series of stomping steps that led to the front of the store. "I don't want to talk about this with you."

"What about Michael Willis? Weren't you and Becky talking about him just the other day?"

Even from her new spot behind the cash register, Abigail managed to shoot a terse glare all the way back to where Paul was retrieving some more books. "You were spying on me and Becky?"

"You and Becky are almost always together and you talk quite a lot."

"What's that got to do with anything?"

Paul gathered another armful of books and carried them to the shelf at the front of the store. Although he wouldn't have dropped one volume in the middle of a hurricane, he fretted with them as a way to avoid his daughter's critical eye. "I have ears," he said. "They're not filled with wax. I hear things." He also saw things, but he decided not to embarrass her with those details.

"Becky's meeting me at Johansen's Bakery. Can I have some money?" she asked while already poking a key to open the cash register.

"Take fifty cents. Not a penny more."

"Fine."

Sliding each book into place and taking his time in the process, Paul waited until he heard his daughter walking to the front door before saying, "If you're still hungry, there's going to be a picnic after Sunday services."

"That's not for two days," she pointed out. "We're not eating until then?"

"Of course we are. It's just that . . . most everyone will be there. The Willis family, for certain."

Abigail lingered at the door with her hand on the knob. She closed her eyes and pressed her lips into a tight line in an expression of anxiety dating all the way back to when she'd been a baby worried about standing upright. "Michael doesn't care if I'm there or not."

"Do you know that for a fact?"

"Yes." When she finally looked over to her father to see his stern expression, Abigail sighed. "No."

"Then you should go to that picnic and ask him to dance."

"He should be the one to do the asking."

"Maybe he's shy," Paul said. "Boys get shy too, you know. And it's not such a terrible thing to ask one to dance. Many of them even like it that way."

"Sure they do," she scoffed. "That's less work for them."

Paul laughed and fell into an easier rhythm of placing the books in their proper order. After taking a moment to lift one to his nose

13

so he could smell the musty pages, he said, "You're right about that, but it never hurts to meet someone halfway. If things go right, it won't hardly matter who took that first step."

"I guess I could go to the picnic . . . if Becky's going too."

"That's the spirit."

"You know what would make me feel better about going?" she asked.

"What's that?"

"If I had a new dress to wear."

"I couldn't agree more. Martha just sent over a few nice ones the other day," Paul told her. "They're hanging next to those waistcoats."

"I was thinking more about the fancy silk ones on the front display."

"I bet you were. Those will fetch a mighty good price, but not if they've already been worn. They'll be damn near worthless once you spill jam or soup on them."

"I won't spill on it, Daddy!" she insisted while coyly trying to shift her arms to hide the faded stain on the dress she now wore.

"You spill on just about everything, sweetie. It's part of your charm."

Judging by the way she stormed out of the store, Abigail did not share that sentiment or find it half as endearing as her father did.

CHAPTER 2

Supper was a simple affair prepared hastily by Abigail and cleared away by her younger brother. David was a slender boy with fair hair, dark circles under his eyes, and long legs. When he was done washing the last of the dishes, David went out to the porch and approached his father, who stood enjoying the night.

"I'm done with my chores, Pa," David said. "Did you bring me anything from the store?"

"Some new books came in today," he said while puffing on a chipped pipe. Even though he didn't look over at David, he had no trouble picturing the boy's wide, expectant eyes.

"I know them books came in!" David squealed. "You said you'd bring me one!"

"Did I?"

The nine-year-old let out an all-too-familiar sound that was part groan and part whine. Before it could shift too far into the latter category, Paul said, "Of course I brought you one! You think I'd forget about my boy?"

"No, sir!" David beamed.

Paul lowered himself onto a chair that had been left in the elements for so long that it had practically grown roots into the porch. It sagged beneath his weight and creaked with every shift of his body but showed no hint of breaking. It protested loudly when Paul reached around to pick up the thin volume he'd set down where it could remain out of sight until now. When he held it out to the boy, he showed an expression that bore an uncanny resemblance to the one David had worn earlier.

Unfortunately David's expression didn't last very long. "Oh," he said. "Did you bring any others?"

"No," Paul replied. "I thought you'd like that one. It's a ghost story."

"Ghosts are scary."

"But it's just a story."

"I'll have nightmares," David said in a voice that was growing into more of a whine.

"All right, then. I saw another one you might like."

"Really? Is it about trains?"

"No. It's about an adventure in the jungles

16

of Peru! That's where the conquistadores landed, you know."

"Jungles are scary."

Paul drew a deep breath. "You've never been to a jungle."

"I know. They're still scary."

"It's just a story. Maybe if you read it, you'll enjoy it and then you won't be so scared about it anymore. That's how men become brave."

David nodded even though he'd obviously stopped listening. Wincing slightly when Paul rubbed his arm, he said, "I just like stories about trains. And horses. They're not so scary."

"I'll look around for something along them lines when I go back to the store tomorrow," Paul said, even though he knew well enough that he'd already set aside a story about a young Arabian thief who tames a wild stallion. "It's just that . . . you're getting close to ten years old, son. There's no reason to be so squirrelly."

At least when David nodded this time, he seemed to be listening to what Paul was telling him. "All right, Pa."

"Will you help in the store tomorrow?"

"Last time I got hurt."

"It was just a sliver in your hand," Paul growled. "Are you still crying about that?"

17

"N-no."

"You'll help me in the store tomorrow and you'll come with me to pick up some new inventory on Monday."

"But I got school on Monday!" David said.

"Not when your father needs an extra set of hands to load the wagon. You and your sister are coming along and that's that."

"Will I get paid for it?"

Paul scowled at the boy and took hold of the front of David's shirt to give him a gentle shake. "What am I gonna do with you? I'll pay you fifty cents but not a penny more. Deal?"

Extending his hand so quickly that he almost threw out an elbow, David replied excitedly, "Deal!"

Father and son shook hands and enjoyed a nice couple of moments before David asked, "What else can I do and get paid for it?"

"Go to bed."

"You'll pay me to go to bed?"

"No," Paul said in a strained voice. "Just . . . go to bed. It's getting late."

David started walking into the house, stopped, and then turned around to approach his father again. He kissed Paul's forehead and then went inside.

Once he was certain he was alone on the porch, Paul started flipping through the book he'd tried to give to David. Since it wasn't going to be put to any use at his house, he'd take it back to the store in the morning. He could think of a few boys who would get a thrill out of the adventurous yarns. In fact, he was hard-pressed to think of a boy other than his own who wouldn't like it. Or perhaps he just didn't know children very well.

"I'm trying, Joanna," he said quietly into the night sky. "I'm trying, but it surely ain't easy. I wonder if you would have an easier time with these two. Aw, who the hell am I kidding? Of course you would."

With that, Paul set the book down and crossed his arms over his full belly. He thought about inventory and numbers that had yet to be written into the ledger in his office. He thought about when the next traveling salesmen were due to roll through town and how much of a discount he could wheedle from them for a bulk purchase. As the steady current flowed through his head and a cool breeze touched his face, Paul started drifting to sleep.

Eventually his thoughts drifted toward the future. He'd heard tell of a vein of gold that had barely been touched in a mine that was being sold for next to nothing. If he found a buyer for his store, he could cash in and possibly become rich after a few months of hard work. There were always ranchers looking for partners down in Texas or back in his old Kansas stomping grounds. Running a spread instead of working on one could set him up for life.

So many different trails to ride after leaving Keystone Pass.

So many destinies to chase.

Tomorrow.

CHAPTER 3

Despite the biblical origins of his name, Paul had never been much of a churchgoing man. His mother and father had dragged him to Sunday worship for most of his childhood, presumably as a way to cleanse his young soul or enrich his growing mind. He couldn't much speak to the success of the former, but the latter didn't seem to take very well. If not for Joanna, he probably would have avoided hearing another sermon for the rest of his days. She'd been a truly joyful Christian. In Paul's experience those were a rare breed whose faith came from genuine inspiration instead of habit or fear of retribution in the hereafter. If she was lenient in some matters, taking the children to church wasn't one of them, and it seemed only proper for Paul to continue doing so after she'd passed on. The children, however, weren't as eager to uphold the practice.

They sat on either side of him in one of the pews at the back of the town's small church. As Paul attempted to sing along with a few of the hymns, David and Abigail shifted fretfully and occasionally swatted at each other. Since they didn't carry their squabble any further than that, Paul let them be.

After Pastor Harlowe was done talking, he smiled at everyone in front of him, let a few other folks pass on some news about birthdays or sicknesses and such, and then concluded the services. Paul and the kids filed out with the rest of the congregation, shook a few hands, and pretended to have been a little more enlightened than when they'd walked in.

"Do we really have to go to this picnic?" David asked.

Paul looked down at his son as if he'd sprouted antlers. "Why wouldn't you want to go to a picnic?"

"There might be bees."

"You know what I can guarantee there'll be?"

"What?" David asked hesitantly.

"Pork ribs, corn on the cob, and pie!"

The boy's face lit up. "Peach pie?"

"Maybe."

"Probably just the same old cherry pie

that Claudia Spencer always makes," Abigail groaned.

"You hear that, Dave?" Paul asked with genuine excitement. "Claudia Spencer's cherry pie!"

Nodding as if he'd just decided his fate as well as that of his family, David declared, "All right. We're going to that picnic." Stretching his arms out to his father, he said, "Carry me."

Paul winced a bit and pushed the boy along to clear a path for the stragglers leaving the church. "You're too big for that, son. You're almost as tall as I am."

That was about a foot and a half from being true, but the point had been made. David shrank as if the wind had been taken from his sails and stuffed his hands into the pockets of his itchy black suit. Before he could slink too far away, David was swept off his feet and carried toward the little field behind the church. Even though Paul had only managed to lift him about seven inches off the ground, the boy reacted as if he were flying.

"Be quiet, Dave," Abigail scolded. "People will hear."

"Don't be so cross," Paul said as he carried his son a few more steps and set him down. "You love picnics."

"Not when he's squealing like a stuck pig."

"*You're* a stuck —"

"Enough of that," Paul said before the siblings came to blows. "Let's get something to eat and play some games."

"Games?" David asked. "Where?"

"Over there by those other boys," Paul said as he pointed his son toward a growing flock of children near a duck pond. "Why don't you go and join them?" When David looked away tentatively, Paul gave him a little push. "Go on, now." After the boy had made significant progress toward the group, Paul shifted his focus to his left.

"Don't say it, Daddy," Abigail warned.

"I see a certain young man over there as well."

"I told you not to say it."

"Michael doesn't look happy being with so many younger boys, and his mood's probably not going to be any better once David gets over there."

She smiled, albeit hesitantly.

Even though he'd been the girl's father for all of her fourteen years, Paul still seemed uncomfortable when he tugged on her collar and pulled her sleeves to straighten a couple of wrinkles in the fabric. "I know this isn't the fancy silk dress you

24

had your eye on, but it sure does become you."

Abigail looked down at the new, bright green cotton dress. Taking hold of her skirts, she gave them a half-hearted twirl and grumbled, "That other one would have been too fancy for a church picnic anyway."

"See? Always a bright side. Just like your mother."

Hearing mention of Joanna brought a much brighter smile to her face. It was a beautiful sight for her father, even if there was a hint of sadness behind the expression. "And I haven't spilled on it."

Tapping the tip of her nose, Paul chided, "Not yet anyway."

That triggered the all-too-familiar eye roll. Abigail suddenly couldn't move fast enough as she spun away from him and made her way toward the older boy who had captured her attention since last spring. She almost made it to Michael Willis's side before allowing herself to be sidetracked by her best friend, Becky.

"You're doing well with them," came a familiar voice from over Paul's shoulder.

After putting on what he thought was a pleasant expression, Paul turned around to face Pastor Harlowe. The pastor was a few years younger than him, but his thinning head of hair tacked on a bit more age than he'd earned. When he'd first arrived in town a few years ago, Harlowe looked more like a rancher than a preacher. Trim and muscular, he'd turned plenty of heads from the available ladies in town. Although still unmarried, Harlowe had been invited to enough home-cooked suppers to lose a bit of his muscle and add a few layers of padding beneath his starched black clothing. His friendly demeanor, on the other hand, was still as engaging as it had been during his first service in Keystone Pass.

"Thanks for the compliment," Paul said, "but I know I'm lacking as a father."

Harlowe dismissed that with the back of one hand. "Nonsense. They're fine children and have been through a lot. You've been there for them and they're better for it. That's plain enough to see."

"Well . . . thank you."

"You've been through a lot as well. How are you holding up?"

"Joanna's been gone a while now," Paul said.

"That doesn't mean it's easy. We all heal at our own pace."

"Yeah." Paul removed his hat and wiped away a few beads of sweat. The summer heat was waning, but he couldn't help feeling as if it were all focused on him at that moment. "That was a nice service today. Real nice."

"Did you enjoy my sermon? I worked hard on it."

"It was good."

"Which part did you like best? The passages on Abraham or my question about Genesis?"

"The Abraham passages. Definitely."

Harlowe placed a hand on Paul's shoulder and kept it there. "Neither was in my sermon today. I was just testing you."

"And I failed." With a shrug, Paul added, "Sorry about that."

"There's no failing where I'm concerned. At least, not with something as fluid as words," Harlowe said. "I knew you weren't listening. You're always distracted when you come to services. I'm just happy to see you in the Lord's house. I hope you take some comfort from just being there."

"I . . . I do."

Grinning like a kid not much older than Paul's own, the pastor said, "I'm glad. And I know you're telling the truth because I already saw what you look like when you're lying."

"Lying to a preacher," Paul sighed as he put his hat back on. "That won't look good when I'm up there being judged."

"I forgive you, Paul. There. Clean slate."

"That easy, huh?"

"Sometimes. Now, why don't you help yourself to something to eat? That is, unless you'd like to talk some more?"

Paul smiled at the other man with genuine, if somewhat tired, warmth. "I am mighty hungry. Also, someone's got to keep an eye on my youngest. Sometimes them other boys play a little rough."

"Don't forget about your other child," Harlowe said while nodding toward the other side of the duck pond. "She might need some watching as well."

While Paul was happy to see Abigail walking next to Michael Willis, he wasn't pleased with the fact that they were making their way around the pond to a cluster of trees where they could easily slip out of sight. " 'Scuse me, Pastor."

"Tend to your flock and I'll tend to mine," Harlowe replied.

Paul stormed across the little field surrounding the church. With snowcapped mountains behind the perfect angles of the structure's roof and steeple, it was a sight that could inspire any man. Watching a beloved daughter wander away with a young man who had the motives of any other young man was enough to inspire a father in a much different way. He was about to unleash some of that inspiration when Paul caught the scent of some fried chicken.

Mrs. Willis stood behind the plate of poultry, stacking napkins into little piles. "Hello, Paul," she said. "Beautiful sermon today, wasn't it?"

"It sure was."

"Go on and take some chicken before it's gone."

Paul might have wanted his daughter to enjoy some companionship, but he'd gladly wring the neck of any boy who sought to take things too far. Before making that intention clear to Mrs. Willis's son, he took a napkin and a nice plump chicken breast from the table. "Thanks kindly, ma'am."

Mrs. Willis gave him a friendly nod and shifted her eyes to the next parishioners to find her offering.

Abigail and Michael had stopped their wandering just a few paces away from the trees, so Paul held his ground. After taking a bite of chicken, he glanced over to where David was playing. As fidgety as he'd been the night before, or any other night for that matter, David was holding his own with the other boys. In fact, he was quick to throw himself into a lighthearted scrap that quickly grew into a mess of flailing arms and laughing children. It did Paul no end of good to watch that. Having another couple bites of chicken improved his mood even further.

Turning back toward the other side of the pond, Paul felt his heart skip a beat. Michael and Abigail were nowhere to be found. Before he could get himself worked up even more, Paul caught a glimpse of Abigail's skirts flapping in the breeze. She was standing behind some trees. With a long, squinting stare, Paul saw Michael was less than an inch away from her.

"Hey!" Paul barked. "You two!"

Neither his daughter nor the Willis boy responded.

"Abigail Meakes!"

She snapped to attention and hopped fully into view. When she saw her father staring directly at her, the girl flushed and averted her eyes.

"Get over here and get something to eat," Paul said. "Both of you."

After a few seconds, Michael stepped out from wherever he'd thought of hiding in those trees. He looked sheepishly across the pond and hurried over to his mother's table. Since neither of their clothes were too rumpled, Paul guessed they hadn't been up to much while out of his sight.

Abigail's fists were clenched and every step she took was heavier than the last. By the time she made it to where Paul waited for her, she was fit to be tied. "I can't believe you did that," she hissed.

"What?" Paul asked with poorly feigned innocence. "I know you like chicken just as much as I do."

"I like turkey, Daddy. You should know that."

"Well, when you were a little girl, you wouldn't eat much of anything other than chicken or mashed potatoes. Surely you haven't grown out of that."

"I've grown out of a lot of things, in case you haven't noticed."

Paul let her sneer at him for a few more seconds before he pulled her close and kissed the top of her head. "Then help yourself to whatever it is you do like."

"Can I eat with Becky? She's right over there."

"Of course."

Abigail took a few angry steps away, turned, and walked back over to her father. "You want me to get you anything, Daddy?"

"Just bring me some pie in a while. I don't much care which kind it is, but you're eating it with your kin."

She nodded and walked away. Paul noticed how she glanced over to Michael Willis. A few fleeting smiles were exchanged between the young man and Abigail, which seemed innocent enough. Even so, Paul made certain to make his fatherly presence known for the rest of the picnic.

CHAPTER 4

The next morning was a quiet one. Most of the time, Paul would welcome such a thing. On this occasion, however, the silence was imposed upon him by his children instead of a pleasure granted by a cool and calm sunrise. Paul awoke, brewed his coffee, ate a simple breakfast of warm oatmeal, and worked with David to get the horses hitched to his cart. Not a word was spoken, but he hadn't quite noticed just yet. After the sleep had been purged from his mind and body, he tried exchanging a few pleasantries with his children.

They responded with stifled grunts.

Paul climbed into the wagon's driver's seat, waited for the children to pile into the cart behind him, and then snapped the reins. "Here we go!" he announced.

Still . . . nothing.

By the time their house as well as the rest of the town was behind them, Paul got a little suspicious. "You want to take the reins, son?"

"Eh."

"Is that yes or no?"

"No."

"Why not?"

"Because!"

Paul scowled and bit back his first impulse to try to snarl even louder than the boy. After a few more seconds of tense quiet, he asked, "You usually like to drive the cart."

"Not today," he said.

"Something wrong?"

More silence. Paul didn't need to turn around to get a clear picture in his head of his son swinging his legs over the back of the cart while wearing the terse little frown he'd perfected over the last several months.

"He's still upset about getting pushed into the pond yesterday," Abigail announced.

When he heard the light impact of a hand against an older sister's arm, Paul could picture that just as well as he could imagine David's sour face. Shifting in his seat, he turned to look over his shoulder and say, "It was all in good fun. Just about every boy there wound up in the water with them ducks."

"But I was the first," David griped.

"You're a trailblazer."

"They were laughing."

"You were laughing too, if I'm not mistaken."

David crossed his arms into an unbreakable chest plate that would be his armor for the next short while.

"All right," Paul said as he shifted forward once again. "That's why he's in a mood. What's your excuse, Abigail?"

"As if you didn't know," she snapped.

"Bring me up to speed."

The little wagon rocked a bit as she made her way to the front and hung on to the sides with both hands. "You treated me like a child," she whispered. "In front of Michael."

Leaning toward her, Paul whispered, "You are my child, Dumplin'."

"Don't call me that."

"You are my child . . . Abigail. And if you can think of one father who would be so quick to let his daughter sneak off into the woods with a boy, I'd like you to introduce me to him."

"Why?" she asked. "So he could tell you how to trust your daughter?"

"No . . . so I could talk some sense into him." Sensing that she was on the verge of scampering to her brother's side and staying there, Paul quickly added, "You're too

35

young to be keeping company with a boy like that."

"Just the other day, you were twisting my arm to talk to Michael Willis. Now you're chasing him away!"

"Talking is one thing," Paul explained. "You should talk to more people than just Becky, and it's natural for a pretty girl like you to talk to a boy. You've had your eye on the Willis lad for a while and I know it makes you happy to share his company. But walking away to be alone with him . . . that's something else entirely."

"I know, but —"

"No," Paul snapped. "You don't know. You can't know. You may think that you do, but you don't."

There was obviously a whole lot brewing behind the girl's eyes, but she kept it to herself. Paul could feel the tension rolling off her like heat from a rock that had been baking in the sun. At the first sign of a cooling period, he said, "I'm only looking out for you, Dumplin'."

"Please don't call me that."

"What about the rest of what I said? Do you understand that, at least?"

Reluctantly she replied, "Yes, Daddy. I just don't know why you changed your mind about Michael that way. We weren't doing

anything in those trees. We were just talking."

"At first you were talking. Later, there
might have been more."

"I don't think so."

"But he was entertaining the notion."

"How do you know?" Abigail snapped.
"You haven't even properly met Michael
yet."

"I know because I used to be a young man
myself and they tend to keep their manners
when they know they're bein' watched.
When they're off alone, their minds tend to
wander . . . along with their hands."

"The only thing he touched was my arm,"
she assured him.

"Good."

"I don't even know what you expected to
happen so close to a church picnic anyway,"
she said in a huff.

Paul smiled and stretched out to wrap an
arm around his daughter. He couldn't reach
much of her from where he was sitting, but
Abigail met him halfway by resting her head
on his shoulder. He believed that she truly
didn't know what else could have happened
with Michael, and he thought a quick prayer
to thank God above for that. Since she
didn't know that, she didn't need to know
how much he'd gotten away with when he

was Michael's age after leading pretty girls away where nobody could watch them.

"You're a good girl, sweetie."

"I'm not a little girl anymore, you know."

"I didn't say little girl. I said you're a *good* girl."

"Right," she said, "but you treat me like I'm little. Littler than him, even."

Paul checked on David to find the young boy sitting at the back of the cart. He'd been watching his father and sister, but as soon as Paul looked at him, the boy quickly twisted around to put his back to them both.

"I guess I always will," Paul admitted. "If your mother was here, she'd understand better and would give you a bit more slack. But . . . she's not . . . so you're stuck with just me."

"Wonderful."

"On the bright side," Paul added, "you'll have two strong men to keep the boys in line when they come to court you."

"Well," she said loud enough for her voice to carry, "more like one strong man and a string bean."

"I heard that!" David said.

"There's some good news," Paul said cheerily. "The boy's not deaf."

For a good portion of the rest of the ride,

David proved to his sister that he wasn't mute either.

CHAPTER 5

The trail went all the way to Colorado Springs and probably well beyond. All Paul cared about was that it first led to a small trading post just under ten miles away from Keystone Pass. After a steep incline where the trail dipped into a shallow slope, the trading post appeared as if it had been hiding until the last moment from anyone approaching from the south. After having made this ride so many times, Paul could have found the trading post in his sleep. Although the children weren't overly excited to see the small cluster of buildings sprouting like weeds beside a crooked stream, David and Abigail were anxious to get inside one of the three stores to see what new sweets had been put on the shelves since their last visit.

"You two stay close to me," Paul said as the wagon drew closer to the trading post. "Don't go wandering off."

"What if Mr. Prescott isn't there yet?" Abigail asked.

"Then maybe you can look around, but you've got to stay close. We're not going to waste a lot of time when we're here to work." Pivoting around to glare at both of his children, Paul added, "And don't think for a second that you'll get out of loading this cart just because we can't find you. If me and Mr. Prescott have to do all of the lifting, you two will be up to your ears in chores for years to come. Understand?"

"Yes, sir," they both said in unison.

Satisfied that he'd sufficiently frightened his young ones, Paul rode straight up to the largest store and climbed down from the driver's seat. His legs ached and his back was stiff as a board after the ride, which had taken the better part of the afternoon. The building directly in front of him was more than just a store. It was also part restaurant, part saloon, and even had a stagecoach ticketing office tacked on to one side. As soon as someone opened the door to step out, he could smell the enticing aroma of beef being cooked in a pan of sliced onions. He suddenly couldn't get inside fast enough.

"Hey there, Paul!" a woman with wispy blond hair said from the small dining room near the entrance. "Knew you'd be stopping by, so I cooked up your favorite. Steak and onions."

"You're an angel, Dorothy."

"Speaking of angels, it looks like you brought a few with you."

The blond woman was still looking at the front door, where Abigail and David had filed in to stand behind their father. While Paul had his sights set on the corner of the main room where a few round tables were set up near the kitchen, both of his children were studying the other half of the room, which was filled with shelves of various merchandise for sale. The store was about twice the size of Meakes Mercantile but felt even larger because of everything that was crammed inside it.

"They're waiting to find new ways to spend my money," Paul said warily.

"Then by all means," the blonde replied, "turn them loose."

"Thank you, Dorothy," both children said.

Glaring at the blonde, Paul said, "You're only telling them that because you own a piece of this place."

Dorothy shrugged. "I'm not about to deny it."

"Is Prescott here yet?"

"He's meeting with Trace about some

wine or such. They'll be bartering for a little while yet."

Trace was the owner of that store and had a piece of the neighboring one as well. David and Abigail knew that and watched their father expectantly. Although they often had a great deal of sway over his actions, Paul was more affected by the enticing aroma of the special that had been prepared in the kitchen.

"All right," Paul sighed. "You two have got until I finish my steak to have a look around."

"Thanks, Daddy!" Abigail said as she rushed to wrap her arms around him. David joined in as well, looking happier than he had for the last few days. After robbing him for a quarter each, they abandoned him to explore the aisles with which they were already so familiar.

Sitting down at one of the tables, Paul asked, "How is Trace?"

"Feeling the pinch from Territorial Mining just like everyone else."

"Uh-huh."

"They made a real good offer, but . . . are you listening?"

Paul froze while tucking a napkin under his collar as if he'd been caught leering into the blond woman's bedroom window. "Sure

I am," he was quick to say. "Mining company. Feeling the pinch. I got it."

"Why don't I fetch you a plate of food?" she sighed. "After that, I know I'll have your undivided attention."

"Sounds like a good plan!"

Dorothy fixed him one of the daily specials with an extra helping of onions and a scoop of mashed potatoes. Since there weren't many other customers in the place at the moment, she pulled up a chair and sat with him as he ate. Instead of discussing the mining company's offer, they came up with more pleasant things to talk about, such as the weather and how their children were doing in school. She did most of the talking since Paul's mouth was almost always too full to form any understandable words. He did speak on occasion, however. In fact, Paul enjoyed talking to someone closer to his age for a change of pace.

Setting down his fork and knife, Paul asked, "What's for dessert?"

"Finished already?" Dorothy chuckled. "I'm surprised you didn't eat the plate as well."

"Throw down enough gravy from those potatoes and I just might."

"I've got a few pies in the oven if you don't mind waiting."

"He can check back later," said another man who'd just stepped into the dining room. "Depending on how well things go, I might even join him."

The man was tall and gangly of limb. He wore a suit that was frayed at the cuffs and a bowler hat to cover a bald spot that overtook more and more of his scalp every time Paul met up with him. The full, well-trimmed beard and the grin beneath it, however, rarely changed.

"Why, if it isn't Leandro Prescott," Paul said as he pushed away from the table and got to his feet. "As I live and breathe. Dorothy, when did you start allowing undesirables like this into your fine establishment?"

"He eats almost as much as you do," she replied while gathering up the dishes that had been left in Paul's wake. "We can't afford to turn away money like that."

Paul stood toe-to-toe with the other man, straightening up to make Prescott's height advantage appear just a bit smaller. Naturally Prescott straightened up as well to look down at him as though he were perched atop a mountain. "Speaking of money," Prescott said, "you ready to part with some of yours?"

"Not nearly as much as you'd like."

"We'll just see about that."

After a bit more posturing, Paul cracked a smile and slapped Prescott on the shoulder. "What've you got for me this time?"

"A few suits that should fetch a good price from some rich banker, a real nice set of silverware and matching china, a dozen lace tablecloths —"

"Get to the good stuff."

Raising his eyebrows, Prescott asked, "You recall that fella from back east selling all those gadgets at such a high price?"

"You mean the one with them picture cards of New York City that looked like the real thing was right in front of your face?" Paul asked anxiously.

"No. The one with all of the things meant to keep ladies feeling pretty."

Paul's excitement faded as quickly as it had arrived. "Oh. The corsets and the box that makes those sparks?"

Draping an arm over Paul's shoulders, Prescott led him to the front door. "I know such things don't appeal much to you and me, but the womenfolk can't get enough of them! Why do you think that easterner was so hard-set on his high prices?"

"What is this stuff anyway?"

"Are you going to pay your bill or should I just wait until you come back?" Dorothy asked from the dining room.

"We'll be back," Prescott replied. "And the man who strikes the best bargain will be the one to pay for the feast. Deal?"

"As always," Paul said.

Dorothy didn't have the first notion how the men came to their agreements about who'd gotten the better of the other. All that mattered to her was that they did and the bill always got paid. Shrugging, she allowed them to step outside without another protest.

"These aren't just corsets," Prescott insisted as he and Paul took their discussion to the wide front porch outside the trading post. "They're specially designed to make a woman not only appear slim but shed unwanted girth through the advancement of modern engineering."

"Engineers?" David said as he stepped from behind a stack of toy wagons and hurried to catch up to them. "Like the ones who drive trains?"

Prescott turned toward the boy and tussled his hair. "Not exactly. You're getting tall!" Looking past David to a short bench at the corner of the building, he smiled and added, "And you're prettier than ever, Abigail!"

When she stood up, she made it look like an afterthought. The reluctant smile Abigail gave him was just as disinterested as the ones she frequently gave her father. "Hello, Mr. Prescott."

His eyes narrowed before he said, "You look about the right size for some of the items I brought for sale today."

"She doesn't need any corsets," Paul said.

"I'm talking about some nice blouses and shawls," Prescott amended. "The kind worn by the women of high society."

Although Abigail's interest was piqued, Paul's obviously wasn't. "I didn't come all this way for shawls. Usually you've got the sort of things I can't get anywhere else."

"What do you think about devices that are said to cure most anything from a fever to back pains?"

"What now?"

"Daddy," Abigail said as she drew closer. "I want to see the clothes."

"And what about the train drivers?" David whined.

Paul waved both of his children into silence without taking his eyes off the salesman directly in front of him. "What's this device you mentioned?" he asked.

"That box with the sparks," Prescott explained. "It's supposed to use electrical current to realign . . . something or other. There's plenty of literature that goes along with it. What's important is that it's been fetching top dollar in all the big cities from the same folks who buy all those other medical machines, like the lanterns with the colored lenses that are supposed to promote peaceful sleep and any other manner of pleasantness."

"Sounds dumb," Abigail mumbled.

"All scientific advancements seem dumb at first."

"Yeah, well, I'm inclined to agree with her," Paul said.

Prescott shrugged. "Me too, actually. All we've got to believe is one thing and that's how much people are willing to pay to take a chance on curing their aches and pains. If you've seen any papers from New York, Chicago, or Saint Louis, you'd know I'm right."

"I've seen plenty of advertisements for those gadgets," Paul said. "And they do fetch a high price."

"My prices aren't nearly so bad," Prescott said with a silver tongue. "Leaves plenty of room for profit on your end."

"What are those corsets you mentioned?"

"I've got some in my wagon. It's parked a short distance from here."

"Why didn't you just use the livery?" Paul asked.

"Because then Trace might get a chance to see my wares before you do," Prescott replied. "I can't abide such fine products landing at this trading post before giving my good friend Paul Meakes a chance to get a crack at them."

Paul stared at the other man with a critical eye. Before long, Prescott added, "I might also have some trouble brewing with some of the tribes in the area."

"Indian troubles?" Paul asked.

That brought David rushing over to them, his eyes wide and his breath coming in excited gasps. "Indians? Where? Do we get to see Indians?"

"Quiet," Paul snapped. "What sort of trouble, Leo?"

"Nothing too dramatic. Just some disputes over a batch of tobacco I sold them. It's a simple matter, but it behooves me to be ready to get moving as quickly as possible." When he saw Paul's eyes dart toward his children, Prescott added, "You can leave them here if you like. I'm sure Dorothy wouldn't mind watching over them. She's got plenty of her own, you know."

Paul nodded. "You two go back inside and mind Miss Dorothy. If you want something to eat, tell her to put it on my bill."

Neither of the children needed any more

reasons to get back into the trading post, where they could resume looking at the store shelves and decide what dessert they wanted to try first.

When his young ones were gone, Paul asked, "You're not trying to unload more stolen merchandise, are you?"

"No!"

"You did that to me once before."

"No need to remind me about that," Prescott said. "I got into much more trouble than you did over the affair. It only happened that once and I swore to you it wouldn't happen again."

"Swear it a second time."

"You have my word, Paul," the salesman said earnestly.

"And what about this trouble you're trying to avoid?"

Prescott let out a slow breath. "I'm not even certain it's anything more than a stretch of bad luck, to be honest."

"What do you mean?"

"I've been doing a fair amount of business in towns along the Arkansas River and several other smaller creeks branching off from it. Lots of trade happening out that way from merchants either going to or coming from the Rockies. Last time I left my wagon in a livery, someone tampered with it. Could have been the last couple of times. I'm not certain."

"You were robbed?"

"Nothing serious and no losses I couldn't recoup quickly enough. It's just made me wary of liveries. Might be the work of some bunch of small-time thieves or a dissatisfied customer looking to exact a refund with his own two hands."

"What was that talk of Indians?" Paul asked.

"There's always been troubles with the savages when it comes to anyone plying their trade or even riding for too long in their territory. Any mining company, railroad, or rancher will tell you as much."

"Of course."

"Being a man who trades with a large number of customers and covers a whole lot of ground in the process, I've run afoul of a few dangerous characters. Whether it's just a small band of robbers, a tribe of redskins, or a few unhappy customers, they're all accepted hazards of a man in my profession. I can take care of myself," he said while flipping open his jacket to show the pistol holstered under his arm. "But it's rarely come to that."

"Just tell me if you're putting me or my store in danger," Paul said.

52

"I'd never do that. You're a good friend and a better customer. The reason I prefer to do my business in the open these days is so I can see any trouble that might be coming along, whether it's aimed directly at me or not. And precautions like the ones I'm taking are the reasons I'm still in business when so many of my competitors have long since gone. Besides, my cautions are only temporary. I'm heading out to Leadville from here and will stay there for a while. When I come back this way again, this little inconvenience will be nothing more than an unpleasant memory."

"Leadville?" Paul asked. "You have something lined up there?"

"I'll be conducting some important business at the Board of Trade. Should be quite profitable."

Paul did plenty of business with independent traders like Prescott. Unlike Prescott, however, most of those other traders only gave a damn about getting their money no matter how many bodies were left behind afterward. He'd been in business for himself long enough to know that a certain amount of risk had to be accepted once a man staked a claim west of the Mississippi River.

"All right," Paul said. "Let's take a look at what you've got. But I expect a discount for the added risk as well as having to change locations."

"And here I was worried about outlaws robbing me," Prescott groaned.

CHAPTER 6

Once he got to Prescott's wagon, Paul felt silly for making such a fuss in the first place. It might not have been in a livery or within the fence line of the trading post, but it was less than a quarter of a mile away from the spot where his children were waiting. It was so close, in fact, that Prescott and Paul walked there without breaking a sweat.

As soon as the back of the covered wagon was opened, both men carried on like every other time they'd met to conduct business. Prescott started with his easy sales first, displaying several items that he knew Paul would snap up. Once the clothing, dishes, and silverware were out of the way, he got to the more exotic items.

"Believe me," Prescott said as he rummaged about inside the wagon. "When you see how much ladies will be willing to pay for these, you'll thank me for bringing them to you."

Once he got a look at the items in question, Paul said, "Looks like another corset to me."

"It's these extra straps here that make the difference. See how they cinch in at three particular spots? That's to increase and decrease blood flow to vital areas."

"Seems damn barbaric to subject a woman to that kind of torture."

"You might say the same thing about any corset," Prescott replied. "The man who built this one is a professor from all the way out in Paris, and he swears his enhancements make a world of difference."

"How much?"

"I've seen them sold for upward of twenty dollars. I'll let you have it for fifteen."

"Just the one?"

"I've got a dozen in stock."

"I'll take 'em all for ten apiece."

"Thirteen," Prescott countered.

"Twelve, and I don't even know why I'm bothering with the foolish things in the first place."

"Because you know you can pull in a healthy profit and you'll be the only store for miles around with any in stock. Make it twelve and a half and you got a deal."

"Fine," Paul said. "What about them sparking boxes?"

"They're around here somewhere. While I'm looking for them, why don't you have a look at some tonics I've acquired? They're good medicine instead of the laudanum-and-hops concoctions that you'll usually find. Nothing but herbs, a few extraordinary spices from the Far East, and vitamin water. Doctors all through California swear by it to fight ailments from gangrene down to a fever."

"That's a harder sell," Paul said. "Especially since that sort of thing is available from the backs of dozens of wagons at any given time."

"Not for the price I can offer. Even after you mark it up for your customers, you'll be able to compete with any traveling medicine show. Just take a —"

A piercing cry shattered the crisp air that had blown in from the north. It was quickly followed by another shout as well as the thunder of hooves beating against the ground.

"Damn it to hell," Paul snarled. "I thought you said your trouble with the Injuns wasn't that bad."

"It isn't!"

"Well, that sure sounds like a war cry to me."

Following Paul around to the front of the

wagon, Prescott climbed up into the driver's seat. "That doesn't mean they're after me."

"Well, it sounds like they're kicking up a mess of trouble at that trading post, which is where my two young'uns are." Having pulled himself onto the wagon as well, Paul reached beneath the seat for the shotgun kept there. "Get me there real quick or I'll start running."

"No need for that," Prescott said as he pulled the lever to release the brake. "These horses are well rested. Just be ready with that shotgun." He then took hold of the reins and snapped them with enough force to send a loud *crack* through the air. The team of four horses dug their hooves into the dirt and got the wagon rolling. In a matter of seconds, they were pointed toward the trading post and headed there with building speed.

Setting his eyes firmly on the small group of horses gathered outside Trace's store, Prescott said, "If those Indians are after me, I'll lead them away so you can get to David and Abby."

"Once they're safe, I'll —"

"Just worry about them young ones," Prescott snapped as his wagon rolled up to the northernmost edge of the trading post.

"After that, I'm sure we'll think of something."

Not wanting to waste another moment arguing, Paul jumped down from the wagon as soon as it slowed and moved away so it could roll on without him. Prescott snapped his reins and let out a loud noise that caught the attention of horses and men alike. There were only two riders in sight and they were most definitely Indians. Although he was no expert on the native tribes, Paul had lived in Colorado long enough to know a Comanche when he saw one. Seeing more than one wearing war paint was never a welcome sight.

"Come on, you savages!" Prescott hollered as he drove his wagon down the path in front of the few structures in the trading post. "You want me? Come and get me!" In case that wasn't enough to catch their eye, he followed up by firing one of his shotgun's barrels into the air. Not only did the thunderous roar bring both mounted Comanches to him, but it spurred his team to move even faster than before. In no time at all, the wagon and both members of the raiding party were riding away from Trace's store.

Paul hurried toward Trace's front door. The first thing he noticed was the shattered window. When he spotted arrows lodged in the door itself, he reached for the pistol at his side. Normally the old Schofield .44 only saw the light of day when it was being cleaned or if it was firing a few rounds into bottles placed atop a fence post. The only time he wore the battered holster strapped around his waist was when he was out for a ride like this one, and that was just in the event he crossed the path of a hungry wildcat or venomous snake. He drew the pistol now, praying his marksmanship wasn't put to the test.

His stomach was in a knot and his knuckles were white around the grip of his weapon as Paul stormed in through the front door. "David!" he shouted. "Abigail! Where are you?"

He didn't get a response right away, and those few seconds of silence were the longest he'd ever experienced. They were mercifully brought to an end when a familiar voice called out to him.

"In here," Dorothy shouted from the next room.

As Paul turned and headed toward the dining room, he noticed the general disorder of things around him. His senses were too jangled to catch every detail, but items were scattered on the floor, tables were knocked over, and various liquids had been spilled to form dirty rivulets within the grain of the floorboards. Some of it stuck to the bottoms of his boots, nearly causing him to slip and fall. Inside the dining room, Paul couldn't see much through the uneven barriers formed by all of the upended tables and chairs.

"Where are you?" he shouted.

"Kitchen."

"Can you come out, Dorothy? Where are my children?"

Although there was no answer to his question forthcoming, Paul wasn't drowning in more silence. From the room behind him came the crash of fragile items, glass jars, and heavy shelves hitting the floor. Paul reflexively turned to look into the main room of the store at a man who stalked down one aisle after pushing over a shelf full of expensive merchandise. He was a dark-skinned man dressed in buckskin britches. His chest was bare except for thick streaks of paint that had been applied to match the crude designs on his face. He wore a leather strap around one upper arm decorated with feathers, beads, and bone similar to the enhancements made to the rifle he carried.

"Wh . . . what are you doing here?" Paul asked.

The Comanche warrior stared at him with eyes that were somehow both fiery and cold. At the same time he was planning three different ways to put Paul into his grave.

Paul raised his gun and did his best to keep his hand from shaking. "What do you want?"

"Step aside," the warrior said.

Since he didn't have much of a plan going in, Paul cleared a path for the Comanche while putting himself between the muscular figure and the dining room. As the warrior made his way toward the front door, he knocked whatever he could to the floor and pushed over any shelves that were still standing. He was almost close enough to open the door and walk outside when another door behind Paul was flung open.

"That's him!" Dorothy said as she emerged from the kitchen. "That's the one who did it."

"Stay back," Paul told her.

"Don't let him go," she said frantically. Her face was wet with tears and a tickle of blood ran from a cut on one temple. "He was the first one to ride into town. He's the one responsible!"

"Responsible for what?" Paul asked through mounting frustration.

"He . . . he's the one who shot Abigail."

Paul turned to look at her again. This time, he noticed the bloodstains covering her apron. He didn't need to think any more after that.

He didn't care that the warrior had the look of a bloodthirsty wolf.

He didn't care that it had been over a decade since he'd fired the Schofield at anything that didn't slither or crawl on four legs.

When he saw that blood and thought about his daughter lying wounded somewhere, Paul simply bared his teeth and charged.

CHAPTER 7

It was probably best that Paul was so enraged that he forgot about the pistol in his hand. Since the Schofield was rarely on his person, it simply registered as a heavy object to his racing mind as his body allowed instinct to take over. His decision to run straight at the Comanche rather than fire a shot seemed to puzzle the warrior as well. The burly Indian had been bringing his rifle to his shoulder and was caught halfway there by the time Paul got to him. Lowering his head, Paul wrapped both arms around the Comanche's midsection to drive him toward the closest wall of shelves.

Somewhere along the way, the Indian pulled his trigger. The rifle sent its round into a wall, and the explosive sound of the shot rang painfully within Paul's ears. As he cursed at the Indian, his words sounded like a dull roar amid the piercing ring and rush of blood inside his head.

The Comanche staggered backward until his shoulders bumped against a shelf that was only standing because it was built directly into the wall. Now that he had steadier footing while propped up between Paul and the shelf, the Comanche pulled an arm free, raised it high, and dropped his elbow down onto Paul's back. The rifle wasn't good for much at such close range, so he let it drop to grab Paul. In a matter of seconds, the Indian's brawn won out over Paul's rage and the Comanche threw the smaller man into one of the toppled shelves.

Landing with a grunt, Paul winced as his senses rushed back to him. The rage was still there, but now it was tempered by fear and pain from all of the parts of him that ached from being so thoroughly battered. "I'll . . . I'll kill you," he snarled.

The Comanche barely flinched. "Stay down," he said in a rumbling baritone, "or you will be the one to die this day."

Paul lay partially wedged between two shelves. His legs were sprawled, and when he attempted to get to his feet, his hands and feet skidded against various items that littered the floor beneath him. As he struggled, he was reminded of what was still clutched within his right hand. Gripping the Schofield tightly, Paul brought it up while pulling its trigger. The man who'd sold him the firearm had instructed him to squeeze the trigger instead of pulling it. Now he knew why. Not only did the pistol buck against his palm earlier than he'd intended, but his round punched through a stack of hatboxes several feet away from where the Comanche was standing.

Although he reacted to the shot, the Comanche moved without a hint of desperation. Every move was clean and concise as he ducked down and moved to Paul's left. His steps were so sure that he hardly even disturbed the mess on the floor around him.

Paul kept firing as he struggled to pull free from the shelf and stand on his own two feet. Burned gunpowder stung his nose, and the only thing he could hear was his own frantic breathing and the quick thudding of his heart. Every gunshot was more muffled than the last until they too were lost in the cacophony. Once he'd gained enough of his senses to realize he'd wasted too many bullets already, Paul forced himself to stop shooting so he could use both hands to prop himself up. After a few slips, he finally managed to pull himself upright.

The Comanche stood calmly in another part of the room. His posture was that of a wary predator, slightly hunched and ready to pounce. His keen eyes were locked on Paul's, watching to see what the other man had in mind for his next move.

Paul felt his blood run ice-cold. Even though he was the one holding a gun and knew he had at least another shot or two, he was at a distinct disadvantage. "You're not taking these women," he said.

Furrowing his brow slightly, the Comanche replied, "What women?"

"The ones you already shot."

"I shot no women."

"The hell you didn't!" Paul roared as he raised his Schofield to send whatever shots he had at the Indian.

That was all the Comanche needed to launch into motion. His head bobbed down and to the side along with the rest of his upper body to move in a swift, fluid rhythm. His legs remained steady beneath him as he darted across the room to circle around toward Paul's left before closing in.

Watching as if from a distance, Paul fired a quick shot as soon as the Schofield was pointed anywhere close to the Comanche. He got a bit closer than his previous attempts, which bought him another couple of seconds as the warrior kept moving to the side rather than straight at his prey. Knowing he was down to his last shot or real close to it, Paul sighted along the top of the Schofield's barrel before dropping the pistol's hammer again.

The Comanche stood less than three paces away. His broad chest rose and fell with every measured breath and he held a knife in a loose, comfortable grip. Paul hadn't seen him draw the blade from any scabbard and wasn't about to give the Indian a chance to put it to use.

"Drop that knife," Paul demanded.

The Comanche didn't speak or make any movement that could be interpreted as a reply.

Thumbing back the Schofield's hammer, Paul said, "I'm warning you."

"You won't shoot me."

"Why?"

"You can't," the Comanche replied.

"Don't think I got it in me?"

In a quick burst of motion, the Comanche sprang forward one step. The movement wasn't enough to bring him all the way to Paul, but it was more than enough to cause him to pull his trigger out of reflex. Paul let out a startled grunt as every muscle in his gun hand tensed. His eyes even clamped shut a split second before he heard the hammer smack against the back of an empty bullet casing.

The Comanche's voice rolled through the air like distant thunder. "You already fired six rounds."

Paul steeled himself and prepared to throw the pistol at the Indian's head. Before he could extend his arm far enough to make the toss, the man that had been his target was already in a different spot. Paul shifted his weight to adjust his aim. His arm snapped forward only a few inches before it was stopped by a grip that felt as solid as cast iron.

Suddenly the Comanche was less than an inch away from Paul's face, holding Paul's wrist as if he was about to pull his arm from its socket. "You have taken enough from us already, white man," he said. "You will not take this place from us as well."

"You . . . took my daughter," Paul said as he strained to pull free of the warrior's grip.

"If she is gone, then you only know a small piece of my people's pain. Now," the Comanche added as he pressed his blade against Paul's ribs, "you will feel even more of it."

Paul's blood went from cold to hot in an instant. His muscles burned beneath his skin, and his breath surged through his lungs as senses that had been muddled before were now sharper than ever. And still, that wasn't enough.

Not only was the Comanche able to force Paul's gun hand away, but he dug the tip of his knife in through the layers of clothing wrapped around Paul's body. Paul dropped his gun to free both of his hands. He grabbed the Comanche's wrist to keep the knife from being driven all the way between his ribs, but even though he slowed the Indian's deadly progress, he could not stop it.

Paul drove a knee up into the Comanche's body. It thumped against solid muscle and barely caused the other man to flinch. He tried stomping his bootheel against the Comanche's feet, but the impact against the floor only caused the knife's blade to scrape erratically against him. His wrist was still held tightly, so Paul shoved away from the Comanche to at least put some distance between himself and the blade. As soon as he thought he'd bought some time, Paul found himself in an even worse predicament.

The Comanche let go of Paul's wrist and lunged forward. In a heartbeat, he was behind Paul and snaking one arm around his throat. With a twist of his forearm, the warrior forced Paul's chin upward so he could press the blade's edge against his exposed throat.

Any movement Paul made from there only dragged his neck against sharpened steel. His mind raced for a way out of danger even as his heart told him there was none to be found.

When he swallowed back a breath, he felt the blade bite in deep enough to send a warm trickle of blood down the front of his neck.

"You there!" Prescott shouted from outside the store. "Let that man go."

Both Paul and the Comanche looked through the front window to find the salesman standing outside with a shotgun at the ready. Prescott stepped in through what remained of the large pane of broken glass. "I said let him go. Right now."

"You will kill us both with that gun," the Comanche said.

"This ain't loaded with buckshot. I've brought down a hawk while it was flying, so I can sure as hell hit a big ugly savage that's standing right in front of me."

Although the Comanche wasn't pleased with the way Prescott spoke to him, he saw some truth to the other man's words. He eased the blade away from Paul's neck but kept it close enough to open him up if he changed his mind. "The other hunters with me will kill you if I do not join them."

"That won't matter much to you when you're lying dead on the floor," Prescott pointed out.

Locking his steely gaze on Prescott, the Comanche released Paul and stepped away. Keeping his head high and his back straight, the warrior walked back to the spot where he'd left his rifle. He stared at Prescott as if he was looking at the vilest thing on earth before stooping down to pick up his weapon. When he straightened up again, the Comanche held death in each hand and looked straight down the barrel of Prescott's shotgun as if it couldn't harm a single black hair on his head.

Paul stood rooted to his spot, waiting to see what would happen next.

"Go on, now," Prescott said. "Get out of my sight."

Pointing the tip of his knife at both of the other men in turn, the Comanche said, "This is not over, white man."

"It is if you know what's good for you."

The Comanche let out a huffing, humorless laugh, walked across the room, and headed straight through the front door.

Paul let out the breath he'd been holding and rushed to pick up his Schofield. He did his best to reload the pistol quickly, but trembling hands made the task somewhat difficult.

"You all right?" Prescott asked.

Paul nodded in a series of quick, up-and-down twitches. After taking a quick look up from what he was doing, he said, "I'll feel a lot better once you stop pointing that shotgun at me."

Looking down as if he didn't know what he was holding, Prescott lowered the weapon. "You sure you're all right? You look kind of . . . bloody."

"Just a few scrapes and shallow cuts. Nothing serious." Paul snapped the Schofield shut and held it at the ready. "Where are the rest of those savages?"

"I chased them off."

"Just to be certain, stand guard at the door. I need to check on my young ones."

The fear that had been etched into Prescott's eyes turned immediately to ferocity. "What happened to them? Are they hurt?"

"That's what I intend to find out. Just make sure nobody tries to come at us again."

"No one's getting by me." Even though Prescott was just a salesman, he spoke those words with the resolve of a hardened killer.

Paul didn't realize how shaky he still was until he started walking through the devastated store. When he got to the front window, he looked outside and only saw Prescott's wagon near a couple of men trying to make sense of what had just happened. The front door was ajar and the restaurant portion of the store was still in disarray. Dorothy was huddled against the counter near the door to the kitchen, where a display of desserts was kept. She rose to stand and approached him with concern etched into her features.

When she started to speak, Paul realized he didn't want to hear what she had to say.

He didn't want to take another step or move any closer to the moment where he might see what terrible harm had come to his children. Before his crippling dread could overtake him, Paul rushed to Dorothy's side and faced it head-on.

CHAPTER 8

"Where is she?" Paul asked. "Where's Abigail? What about David? Is he all right? Where are they?" Once he started talking, Paul couldn't stop. He didn't even know what else he was saying until Dorothy placed a hand on his cheek and looked him straight in the eye.

"Take a breath," she told him, "and put the gun down."

Even after Paul reminded himself that he was still gripping the Schofield as if he was about to walk into a fight, he was reluctant to put it back into its holster. "Just take me to them," he said.

The kitchen was less than a few paces away and Paul could already hear the hushed voices of his children coming from that direction. Before he could get to them, Dorothy took hold of him and asked, "Are those men coming back?"

"I don't think so."

"No," Prescott said with certainty. "The first bunch of them rode off when I charged in with my wagon, and that last one already beat a path away from here."

"Good," she sighed. "Now go into the kitchen and see those kids of yours. They're petrified."

So was Paul, but he didn't have the luxury of saying as much. Of course, he didn't need to say it since his actions spoke for him just as well. "Are they all right?" he asked in a hushed tone. "If even one of them is . . . I just . . . I don't think I could . . ."

"They're both alive and well."

"But you said Abigail was . . ."

"I know," Dorothy said. "Just get in there and see for yourself."

Now that he knew he wasn't going to walk in to be confronted by the sight that was every parent's nightmare, Paul couldn't get to the kitchen fast enough. He charged through the doorway, calling their names while searching for any sign of them. At first, he couldn't see anything. Then he saw his son's head poke up from behind one of the two iron stoves at the back of the room.

"Are they gone?" the boy asked.

Paul hurried over to him and scooped the boy into his arms. "They're gone, son. Did they hurt you?"

"No."

"What about your sister? Where is she?"

Even better than hearing good news from David, Paul heard it from Abigail herself as she spoke up in a shaky but beautiful voice. "I'm here, Daddy. In the pantry."

Paul looked over to a wide cupboard that reached almost all the way up to the ceiling. One of its doors opened thanks to the trembling hand pushing it from the inside. After opening both doors wide, Paul kneeled down so he could place his hands on the bloody rags that had been tied around her left thigh. "What is this?" he asked while studying the wound.

"She was shot," David replied.

Dorothy was in the kitchen as well and she quickly said, "He told me the same thing and I nearly lost my mind with worry."

Paul didn't have to think too far back to remember the sight of her in that very state.

"I saw the blood and her lying on the floor," Dorothy explained, "and I thought the worst. I'm sorry for alarming you the way I did."

Looking at his daughter, Paul said, "Tell me what happened."

"The Comanches rode in and circled the trading post," Abigail said.

David was quick to add, "I knew they were

Comanches, Pa. I read about them."

"Good, son."

"They rode around and made a lot of noise," the girl continued. "Me and David went to the window to see what was happening and one of them shot at the store."

"With an arrow!" David said while holding up a pair of thin lengths of broken wood. "This arrow!"

"Good Lord!" Paul said as he snatched the broken arrow away from his son.

Dorothy was reaching down into the cupboard to take Abigail's hand. "They were shooting out every window they could find. I doubt they even knew anyone was standing behind this one at the time. These two got away from me before I could stash them away, and as soon as she was hurt, I brought them in here to hide."

Paul set the arrow pieces on the nearest table so he could help get his daughter out from where the kitchen's dry goods were stored. By the time they'd gotten Abigail on a chair and in a position that wouldn't aggravate her leg, he figured she'd be more comfortable if he left her lying on a pile of flour sacks with bags of oats to use for pillows.

"I'm gonna take a look at this," he said while tugging at the end of the material that had been wrapped around Abigail's upper leg. "Ready?"

She'd always been a hearty child, but she didn't do well at the sight of blood. Closing her eyes, she gripped her father's arm tightly and nodded.

Dorothy hovered nearby, wringing her hands. "It's just one of my aprons that I tore up to use as dressing," she said. "It's all I could find after . . ."

"After I took the arrow out," David announced.

Stopping in the middle of untying the knotted cotton strip as delicately as he could, Paul looked at his son and said, "You what?"

"She was screaming," David replied meekly. "I had to do something."

"I thought you were afraid of things like this," Paul said while getting back to his work.

Speaking as if he was stating the most obvious thing under the sun, the boy said, "She's my sister."

The material was soaked with blood that caused it to stick to Abigail's skin. Paul removed it with careful tugs that caused her to twitch and fret.

"I'll get some water," Dorothy said. "Should make it easier to get that dressing off. Looks like that wound could use a cleaning as well."

"Wait!" Prescott said from the doorway.

Paul almost went for his gun. Until that moment, he hadn't even realized the salesman was so close.

Beaming, Prescott announced, "I've got just the thing!"

"Should I not get any water?" Dorothy asked after Prescott had run from the kitchen to bolt through the dining room.

"Go on and get it," Paul said. "David, tell me what you did to your sister."

"Don't be mad at him," Abigail said. "He was just trying to help me."

When the siblings weren't snapping at each other with barbed comments and balled fists, they were defending each other like a couple of outlaws doing whatever it took to keep their gang out of trouble. At times, Paul couldn't decide which irritated him more.

"I was talking to your brother," he said since he didn't want to hear what Abigail thought would calm him down the quickest. "You just sit back and let him talk. Go on, David."

Cowed by all the raised voices, David kept his head down as he said, "After the window broke, Abby fell down. There was something stuck in her leg, so me and Miss Dorothy helped bring her back here where we could hide."

"I already heard that much," Paul said while continuing to peel away the dressing wrapped around his daughter's leg. "Tell me about the arrow."

"It barely got her," the boy said. "Went all the way through. I read in that book I told you about that it's not good to just pull an arrow out. It could rip someone up real bad inside, so I broke it in two and pulled it out. There wasn't any mess or nothing, I swear."

Now that he'd removed the makeshift bandage, Paul could see the blood smeared over his daughter's skin. Dorothy had already returned to hand him a wet rag. He took it, squeezed some of the excess water onto the wound, and asked, "Does that hurt, Dumplin'?"

"No," Abigail replied. "Not too much."

As Paul dabbed at the wound, his son continued talking at an increasingly excited pace. "After I snapped part of the arrow off, it came right out. Then Miss Dorothy came along to wrap us both up on account of the bleeding."

"What do you mean, both of you?" Paul asked. He looked over to his boy and saw more shredded material had been wrapped around David's hand. "You were hurt too?"

"It's not so bad," David replied. "But it still hurts."

"He's probably more frightened than anything else," Dorothy told Paul as she comforted the boy with a few pats to his shoulder. "When he pulled the arrow out, he cut himself on the point. That's all."

"But . . . it still hurts," David said.

Relieved that his son's grievances were still of the typical sort, Paul smiled at him and said, "I'm sure it does. Let's see."

Although he'd seemed sick to mention it just a few moments before, David was more than willing to rip away the loose bandages wrapped around his hand so he could show the long red scrape to his father.

Paul took a moment to look at his son's hand. Apart from the scrape and a bit of dried blood, there wasn't much to see. "This looks fine. How about you just wrap it back up again?"

"All right."

Now that Abigail's leg was clean enough for him to see the wound for what it was, Paul felt a whole lot better. It was obviously painful for her and she would need to get stitched up, but the arrow had gone through a thin layer of flesh without doing much in the way of damage. Dabbing at the gash on the top part of her thigh, he asked, "Does that hurt?"

"Yes, it hurts!" Abigail said as she squirmed. "Leave it alone."

More people were filing into the store and men's voices drifted in from several directions. Some made their way through the mess in the next room while others wandered up and down the street to survey the broken windows that the Comanche raiding party had left behind. One voice separated itself from the rest as it continually demanded people to step aside and let him pass. Finally, after a series of hurried steps, Prescott rushed into the kitchen holding a small liquor bottle in each hand. "Here you go," he said breathlessly. "And since you're friends . . . free of charge!"

"My girl ain't drinking that," Paul said. "She can handle the pain just fine without whiskey or the like to dull her senses."

"I'm still in pain," David said anxiously. "I'll have some."

"All right, then, my good boy," Prescott said as he handed one of the bottles over. "Here you go. Drink up."

Paul jumped to his feet and hurried over to his son, who'd sat down nearby. Even though he reached David quickly, he wasn't fast enough to prevent the boy from taking a long sip from the bottle. When he snatched the bottle away, a stream of dark liquid sprayed from the top of the bottle as well as the mouth it had just been tipped against. "Spit that out right now," Paul demanded.

Too startled to move and too confused to disobey, David simply opened his mouth and let the drink he'd taken dribble down his chin and onto the front of his shirt.

"What is wrong with you?" Prescott asked. Judging by the look on everyone else's face, they were all thinking along those same lines in regard to him.

"I won't have my son drinking whiskey or some other kind of liquor just because he scraped his hand!" Paul said.

Prescott looked at the other bottle in his hand as if he had to check its contents for himself. "This isn't whiskey," he said. "Or any other liquor for that matter. Why would I hand something like that over to your boy? The least I would do is ask before taking such an action."

"Then what is it?"

"It's that healing tonic I told you about. Herbs and vitamins that strengthen the body and mind against all manner of ailments."

"What else is in it?" Paul asked suspiciously as he sniffed the bottle he'd plucked

84

from his son's hand. "Opium? Hops?"

"It's actually more water than anything else," Prescott confessed. "The vitamins and such come in the form of a powder that is dissolved into it, which gives the water its enticing color."

Enticing wasn't exactly the way Paul would describe the liquid's color, but it didn't smell like anything with much kick to it. "Drinking this is supposed to help with a knife wound?"

"Not as such, but it can't hurt," Prescott admitted. "The vitamins will strengthen the system. Poured directly onto the wound will put the healing herbs right where they need to be, however."

"Sounds helpful," Dorothy said.

"And you say this is mostly water?" Paul asked.

"Pretty much."

Now that his blood had stopped boiling, Paul felt as if he was about ready to collapse. As far as the tonic went, he reminded himself that Prescott wouldn't do anything to harm a child. "The lot of you can drink whatever you want," he sighed. "I'm going outside to make sure those Indians aren't coming back."

"They're gone," Prescott said. "Trust me. It's not like there's anything left around here

85

for them to break."

At that moment, a narrow door at the back of the room creaked open. The sound startled both Paul and Prescott so much that they drew their weapons and took aim at that end of the kitchen.

A narrow, pale face peeked halfway from behind the door as a set of bony fingers gripped its edge. "Did you say they're gone?" he squeaked. "Are you sure about that?"

"Yes, Trace," Dorothy said. "They're gone. It's safe for you to come out."

The owner of the largest portion of the trading post stepped out from a small closet filled mostly with brooms and buckets. He wore a rumpled white shirt, gray pants, and a greasy apron tied around his waist. Dust covered him from head to toe, most likely from cowering in the closet. "Glad to see you folks are all right. I suppose I'll take a look at what those savages did to my place."

Paul, his children, Dorothy, and Prescott all watched as Trace strolled through the kitchen. Stopping short of the door to the dining room, he said, "You all seemed to have everything well in hand before, so that explains why I tended to . . ."

"The broom closet?" Abigail asked.

"That's right." Trace then turned around

and looked at Prescott. "You got any of that healing tonic left?"

"Plenty."

"Good. Save me a few bottles." With that, Trace left.

It did Paul a world of good to laugh at such a bold display of cowardice.

CHAPTER 9

If the visit to the trading post had been as uneventful as it was supposed to be, Paul would have made it back home well before nightfall. Since Abigail needed a bit of time to rest, Paul and David helped clean up some of the mess the Comanche had left behind. They would have been kept busy if they'd stayed until the next day, but Paul loaded up his wagon and headed back to town before it got to be too late. By coaxing his team a little harder, he managed to catch sight of Keystone Pass as the last glow of sunlight was fading away. Familiarity with the trail and pure necessity allowed him to make the rest of the ride in darkness.

David and Abigail had been mostly silent all the way home. When he rolled to a stop and set the brake in front of his house, Paul looked over his shoulder and said, "This is where you get off, boy."

"No," David said. "I want to come with you."

"You'll stay put."

"But why?"

"Because I said so! That should be enough for you," he barked. With that, Paul snapped his reins to get the wagon moving again.

They were halfway down the street that cut the town in half when Abigail said, "He doesn't like being alone."

"Well, he'll just need to get used to it."

"He helped me at the trading post. He wants to help some more."

Paul drew a deep breath. "I know," he said as he pushed that breath out again.

After a few more moments, Paul turned a corner and steered toward a narrow building stuck between a dentist's office and the funeral parlor. Paul didn't need to see the hours painted on the front window of that building to know the doctor's office was closed for the night. He made a sharp turn down a wide alley and rode to the lot behind the office.

"Ummm . . . ," Abigail said softly. "David followed us."

"I know that too."

"Don't be mad at him."

"I'm not." Raising his voice, Paul asked, "Do you really want to help?"

Almost immediately, the boy replied, "Yes, Pa!" as he ran to catch up to the wagon. Since he'd been walking behind it all the way from their house, his normally limitless supply of breath was coming in heavier gulps.

"Then go on up those stairs, knock on the door, and tell Doc Swenson about your sister."

David looked up at the top of the narrow stairs attached to the back end of the doctor's office. His eyes widened and his mouth hung open as if he were gazing into the black maw of a monster's cave. "I . . . I want you to come with me," he said.

"No," Paul replied sternly. "Go up there and do as I told you."

Although he was reluctant to disobey his father's command twice in one evening, David also wasn't in a hurry to climb those stairs. He nearly jumped out of his skin when Paul snapped, "Get moving, boy!" Using one fear to temporarily overcome another, David took off running and climbed the stairs amid the loud knock of his boots against weathered wooden planks.

"I wish you'd let up on him sometimes," Abigail said.

"And I wish you'd let me do the fathering without blindly taking his side."

"I hardly ever take his side," she pointed out.

"No. Just when I least want you to."

"You don't ride me the way you do him."

"Yeah," Paul said as he watched his son finish the climb and timidly approach the door. "But you ain't gonna grow up to be a man. Unless I spur him on every now and then, neither will he."

After a short series of frantic knocks, David pulled his hand back as if the door had grown fangs and bitten him. Soon the door was opened by a man of average height dressed in a long nightshirt. He nodded as David talked to him, patted the boy's shoulder while saying a few things to him, and then walked back inside. David wore a beaming smile and came down the stairs two at a time. "He's unlocking the front door," he said before he'd reached the bottom stair.

Paul climbed down from the wagon, walked around to the back, and scooped his daughter into his arms.

"I can walk on my own," she said.

"I'm sure you can, but you shouldn't. Besides, you used to love it when I carried you."

She not only rolled her eyes at him, but threw in a heavy sigh to boot. Her indignity only lasted until she'd been brought to the front of the office, where they were met by the man in the nightshirt. Doc Swenson was less than an inch shorter than Paul and had a thick crop of dark red hair sprouting from his scalp. At the moment, the crop was poorly tended and flattened on one side. "Pardon my appearance," he said. "I was sleeping."

"I can tell," Paul replied.

Shifting his attention to Abigail, the doctor asked, "What happened here?"

Thanks to a good amount of help from his son, Paul told him about the Comanche raiding party that had descended upon the trading post and was finished by the time they'd been shown to one of the small examination rooms in Swenson's office. The doctor put Abigail on a bed covered in starched linens and peeled away the dressing on her leg so he could get a look at the wound. After using a damp cloth to wash away some of the blood, he asked, "How did she receive this injury?"

"She was shot by an arrow," David told him. "A big one!"

"The wound itself appears to be superficial, but I'll need to stitch it shut."

"That's what I thought," Paul said. He placed a hand on his son's shoulder and said, "Let's give the man some room to work."

As eager as he'd been to follow his sister before, David was more than willing to leave her once the doctor had a needle in hand. Once outside, however, he came to a halt that couldn't have been more abrupt if he'd been tied to a chain. "Is she going to be all right, Pa?"

"She's already made it through the worst of it. Sooner or later, everyone has to get himself stitched up for something. She'll pull through just fine."

"Does getting stitched hurt?"

"Sure, but it ain't bad." Seeing the exaggerated wince on his son's face, Paul took hold of the boy's shoulders so he could look straight down into his eyes. "Pain ain't a bad thing, son. It just . . . is."

"But I'm —"

"You can't be afraid of something like that," Paul said sharply. "Nobody lives a life without pain. Not a life worth living anyway. You can't be afraid of pain. You can't be afraid of the nighttime. You can't be afraid of dyin'."

Despite his father's insistence to the contrary, David looked to be growing more afraid by the moment. "How can you not be afraid of those things?"

"Because they're all going to happen to all of us sooner or later. There's nothing to be done about it. You just have to get on with your life and stop shivering like a dry leaf every time you see a shadow."

David frowned and hung his head. "I know, Pa. Everybody dies. Just like Mama."

Paul hunkered down to his son's level. "Some things may be scary, but that won't make them go away. And other things . . . most other things . . . are only scary because you make them scary. You understand?"

The boy nodded. He didn't understand but was as close to it as he would get that night. For the next hour or so, David was content to simply sit outside with his father and watch the stars appear in an ever-darkening sky. He was just starting to nod off when Doc Swenson stepped outside. His nightshirt was tucked sloppily into the trousers he'd thrown on and he wiped his hands dry on a frayed towel.

"She's tuckered out," Swenson reported, "but she'll live."

"Any problems?" Paul asked.

"There may be some sort of aggravation around the wound, but I doubt it's anything serious. Bring her back here in a day or two so I can have a look. As far as the stitches go, she took them better than some grown men I've had in my office."

Paul smiled proudly. "How much do I owe you?"

"We can settle up later. The three of you just got back from a long day's ride and must be ready to fall over."

"I've got the money on me now. If it's all the same to you, I'd like to square up with you and then get some sleep."

Swenson and Paul settled the bill for a small amount of money and the remainder in credit at Meakes Mercantile. Paul carried his daughter to the wagon and into her bed without her waking up for more than a few dreary seconds. David insisted on sleeping on the floor in her room, and Paul had no reason to object. After both children were tucked away, Paul stood outside Abigail's room to watch them for a spell.

When Joanna was alive, she'd been the one to watch the children that way. Paul never saw the sense of it. As long as they were where they should be and not making too much noise, he was satisfied. Even now he looked over them with a steadfast eye to make certain no harm befell them. He lingered because that's where Joanna would have been standing if she was alive.

Right in that very spot.

When he closed his eyes and drew a slow

breath, he could almost smell the sweet, fresh scent of her hair.

CHAPTER 10

The next day, bright and early, Paul and David unloaded the wagon. David went to school as Paul stocked the shelves in his store. When David came back from school, he dallied about as much as he could and then finally helped his father.

They went home. Supper was made, the dishes were cleared away, and the floors were swept. Abigail remained in bed most of that time. Paul brought her some water, made sure she was still breathing well enough and her wounds weren't bleeding, and then let her be. David did some reading. Paul put him to bed and Abigail still slept.

The day after that was much the same, but Paul wasn't content to let his daughter sleep. While David was answering nature's call outside, Paul stood at Abigail's bedside and gave her a shake.

"Come on," he said sharply. "Time to get up."

". . . tired," she groaned.

"I'll bet you are. You slept too much. I shouldn't have let you be so lazy yesterday, but I spoil my little girl. No need to tell you that," he chuckled. "Ain't that right, Dumplin'?"

When she didn't respond to that in any way, Paul knew something was wrong. He dropped to one knee and shifted so he could put his face only a few inches away from hers. "Abigail? Wake up, sweetie."

She stirred. Her eyes shifted beneath their lids. She pulled in a few quick breaths but didn't even try to sit up.

Paul grabbed her shoulders and shook her. "Abigail! Wake up."

Her mouth opened, but all she could get out was a soft, panting groan. Sweat glistened on her brow, and when he felt her skin, Paul's heart skipped a beat.

"What's the matter with you?" he said as a way to air out some of the thoughts racing through his head. "Why are you so damn hot? Can you hear me? Abigail! *Abigail!*"

Her eyes opened, but she seemed to have trouble focusing on any one thing.

Lifting her to a seated position, Paul held her there with one arm behind her back. He used the other hand to force her eyes open so he could get a look at them. Normally such a task was a joy. When he saw barely any recognition from her and plenty of red smeared within the whites of those eyes, he felt anything but happiness.

There was nobody close enough to respond to his voice, so Paul laid her down again before rushing outside. Along the way, he grabbed a cup from the kitchen, which he filled at the pump out back. Paul was in such a hurry that most of the water wound up on the floor or his shirt by the time he made it back to Abigail's side. He set the cup down and dipped a trembling hand into it so he could dab his fingers onto the girl's brow. "Come on, now," he said in a fierce whisper. "Look at me like you used to. Just one look and I'll be happy."

She looked at him weakly, which was just enough to let him know she was still in there somewhere.

"D . . . Daddy?"

"I'm right here. How do you feel?"

"Dizzy."

"You've got a fever," he said while picking up the cup of water and trickling it directly onto her face and neck. "Lie on your side. I'm getting a look at that wound."

"But . . . it doesn't hurt."

"Just sit still." Paul lifted the hem of her nightgown until he could see the fresh bandages wrapped around her upper leg. The dressing wasn't soaked through with blood, which he took as a good sign. After only getting a portion of the bandages off, however, he saw something that wasn't so good.

"Is it all right, Daddy?"

Paul wrapped the bandages loosely in place and pulled down her sleeping dress. "I'm taking you back to Doc Swenson."

"Why?"

"Hopefully it's nothing," he said as he picked her up and headed outside. She didn't seem to hear him very well, which was for the best since Paul scarcely believed what he was telling her anyway.

The expression on Doc Swenson's face was nothing like the one he'd worn a few nights before. Before, he'd been easygoing with just a hint of tiredness showing around his eyes. Now his eyes were sharp as tacks and his scowl dug deep trenches into his forehead. "How long has this been going on?" he asked.

"Has what been going on?" Paul snapped. "I only just noticed."

"The fever, Mr. Meakes. How long has

she had the fever?"

"Since last night."

"And what about the inflammation around her wound?"

"The what?"

Abigail lay on the same bed where she'd received her stitches. This time, however, she was drenched in sweat and growing pale. Paul might have been fretful, but he was thankful when he was dragged out of that room.

"Mr. Meakes," Swenson said as he took Paul through the front door, "please calm down. Your daughter isn't doing very well and you spouting off that way isn't helping."

"I'll calm down," Paul said as he stepped outside the office, "once you tell me what's going on with my little girl."

After closing the door behind them, Doc Swenson said, "I want to check a few things. I'll need to watch her for a while. It would be best if she stayed here with me for a while so I can check in on her whenever necessary. She'll most likely vomit whatever she's been eating. If not, I'll want to try to get her to vomit, so it would be a big help if you could bring me some clothes for her to change into just in case these get too dirty."

Paul started shaking his head, which

didn't help to clear it. Soon the movement only made things worse and he reached for the closest thing that might support his weight. It wasn't until he allowed his head to hang forward that he realized he was looking straight down into a water trough. Watching his own reflection as he spoke, Paul asked, "You know for certain she's going to get worse?"

"I . . . have my suspicions."

"Just a suspicion?"

As if sensing the trace of hope in Paul's voice, the doctor quickly said, "It's a very well-founded suspicion. More of a professional . . ."

"Educated guess?"

"If you like."

"And what's your guess?" Seeing that the doctor was searching for his next words very carefully, Paul said, "Just tell me. It ain't like I could feel much worse."

"I'd rather not." Before Paul could rip into him, Swenson added, "That's just because I'm not completely certain and would hate to get you all worked up over nothing."

"You'd hate to get me worked up?" Paul scoffed. "I'd say that ship has sailed."

"Please. Just give me a bit of time to see a few more things. To be completely honest with you, I shouldn't have even told you as much as I already have for just this particular reason. Acting on a false diagnosis does us as much good as chasing a shadow. Or . . . a dog trying to catch its tail."

"I know what you're trying to say. How much time do you need?"

"Give me a few days," the doctor said.

"Will you know anything by tomorrow?"

"Possibly."

"Then that's when I'm coming back. My little girl is in there," Paul said. "You can't expect me to stay away much longer than that without a damn good explanation."

"The more time I have, the more certain I can be," Swenson said. He then rolled up his sleeves and ran his fingers through his hair like any other man who was about to get to work. "I appreciate the breathing room. Tomorrow I should have something more to tell you."

"You'd better."

CHAPTER 11

It was one of the roughest days Paul had trudged through since Joanna had been in labor with their son. As soon as the midwife had shooed him out of their home, Paul spent the day and a good portion of that night fretting in his store and sweating through his clothes. All he could think about was the pain that had been seared into his beloved's face when he'd been forced to leave and the cries of agony that had filled their home. When Paul was finally brought back to see her, Joanna was spent and David's cries were the only ones to be heard. Even though she'd eventually gotten up and to her feet again, his wife was never the same. She'd left something of herself behind that day that never quite came back again. Not long after that, she was gone for good.

Paul would be damned if he was going to let another loved one wither away like that.

Much like that long day nine years ago,

Paul spent most of it in his store. Part of him was anxious to be told it was all right to return so he could see how his kin was doing. Another part wanted to keep his distance where he was safe from hearing anything at all. Ignorance might not have been bliss, but it allowed him to take a few more breaths before being overwhelmed.

Half an hour after he would normally have gone home, Paul put the sign in his window announcing his store was closed. "To hell with this," he grunted. "I'm going over to that doctor's office whether he likes it or not."

David was nearby and nodded meekly.

Recognizing the sheen of sweat and pale hue to the boy's skin, Paul went over to him and placed a hand on his forehead. "What's the matter with you, son?"

"Nothing. I swear."

"Don't tell me that."

"You don't like it when I say I don't feel good."

Paul winced at that as he recalled several instances when he'd scolded the boy for playing possum just to get out of any number of obligations or chores. "I won't be mad," he assured him. "Just be true."

"I feel dizzy," David said. "And kind of warm."

"You want to go home?"

David nodded, lowered his head, and trudged along beside his father as if it took every bit of his concentration and effort just to keep from stumbling into a post or off the boardwalk completely. Paul kept a hand on his son's shoulder to keep him steady while staring straight at the path in front of him. Every now and then, they would pass a familiar face or get a polite wave from a neighbor, but Paul ignored them. Considering his brusque mannerisms, nobody was particularly surprised by such reactions.

After putting his son to bed, Paul went to Doc Swenson's office. He opened the door, strode inside, and took no notice of the slender woman in her early forties who walked up to greet him.

"Excuse me," she said while trying to step between Paul and the hallway leading to the examination rooms. "What's your business here?"

"Doc!" Paul shouted so he could be heard anywhere within the office or the living space above it. "It's Paul Meakes. I'm here for news about my girl."

Before he could finish that statement, the doctor emerged from the room where Paul had last seen Abigail. "There's no need for raised voices," Swenson said. "Your daughter is resting. I suggest you allow her to do so."

"Is she better?"

"Honestly, it would do everyone the most amount of good if —"

"Don't try to appease me and don't try to chase me away," Paul warned. "I gave you time to do your doctoring, so tell me what you learned or I'll take her to someone who can."

"She shouldn't be moved."

"Why?" Paul asked. His question fell upon deaf ears because the doctor had already taken notice of David and was crouching down to place his hands on the boy's face. Paul placed a hand on Swenson's shoulder and pulled him back. "Answer my question, damn it."

"I need to keep a close eye on her. The boy too."

"Tell me what's wrong with them."

"Please, just bring him in here. I'd like to take a look at him. I'm concerned about something."

"You're concerned?" Paul said in an exasperated tone of voice. "What do you think you're doing to me?"

The doctor placed a hand on his shoulder and spoke in a low but steady tone. "Paul, it won't do any good if I tell you something

107

about the well-being of your children unless I know exactly what's going on with them. And I won't know what's going on with them until I can get a look at both of them. Right now."

No matter how much Paul wanted to stand his ground and demand his answers right then and there, he recognized the truth in Swenson's words as well as the determination in the doctor's eyes. Whatever was wrong with Abigail and David, Swenson wanted to uncover it just as much as he did.

"All right, then," Paul said grudgingly. "I'll fetch David so you can have your look. But after that, whether you find what you're after or not, I want to know what the hell is happening here."

"Agreed. Now please . . ." Swenson said as he stepped aside and motioned Paul toward the door.

Paul marched outside, thumping his boots against the ground with every step, but David wasn't where he'd left him. "David!" he called out. "Come over here this instant."

Still, he got no response.

When Paul got home and still couldn't find his son, he nearly threw a fit. His next stop was the store, where he found David tucked away in the corner with all of the books. "Come along with me," Paul said.

"Where are we going?"

"Can't you just mind what I say?"

Hanging his head, David trudged over to his father. After they'd walked a short way from the store, Paul told him, "We're going back to Doc Swenson's."

David perked up immediately. "To visit Abby?"

"We can check in on her, but that's not why we're going. The doc wants to get a look at you."

"Will it hurt?"

"Why would it hurt?"

"I don't know."

"Stop fretting," Paul snapped. "Do what you're told and don't talk back. If the doc tells you to do something, no matter what it is, you do it. Understand?"

"Yes, Pa."

After a few more steps, Paul picked up the boy and carried him. David was too big to be carried that way for long, but he relished every moment. "You know I'm only doing this for your own good, right?"

"Yes, Pa."

"Everything's gonna be all right. I promise."

David smiled and rested his head on Paul's shoulder. It wasn't a long walk to the doctor's office and Paul wasn't anxious for it to end. When it did, he set the boy down and led him inside.

"There he is!" Swenson said as though Paul had been gone for the better part of a week. "Come over here and let me get a look at you!"

When David looked up to him, Paul gave him a little push. "Go on, now," he said. "And remember what I told you."

"I will," David sighed.

The doctor placed a hand on the boy's back so he could steer him down the hall to the room directly across from Abigail's. Once they were inside, the door was shut.

Feeling somewhat abandoned, Paul stood near the front door for a minute or two. He checked his watch, paced for a few minutes, and finally picked a chair to sit in. After settling in for all of four minutes, he checked his watch again and crossed his legs in the opposite direction. His eyes wandered around the office walls, where he found cracks that needed to be repaired, spots where termites were going to be a problem, and a few stains marking points where water had dripped in after a hard rain.

When a wind blew, Paul could feel the slightest trickle of cool air that had snuck in through a warped window frame or a door that hadn't been cut to fit precisely within its jamb. All the while, he heard the muffled voices of his son and the doctor as Swenson checked whatever it was he needed to check. Once boredom left him, anger began taking hold within Paul's idle mind.

That doctor was being paid by Paul for a service and Paul had every right to know what was happening. If he wanted to storm into whatever room Swenson was using, he'd paid for the privilege.

The more Paul thought along those lines, the more convinced he became that he was absolutely right. When he got to his feet, eyes set firmly upon his target, he was ready to barge into the examination room and be heard. A second later, he worried about what he might hear. A few seconds after that, Paul sat down to once again brood in silence.

As soon as he resigned himself once again to waiting, Paul heard one of the doors down the hall open. Instead of his daughter walking on her own accord to pay him a visit, Paul saw Doc Swenson walk down the hall toward him. The expression on the doctor's face was near unreadable.

Walking straight past the chair where Paul was seated, Swenson said, "Let's get a bit of fresh air, shall we?"

Paul stood up and followed the doctor

through the front door to the porch in front of the office. Once there, the doctor removed a dented cigarette case from his pocket and opened it. "Care for one?" he asked while offering the case to Paul.

"Thank you, no," Paul replied.

"I'm sorry to keep you waiting so long, but I appreciate your patience."

"To be honest, that patience is running a bit thin."

"Can't say as I blame you. If they were my children, I'd be champing at the bit to hear something one way or the other."

"You got that right."

The tip of Swenson's cigarette flared as he pulled in a long breath. The tobacco, although of a high quality, didn't do much to soothe him. Finally he flicked some ash to the ground and said, "I don't know a good way to tell you this, Paul, so I'll just come out with it."

Part of Paul was glad to hear that and the other part just wanted to pretend there was no news to be told. "What is it, Doc?" he asked, even though the part of him that didn't want to know was growing by the second.

Despite his recent promise to do otherwise, the doctor took a moment before saying another word. After steeling himself, he straightened up and looked Paul squarely in the eye. "They're poisoned."

"Wh . . . what?"

"That wound of Abigail's shouldn't be as bad as it is right now. It was properly cared for as near as I can tell and I've seen plenty of wounds like it. The stitches were a simple affair and wouldn't explain the symptoms that have cropped up since then."

"What symptoms?"

"Her fever," Swenson replied while ticking them off on his fingers. "Her dizziness. The way she drifts in and out of consciousness. Her sweating. Her shaking. It took a short while for me to know for certain, but I was able to narrow my choices. Now that I can see the condition of the wound, I have a better idea of what we're dealing with."

Paul shook his head as if he could somehow rid himself of what he'd just heard. "I want to see her. Take me to my little girl."

"Of course."

Swenson led him to Abigail's room. She was sitting up, which was better than the last time he'd seen her. Unfortunately the pallor of her skin and the vacant look in her eyes were much worse. Forcing a smile onto his face, Paul sat on the edge of her bed and stroked the side of her head. Her hair was drenched in cold sweat. "How you feeling, Dumplin'?"

"Is that you, Daddy?" she asked while looking around as if Paul were nothing more than a ghost.

"Course it is. Who else would it be?" Since she didn't seem willing or able to answer that one, Paul posed another question to her. "Can you hear me?"

"Yes."

"Do you feel sick?"

"Like before . . . but worse."

When Paul felt a hand on his shoulder, he looked back to see Swenson motioning for him to leave the room. Paul nodded and said, "I just want to see your leg, honey. Is that all right?"

Too tired to speak, Abigail nodded.

Her sheets and blanket had already been folded down, leaving only an oversized nightgown to cover her. Paul eased the hem up just enough to see his daughter's wounded leg. The stitches still looked fine, but the skin surrounding the entrance and exit wounds was inflamed and shot through with dark jagged lines.

"How does it look, Daddy?"

"Fine," Paul said as he quickly pulled the nightgown back into place. "It looks fine. You're gonna be fine. I promise."

That was good enough for her and she

114

closed her eyes to get some semblance of rest.

After leaving the room and shutting the door, Paul faced the doctor and asked, "What did you mean when you said *they'd* been poisoned? Was that just a slip of the tongue?"

"I'm afraid not. Your son is displaying some of the same symptoms, but in earlier stages. It looks to me as if he'll be in the same boat as Abigail before much longer."

"What could have done this?"

They stood in the hallway when Dr. Swenson said, "You mentioned Abigail getting shot by an arrow."

"That's right. The raiders were Comanche."

"Are you certain of that?"

"As certain as I can be," Paul replied. "I've seen a good number of Indians, but I'm no expert. Why?"

"Because the braves of some tribes have been known to dip their arrowheads in poison. Sometimes it's to help bring down a large or particularly aggressive animal, but mostly it's to help tip the scales in their favor when they're out to hunt creatures of a two-legged variety."

Thinking back to the day when those Comanches had ridden through the trading post, Paul gritted his teeth and clenched his fists. "Damn. I thought them raiders were just out to do some damage."

Dr. Swenson slowly shook his head. "The army has been stepping up their efforts to eradicate the tribes all throughout the country. Perhaps those tribes have stepped up their efforts to fight back as well. There's one way for me to be absolutely certain."

"What?" Paul snapped. "Tell me. What is it?"

"If I could get a look at that arrow . . ."

Paul spun around and nearly busted the door behind him off its hinges in his haste to get through it and into the room where his boy had been taken. As soon as he saw his father, David hopped off the cot where he'd been sitting. A second later, after seeing the expression on Paul's face, the boy shrank back.

"You pulled the arrow out of your sister. Is that right?"

"Yes, Pa," David said proudly.

"What did you do with it?"

"I got rid of it."

"Why?" Paul groaned without truly expecting an answer.

"Because," the boy replied. "It was scary."

When Paul's hands clenched once again into fists, his fingernails fit into the grooves he'd already dug into his palms. Perhaps sensing how frayed Paul was feeling at that moment, the doctor stepped forward and asked, "Do you recall what it looked like, David?"

"It was . . . an arrow."

"What about the arrowhead? The tip. Was it a strange color or was there something on it?"

David nodded. "There was! Abby's blood was on it. Does that help?"

"Forget him, Doctor," Paul said through clenched teeth. "He's useless. What else can I do to help?"

"Think, David," Swenson pressed. "What did you do with that arrow? It's very important."

The boy closed his eyes. Tears welled in them, seemingly wrung out of his nervous little body the harder he tried to appease the adults in that room with him. "After I pulled it out, I tossed it away. That's it."

"Did anyone else come to collect it?"

He nodded slowly at first but quickly built up a head of steam before snapping his eyes open and looking back and forth between the two adults waiting for him to speak. "Someone did collect it! One of the ladies who works there. The one that showed me and Abby where to hide."

"The one who served our food?" Paul asked.

"Yes!"

"What did she do with the arrow, son?"

"I don't know. She just came to take it away. Does that help?"

Since Paul was slow to answer, the doctor rubbed the top of David's head and told him, "Yes, my boy. That's very helpful."

Swenson could have stood there tousling the boy's hair all day long and he wouldn't have drawn David's full attention. The boy was staring at his father, all but crawling for Paul's approval.

"Stay here and rest," Paul said. "Me and the doc have to talk."

"Yes, Pa. I will." David practically threw himself back onto the cot as if that act alone was enough to set everything right again.

Paul couldn't get outside fast enough. Even after leaving the office, he continued walking for several more paces and stopped just shy of stepping in front of an oncoming wagon being pulled down the street. He turned around as Dr. Swenson closed in on him.

"You need to sit down," Swenson said. "You're not looking so good."

"Yeah? Well, my children look even worse. I can't abide by that for one more moment."

"What your children need is for their father to care for them properly."

Scowling at the tone in the other man's voice, Paul said, "The best way for me to do that is to see that they're tended to by someone that can get them well again."

"I know you're upset, Paul. It would be most helpful to show a brave . . . and kinder . . . face to those children. Especially David."

This wasn't the first time he'd ever thought about that. Unfortunately he came up just as short on solutions now as he always did. When that happened, his only recourse was to devote himself to something he could more easily wrap his head around. "What do you need to make them better, Doc? Just tell me that much."

Dr. Swenson sighed as if he'd chosen this moment to let himself feel the fatigue that had been building over the last several hours. "What I really need is that arrow."

"Can't you just treat the poison?"

"I could if I knew what sort of poison it was. There's snake venoms, plant oils, herbal toxins, fungus, as well as any number of chemical mixtures. Considering the source and symptoms I've seen, I can narrow the field somewhat. Still, if I administer the wrong treatment, there's a chance that I could only make things worse. If I had the arrow, I could figure out what those children were poisoned with."

Paul had to fight to keep himself from being overcome with rage. "Why would a bunch of savages want to poison innocent children?"

"Sounds like they were just shooting into windows. Most likely, they were trying to cause damage and mayhem as a way to lash out for whatever injustices they think were set against them."

"Injustices are one thing. This is just . . . evil."

"To them and to the cavalry soldiers riding the plains, this is war. War, in itself, is evil. I've heard tell of the army setting the torch to entire Cherokee villages. In return, the tribe sends its braves to ride through a town and fire burning arrows into any building they see. Some tribes were infected with diseases passed on in any number of ways, so this could be a way to answer back to that. Nothing in war stands up to reason," Swenson concluded. "It's all terrible. Just . . . terrible."

No explanation would have appeased Paul's anger. Since dwelling on the subject only stoked his flames that much higher, he forced himself away from the whys. Whys never helped anyone, even when they made perfect sense. He knew why his Joanna had been taken from him, but it didn't make the space on the bed next to him any warmer at night.

"So I'll go get that arrow," Paul announced.

"How? The boy said it was tossed away."

"I'll ride back to that trading post. Someone may have kept it after all. Or maybe if it was thrown onto a heap somewhere, I can look through that heap to find what I'm after."

"Or it could just be lost," Swenson pointed out.

"Either way, I'll be doing more good there than here."

"That's not necessarily true. Those children can use all the care they can get."

"All of that caring and tenderness was never my strong suit, Doc. If there's even the slightest chance I can find that arrow and bring it back, I will. How much time do I have?"

The doctor rubbed his ear before saying, "They're not in any mortal danger right now, but that could change. I'd hate to have you gone if —"

"A week," Paul cut in. "I've got that much time at least?"

"I'd say so, for certain. But that doesn't mean their condition won't change. I don't know what I'm dealing with, exactly, so they might get worse in a few days. Or hours."

"Then I'll just have to ride as quickly as I can."

Chapter 12

Unlike the other times when he had business to conduct, Paul didn't put much thought into what he might need for the ride to the trading post. He had nothing to sell, nothing to buy, and no haggling to plan. He didn't even need to worry about a team to hitch to his wagon. All he did was saddle up the youngest of his horses, toss a few supplies into his bags, and check the sky to see how much light remained. The sun was already dipping below the western horizon, which meant he should put his journey off until tomorrow. But Paul didn't have that kind of patience and he decided to get as far as he could in whatever portion of the day was left.

He had one foot in the stirrups when he paused and checked something else. The old Schofield was in the house. Even though he rarely put the pistol to much use, his hip felt bare without it. Not wanting to squander his time, he hurried into the house, grabbed the gun belt, and strapped it around his waist. There were a few extra bullets in a drawer, which he collected on his way out. He also stuffed some money into his pocket without counting what he had and hurried outside to climb into his saddle. He then snapped his reins and headed out of Keystone Pass.

Paul rode over terrain that he knew so well after having covered it so many times before. As the sun dropped lower, he barely took notice. When night truly fell, he pulled back on his reins and rode a bit farther at a slower pace. He pressed on even when it seemed dangerous to do so. Some bit of light was cast from the moon and stars, but not nearly enough for any man to see the bumps, ditches, half-buried stones, or any number of other dangers that could end a ride on a bad note.

Only when it was absolutely necessary did Paul stop riding and make camp. He knew where a watering hole was without having to see it. Even though his horse and his own body were grateful for the rest, his heart ached at having to stop when his children's suffering went on.

He slept fretfully.

The following morning, he awoke early.

He stretched his back, saddled his horse, and rode on.

The sky would have been a beautiful sight to anyone willing to see it. Paul wasn't one of those men, so the warm reds and brilliant yellows above him passed unnoticed into more common whites and blue. His destination wasn't much farther, so he tapped his heels against his horse's sides to get there as quickly as possible.

At that time of day, the trading post was busy. In fact, it was busier than normal as Paul rode up to Trace's store, climbed down from his saddle, and tied his horse to the closest hitching post. The folks who were walking in or out of the largest store or simply lingering outside it looked to him with a friendly greeting in their eyes. As soon as they saw the grave purpose etched into Paul's features, however, they kept quiet and cleared a path for him.

The store was much improved over the last time he'd been there. Trace had even found inventory to restock a good number of his shelves that had been emptied by the rampaging Comanche. Surely there had been plenty of worse Indian attacks, but nobody could have convinced Paul of that.

"Well, now!" Dorothy said cheerily from the dining room, where she was tending to a few tables. "If it isn't our favorite customer. In case any of you folks don't know, this man stood tall when those savages tore through here and helped drive them away."

Most of the customers showed Paul impressed smiles and the rest were too busy eating to pay him any mind. Paul ignored all of them as he walked straight up to Dorothy and said, "I need a word."

"Of course. What is it?"

"Not here."

Realizing his visit wasn't purely social or even of the normal variety, she cleaned her hands on the front of her apron and nodded. "Come with me back to the kitchen."

He followed her while his head was flooded with unwanted memories sparked by the most common sights and sounds around him. Even familiar smells jabbed at him like rusty nails poking an open sore.

"You look spooked, Paul," Dorothy said. "Are your young ones all right?"

"The doctor says they were poisoned by the arrow that was fired into the store."

Her eyes widened. "Good Lord. But . . . I thought only your girl was hurt."

"She was, but David cut his hand on the arrowhead when he pulled it out of her."

"That's right!" she gasped. "Oh, that's terrible."

"The reason I came back here was to retrieve that arrow," Paul said. "Any chance it's still around here somewhere?"

"I know I haven't seen it. Let me get Trace. He'd know where to look." She turned away from him and walked all of ten paces to the very back of the kitchen, where she found the owner of the store stocking supplies. Explaining the situation to him while all but dragging Trace to where Paul was waiting, Dorothy was out of breath by the time she'd finished.

"They was shooting poisoned arrows at us?" Trace asked.

Paul's voice was terse as he replied, "Apparently so."

Trace's eyes darted to and fro as if he was reliving every second of the raid. "That means . . . we could've all been killed!"

"But you're not even hurt. My David and Abigail are the ones still in danger while the lot of you celebrate like we won a war the day them Indians rode through this place. Now just tell me where to find that damn arrow so I can be on my way!"

"You mean . . . the arrow that hurt your little girl?"

"What other arrow would I want?" Paul said angrily.

"I suppose it don't matter much since I

got rid of them all."

Cocking his head to one side, Paul stepped up close to the store owner. "Got rid of them . . . where?"

"Out back. I . . ."

Paul turned his back on the other man and left the kitchen in a rush. He felt at least half a dozen emotions course through his body, and every last one of them was powerful enough to set his head to spinning. Somehow he made it outside and around to the back of the store before he lost control altogether. Now that he had something to focus on, he collected himself and put his mind squarely to the task at hand.

Behind the store were a few sheds, a short row of outhouses, a corral, and a livery stable. Ignoring the outhouses, Paul started his search at the closest shed. It wasn't long that he regretted charging outside before getting just a bit more direction from the folks who knew where he should look. The first shed was partly filled with shipping crates. The next had tools used for keeping the grounds and buildings. The third was locked.

"Paul, hold on just a moment," Trace said as he approached.

Still tugging on the door to the third shed,

Paul said, "This one's locked. Is this where you put that arrow?"

"You didn't let me finish."

"You're right. Sorry. I've been burning the candle at both ends, driving myself insane ever since my children fell ill. Pile on top of that a lack of sleep and hardly anything to eat and I'm not exactly thinking straight."

"It's understandable," Trace said. Although he seemed somewhat relieved to hear Paul speaking in something closer to a normal tone, he was still uneasy about something. "That arrow . . . there were several of them, actually."

"Great! That'll make the doctor's job even easier."

"You've got to understand. I . . . that is, I didn't . . ."

The purposeful scowl returned to Paul's face, and his voice seemed even more ominous when his hand drifted toward the gun hanging at his side. "I've had my fill of you, mister. Show me where you put them arrows right now or so help me, I'll make you wish them savages had put you in the ground when they rode through here."

"You see . . . I really can't . . ."

Paul's hand closed around the grip of his pistol. "I don't wanna hear nothing about *can't* right now, Trace."

"I need to tell you —"

"Just take me to where you dumped that arrow. Right now."

The tone he'd used was the same as the one that could be heard in Paul's voice when he'd reached his limit with one of the children, and it appeared to have as good an effect on Trace as it did on Abigail and David.

Since he couldn't spit out a complete sentence anyway, Trace flapped his arms in exasperation and stomped past Paul on his way to the livery stable. Rather than go inside the dusty little structure, Trace walked around to the lot behind it. There wasn't much to be found there apart from a stack of ripped burlap sacks, some busted crates, and a pit of blackened trash.

"Here you go," Trace said. "I tried to warn you, but . . . see for yourself."

Paul stepped over to the crates.

"Not there," Trace said.

"I'm not in the mood for guessing games. Just tell me."

"I'm pointing right at it if you'd just stop barking at me and listen to what I'm trying to say!"

Although Paul did see Trace pointing, he hadn't paid it much mind because the store owner's finger was jabbing at the dark spot on the ground instead of anywhere the arrow could have been kept. Unless, of course . . . "You buried it?" he asked.

"No. I burned it. Burned all of them that were left behind."

Paul's entire body slumped forward until he had to use one arm to prop himself up against the stack of crates.

CHAPTER 13

"Why would you do that?" Paul moaned.

Confused eyes darting back and forth, Trace asked, "Do what? Burn the arrows?"

Suddenly Paul sprang back to life. Where he'd slumped before, he now stood taller than ever so he could grab the front of Trace's shirt. "Yes," he snarled. "Why would you burn them?"

"Why would I keep them? Any of us could have been killed by those very arrows. Why would I want to keep a reminder of that around? To sell them as bloody trinkets like some kind of ghoul?"

Ghouls of that sort had occasionally come to Paul's store selling all kinds of horrific wares. Arrowheads were the least of them. Among the samples were bullet casings from battlefields, knives supposedly taken from dead soldiers, pistols pried from the lifeless hands of outlaws, as well as count-less other mementos from another soul's worst day. Paul had taken great pleasure in showing those salesmen to the street, and so, reluctantly, he let go of Trace.

Tugging at his clothes to remove some of the rumples, Trace said, "I'm sorry, Paul. I tried to tell you."

"I know you did."

"After the way I behaved when the attack happened, I thought I was doing the proper thing by wiping away anything those savages left behind. After all, that's why they came through here. To make us afraid. Leave their mark."

"Yeah."

Trace snapped his fingers. "Maybe there's hope!"

Although he waited to see what Trace had in mind, hope was the furthest thing from Paul's troubled mind.

Grunting as he lowered himself to his knees, Trace stuck his fingers deep into the pile of soil and ash. "I set the fire myself. It was hot, but not hot enough to melt rock. I imagine them arrowheads are still in here somewhere."

Paul dropped to one knee so he could dig as well. At first, all he felt was dry dirt, soft ash, and sharp wooden splinters. After pushing down a little deeper, his fingers scraped against something with a bit more substance. Judging by the expression on Trace's face, he'd made a similar discovery.

"I was right!" Trace declared. He then pulled his hand from the ground to get a look at his prize.

Paul did the same. Sure enough, he held a deadly sculpture of stone that had been chipped into an all-too-familiar shape. His son had found a few of these as well when digging through other mounds of dirt over the years, and his smile wasn't much different from Trace's.

"I think this might be just what you need," Trace said in between blowing on the arrowhead to clean it off.

The arrowhead in Paul's hand was filthy. He blew on it once before using his hand to brush off the chunks of dirt clinging to it and ash that remained stubbornly smeared onto its surface. Soon he felt something bite into his finger. When Paul looked at his hand, he saw a thin cut running across his first three fingers.

"Watch yourself," Trace said. "They're sharp."

"Yeah," Paul grunted as he thought about a similar cut on his boy's hand. "I know."

"This one here's in pretty good shape. It's charred and all, but with a bit of cleaning it could be as good as new."

"This one looks about the same."

"Then why don't you seem very pleased about it?" Trace asked. "Isn't this what you were after?"

"Only partly. Any one of these could be the thing that harmed my little ones, but . . ."

"Take them all!" Trace insisted. "Please."

Paul shook his head even as he brought his find up to within an inch of his eyes for a closer look. "The thing is, I needed the poison on the arrowhead more than the thing itself. If the rest buried here are anything like these two, they've been burned clean and wiping them off will only finish the job."

"Then don't wipe them off. Paul, just take them. We'll dig up the rest and you take them back to the doctor so he can do . . . whatever he does. Neither one of us is a doctor, so we can't begin to guess what that may be. Just do your part and let me help you however I can!"

"Don't fret about this, Trace. There was no way you could have known to save one of these damn things in pristine condition. I would've gotten rid of them as well if it was my store that had been attacked."

"But . . . after the way I acted when it happened." Trace lowered his eyes. "If I would have done something different other than act like a coward, this whole mess may have been different."

"May have," Paul said. "Lots of things *may have* been different, but most likely they would have been pretty much the same. From everything I heard, there wasn't much you could have done where my young ones were concerned."

"I know, but —"

"Just stop. Things could have been a lot worse. They may have been downright terrible if we'd put up more of a fight. Them Comanches were already on their way out, and standing up to them more than we did would probably have just forced them into a corner. You and I both know that ain't a smart thing to do."

"I guess so."

Paul closed his hand around the arrowhead. When he felt the sharpened edge touch his palm, he was tempted to grip even tighter so the chipped stone would cut him good and deep. If he couldn't help his children, it only seemed right for him to share their fate.

Before following through on such a desperate notion, Paul blinked his eyes and loosened his grip. "Guess I'll take these back to Doc Swenson just like you said."

Trace extended his hand to offer over the arrowhead he'd uncovered. Just as Paul was about to take it from him, Trace snatched it back. "I just thought of something! Well, two things actually."

"What?"

"First of all, come with me to the pump," Trace said as he jumped to his feet. "You were scratched by one of them arrowheads that are supposed to be poisoned. You'll wash off that hand right now."

"It ain't that deep," Paul said as he stood up. "The poison has probably been burned off anyhow."

"Be that as it may, it doesn't serve you to take any chances. Come along with me. I won't hear another word about it."

Having seen as much of the charred spot on the ground as he could stomach, Paul followed the other man over to the water pump directly behind the largest store at the trading post. He went through the motions of working the pump's handle and then moving his hands beneath the chilly trickle of water that came from the spigot. The water felt good but didn't offer much comfort. "What was the second thing you thought of?" he asked.

"This here arrowhead," Trace said as he washed it off beneath the water once Paul was through. "It's Comanche and so are the men who fired them."

"We already knew that."

"Exactly. So if you're in the market for something and you've plumb run out at your regular supplier, the trail doesn't just go cold. We're businessmen, Paul. More than that, we're store owners! If you needed something that you thought I could supply, only to find out that I didn't have it any-more . . . what would you do?"

"Take what I could and make the best of it," Paul sighed. "We already spoke about that too."

"No! You'd go to another supplier!"

"I should ride around looking for other spots those Comanches have attacked and hope someone there saved an arrow or two?"

"Granted, that was the next thing I thought as well," Trace admitted. "But that would take too long and there's no guaran-tee of success. The only guaranteed place you'll find some of that poison you need is at the source!"

Paul furrowed his brow. "You mean the Comanches themselves?"

"Yep. That is, unless you know someone else that might be mixing up a batch of ar-row toxin."

"Why would they want to help me?"

"I know of two villages not far from here where a good number of Comanches have made their home," Trace explained. "I've dealt with folks from both of them settlements on a few occasions and have found them to be accommodating if not altogether friendly."

"That's not how I would describe the men that attacked this place," Paul said.

"Right. So if you go to one of those camps and it looks like they're on the warpath, move along to the next one. If the other one looks the same or worse, come back here and we'll come up with something else. While you're riding, ask anyone you find if they were attacked and if they know anything about that poison. Not every Comanche is bloodthirsty. Plenty of them will want to help save a child's life."

"Sounds like a whole lot of riding."

"You got anyplace better to be?" Trace asked with a smirk on his face.

"If my children are hurting, I should be with them!"

"But if you can help them —"

"I know," Paul snapped. "I just don't want to waste time when there may be precious little of it."

"Do you really think this would be a waste

of time?"

"My head's been racing for so long I barely know what to think anymore. I've given up on trusting the first thing that comes to mind."

Trace patted Paul's back. "You're in over your head. Any man raising young ones without a woman to lend a hand would know how that feels. So don't trust the first thing that comes to mind. This came to my mind and I think it's your best shot. Why ask a doctor to make sense out of something he scrapes off an arrowhead when you could just hand him a portion of the poison itself?"

"But if I'm wrong in going, it may cost me time with my children."

"So . . . they're dying?"

"Could be," Paul said.

"They're with a doctor who's doing everything he can for them. You took the job of getting some of that poison to make his job easier. If you gave up before trying every last way you could to get that job done, you'd regret it your whole life. How costly do you think that would be?"

As Paul's thoughts settled in his mind like so much swirling grit in a pond full of restless fish, he saw the sense in what he was being told. In fact, the truth of what Trace was telling him was so evident that Paul felt like a fool for not jumping at the idea right away. Perhaps sensing that, Trace said, "You're tired. Maybe it would be best if you got some rest."

"No. I'll go now. Thanks for pointing me in the right direction."

"I've got to do more than point you. I need to draw a map. I'll also have Dorothy put together some supplies for your trip. That'll take a bit of time, so do yourself a favor and stretch out while we work." Before Paul could protest, Trace added, "It's either that or make yourself a nuisance by getting underfoot the whole time."

"You made your point. I'll be over by my horse when you're finished. And, Trace?"

"Yeah?"

"I'm much obliged to you."

Trace shook his head and walked back to his store.

As soon as he found a tree near his horse, Paul sat against it, stretched out his legs, and took a few moments to check for holes in his eyelids.

CHAPTER 14

What had been intended as a short nap turned into something a bit longer. When Paul was awakened by the thump of Trace's foot against his side, the sun was noticeably higher than it had been before. Although there were some kinks in his joints and back after napping in something other than a bed, Paul was grateful for the reprieve. "How long was I asleep?" he asked.

"Not long enough, by the looks of you," Trace said. "Dorothy wanted to leave you be for a while longer, but I knew you'd be wanting to move along as soon as possible."

"Appreciate it."

"You'll appreciate this even more," Trace said as he handed over a folded piece of paper.

Paul took the paper and unfolded it. Apart from the writing on its surface, he quickly noticed the small amount of money tucked into the crease. "What's this for?" he asked.

"A small fund to keep you moving along."

"That's not —"

"Keep it," Trace said quickly. "It's not charity and it's not a gift. Believe it or not, you're not the only one concerned about those children of yours. That money and that map is me and Dorothy's way of helping them get well. If there's any cash left when you're through, pay me back the next time you come here with business to conduct."

Although he felt peculiar about taking a handout from anyone, Paul knew that arguing with Trace would only take up more precious time. So he closed his hand around the money, tucked it away, and took a look at the map that had been drawn for him. "There's three spots marked here," he said. "I thought you only knew of two Comanche villages."

"I do. Dorothy came up with the third. She was just there about a week ago to buy some blankets and such. There weren't any hostilities that she noticed, so you might want to start with that one."

"What about the other two? Any one of them more hostile than the rest?"

"Neither one of them was hostile the last time I saw them," Trace said. "Then again, it's been a good long while since I've been out that way. The best advice I can give you is to be careful no matter where you go. Do you have a pair of field glasses?"

"No."

Trace held up a finger as if he were telling a young boy to stay put. Paul followed the order he'd been given as the store owner turned on his heel and raced back to the main building. Preparing his horse for the ride didn't take long, and before he could climb into the saddle, Paul saw Trace rush back over to him.

"Here," Trace said while handing over a set of field glasses, "take these."

"But these are expensive! I know that for a fact."

"Don't be so full of yourself. I'm not giving them away. I *know* how much they cost. I already feel bad enough that those two children got hurt on my property, so the least I can do is look after the man trying to help them. The best way to keep him safe is to let him get a look at them Comanche villages without getting too close."

"And what happens when I find a village that may have that poison?" Paul asked. "I'll have to get pretty close to get my hands on some of it."

"Could be that one of those chiefs may hand over some of it just to be helpful. Most of them Indians have struck me as good enough souls. If those raiders were just a couple of rogues, there's no reason someone else might want to keep a few innocent children alive. And if they're not feeling overly generous, I'd imagine someone could be convinced to part with some of what you need for a bit of that money you're carrying. You and I have been in business long enough to know that just about everything under the sun has a price tag on it."

Paul couldn't help cracking a smile. "I'm worried about retrieving a poison-tipped arrow from a group of marauding Comanches and you're spouting off about sales practices? That's a bit of a reach — don't you think?"

Shrugging, Trace replied, "It's the best I can come up with. Truth be told, you're doing something I'd never have the courage to do. I can tell you where to find some Comanches around here, give you a few ideas of how to approach the problem, and supply some tools for the job, but that's about it. Wish I could do more."

"You've done plenty." Paul drew a sharp breath and let it out as if he were snuffing out a candle. "Now it's time for me to keep doing my part. I've already talked enough about wasting time, so all that's left is to stop wasting it. I'll take the field glasses and I'll bring them back to you. If they're in any worse condition than they are right now, you'll charge me the difference."

"Of course I will! What kind of business-man do you take me for?"

"You're a good one . . . and a better friend."

When Paul stuck out his hand to be shaken, he was nearly knocked off his feet by an enthusiastic bear hug from Trace.

"Be sure to let me know what happens," Trace said in a voice that was muffled by the hug. "Both to you and your young ones."

"I will. Now you'd best let me go while I have enough wind in my sails to keep moving."

CHAPTER 15

According to the map he'd been given, the first village was less than a day's ride away. Paul pushed his horse to the limit for as long as he dared to make the trip with as much time to spare as possible. While his efforts might have shaved some time off the ride, getting lost amid a tangle of crossing trails didn't help him one bit. Actually calling the barely visible ruts in the ground *trails* was being mighty generous. As the sunlight began to fade, Paul found it next to impossible to follow one for very long before he lost it and was diverted to another. Thanks to either a keen sense of direction or a good dose of pure luck, he found the rock formation marked on the map and the hills just beyond it.

In a matter of minutes, there would be no sunlight left. Rather than race ahead while he could still see the path in front of him, Paul dismounted and led his horse by the reins toward the village. He kept his eyes peeled for any sign of another rider, a wandering child, a woman walking home after washing some clothes, or anyone else from the village who might alert the others to his presence.

He found no one.

The hills he'd been looking for were so slight that he barely knew he'd been climbing them until he saw teepees scattered on the ground at the bottom of a gradual incline less than a hundred yards away. Paul dropped to one knee as his heart thudded in his chest. He'd already been carrying the field glasses in one hand, but he still had to fumble to get them to his eyes so he could look through them. Unfortunately, in the growing darkness, all he could see through the lenses was even more darkness.

He cursed under his breath and then winced at the sound he'd just made. Hunkering down even more, Paul stared at the village below while straining to force his eyes to acclimate even quicker to the darkness. Just as he was trying to think of another way to hide himself from anyone in the teepees below, Paul felt a tug from the reins gripped in his other hand. He let out a breath and swore one more time. Since he'd somehow forgotten that his horse was standing tall at the top of the hill while he did his level best to keep from being seen, Paul gave his knees a rest and stood up as well.

"So much for trying to sneak anywhere," he grumbled. Turning to the horse, he patted the animal's nose and said, "Next time, remind me to tie you off somewhere before I make an ass out of myself . . . again."

The horse had nothing to say to that.

Paul felt a measure of relief that he'd botched his attempt at stealth so completely. At least the pressure was off so he could walk into the village like a normal person. After putting away the field glasses and double-checking that his Schofield was loaded, he did just that.

The walk was much easier than the last portion of his ride had been. Not only was he better able to see anything that may be in his way, but his eyes became fully accustomed to the thick blanket of shadow settling over the Colorado landscape. Another factor allowing him to breathe easier was that he no longer had to worry about trying to sneak past any number of eyes that knew every bump and slope surrounding the village. That ship had already sailed, so Paul could just make the rest of the walk at his own pace.

For a while, he thought the Comanches in the village were too busy laughing at him to do anything else. Nobody came to meet him and nobody made their presence known. When he got within twenty yards of the village's perimeter, Paul grew nervous again. He still saw no movement, which could very well mean that someone was coming up behind him with knife drawn or taking aim at him with a bow from a distance. Since there wasn't much to be done about it now and nowhere for him to hide, Paul kept walking.

When he approached the closest teepee without seeing the first hint of life, Paul's hand found its way nervously to his Schofield. He stopped in his tracks and took a moment to look for anyone in the vicinity.

The longer he looked at the darkened teepees, the more they blended in with the surrounding landscape until his eyes could hardly pick them out anymore. Not a single fire crackled within the settlement, and the only movement to be heard was the occasional scrape of Paul's horse's hooves against the ground as the animal shifted its weight.

"Hello?" Paul called out.

His voice was swallowed up by the night like water that had been spilled from a canteen onto a cracked desert floor. Of all the different possibilities racing through his mind on his way to the village in regards to what would be waiting for him, this wasn't one of them. Paul had considered being captured by braves, embraced by a benevolent chief, or haggling with a reluctant trader. Faced with a fat load of nothing, he found himself at a loss.

"Anyone here?"

Since his words had the same effect as his previous ones, Paul felt almost as foolish as he had when trying to sneak up to the village with a horse ambling along behind him. He didn't know what else to do, so he approached one of the smaller teepees and pulled back the flap covering its entrance.

The pointed tent was empty.

The one beside it was empty as well.

One by one, Paul checked the teepees. There were fewer than a dozen of them, so it wasn't a very big job. Although it was too dark to see every last detail, there was no mistaking the hollow rustle of tanned skins wrapped around nothing but cold air and dirt.

By the time he reached the other side of the settlement, Paul was even more confused than when he'd arrived. Having a group of Comanches move on from one spot to another wasn't anything extraordinary, but he was fairly certain they would have taken their village with them. Also, this was supposed to have been the place that Dorothy had visited a week before.

"I suppose this isn't necessarily a bad thing," Paul said to his horse as a way to fill the eerie silence that had wrapped around him like a cloak. "Mark one place off the list and move on to the next."

Even though he had no reason to suspect all those Comanches had hidden themselves just for his benefit, Paul wasn't going to spend any more time inside the village. He led his horse away, rode slowly for a short stretch, and then found a spot to lay out his bedroll. What little sleep he got that night was anything but restful.

The next morning, Paul was up at dawn and riding at an easy pace as he gnawed on some jerked venison for breakfast. He washed it down with water that had almost become ice during the night, which snapped his eyes open just as surely as if he'd splashed the water onto his face. According to the map, the next closest village was five miles southwest of the one he'd found the night before. Since he wasn't entirely sure how far he'd gone before making camp,

Paul was on his guard every step of the way.

His eyes darted constantly in search of other riders or figures in the distance watching him pass. Every sound he heard apart from the ones made by his horse caught his attention and tightened his grip on the reins. Before relaxing, he always patted the Schofield at his side both as a way to display the weapon to anyone who might be watching and to give some assurance to himself by its presence on his hip.

When he spotted a high ridge overlooking the trail ahead, Paul steered toward a narrow slope leading up to the top. Less than halfway along the ascent, the path became too narrow for his horse, so he tied it off to a shrub and made the rest of the climb on his own. It wasn't an ideal lookout point, being covered with jagged rocks and thick foliage, but Paul managed to stick his nose out far enough to get a look at the terrain stretched out before him.

The village he spotted looked to be just under a mile away. It was larger than the first one he'd found and seemed to be just as quiet. Paul dug out his field glasses, put them to his eyes, and gazed down to verify his first impressions. As it turned out, he wasn't entirely wrong. On his first sweep, he saw nothing among the long, neatly arranged rows of teepees. When he took another look, something darted between two of the interior rows. Paul remained focused on that area until he saw the movement again. Whatever it was, it was too small and too swift to be human. After waiting another couple of seconds, he saw it hop out from one teepee to stand in the row between it and its neighbor.

Wagging its tail, the dog paced in a small circle before picking a spot on the ground and digging at it. Several seconds later, it plopped its back end onto the spot it had scraped and looked up with its tongue lolling from its mouth. When the dog's gaze found him and stayed there, Paul froze.

Could the dog be some kind of guard meant to watch for intruders? If so, what would happen now that it had found one?

Paul was already mostly hidden behind the growth atop the ridge, but he suddenly felt very exposed up there. The instant he tried to ease himself down to one knee, the dog popped up to all fours and barked.

Paul froze again. This time, he was caught halfway between standing and kneeling. For a man far from his twenties, it was not a comfortable position to hold for more than a few heartbeats.

The dog barked again, its tail wagging and

its tongue flopping in and out of its mouth with every quickened breath. Instead of watching it, Paul lowered the field glasses so he could get a wider view of the rest of the village. As far as he could tell, there was nobody nearby to respond to the dog's voice. He looked instead to the land surrounding the village to find only a few more small creatures scurrying to and fro in their ignorance of any human dramas playing out in the world around them.

Straightening up again, Paul let out a relieved breath as his knees returned to a more natural position. He didn't know a lot about the Comanches other than a few of their trading practices, where to find a handful of friendly hunters during certain times of the season, and to give them a wide berth when their feathers were ruffled. Since he didn't have time to learn any more than that, Paul turned around and made his way back to his horse so he could take one of the few viable options open to him. He climbed into his saddle, rode back to the main path, and headed straight toward the village.

The Comanche settlement looked even larger than it did from above. Rows of teepees formed straight lines like the pointed tops of a barricade surrounding an army fort. Upon reaching the edge of the village, Paul was greeted only by the dog, who seemed more than happy to make his acquaintance.

"Are you the only one living here?" Paul asked.

The dog stood on its hind legs and playfully swatted at Paul's horse with its front paws. Panting loudly, it opened its mouth and barked once through the closest thing a dog could manage to a smile.

"You seem friendly enough." Raising his voice, Paul asked, "What about the rest of the folks around here? Are they willing to be just as courteous?"

After waiting for a short spell, Paul became convinced that he wasn't going to elicit a response that way. He flicked his reins and rode down one of the middle rows through the village. Although he tried to keep his mannerisms calm, Paul felt every muscle in his body tensing to the point of snapping off bone the deeper he rode into that village. Just over halfway within the settlement, he drew a deep breath, dismounted, and approached one of the largest teepees.

Every step he took, Paul feared would be his last. When he made it to the entrance flap, he pulled it open and gingerly looked inside. The teepee was just as empty as the ones in the previous camp he'd found. That discovery, although not a welcome one, allowed him to relax just a bit. He checked a few more of the closest teepees and then climbed back into his saddle.

The dog sat nearby, watching Paul expectantly.

"I suppose if anyone was here, they would have said something by now. It's not as though I'm such a fearsome man." Once again raising his voice so it could be heard throughout as much of the village as possible, Paul added, "Or perhaps the Comanches have taken to hiding rather than showing their faces in the light of day?"

The moment those words left his mouth, Paul cursed himself as a fool. His challenge was a last-ditch effort to draw a response, but he quickly decided that wouldn't have been the response he would have wanted. Fortunately no one came to show him how a Comanche deals with a braggart, and the dog didn't understand a word of what had been said.

Paul flicked his reins again and rode out of the village. Even after the teepees were behind him, he still didn't feel comfortable. It took every bit of courage he had to stop and twist in his saddle to get a look over one shoulder. The rows of braves he'd feared to see weren't there. The only set of eyes looking back at him did so from beneath the dog's brushy brow.

"You hungry?" Paul asked.

The dog lowered its head and tail while slinking closer to Paul's horse.

Paul dug into a saddlebag, tore off a piece of venison, and tossed it to the ground. "There you go, boy."

Devouring the treat in a few quick chomps, the dog looked right back up at him with its tail wagging in a blur of motion.

"That's all I've got," Paul said while moving along. "It doesn't serve any businessman well to give away too many free samples."

That bit of insight was lost on the dog but did nothing to dampen the animal's spirits. It followed Paul anxiously, never losing hope that another bit of venison might come its way.

The ride to the third camp didn't cover a lot of distance, but the terrain was rougher to traverse. It consisted of deep streams overflowing with waters coming down from higher ground, flat rocks, and drop-offs that could easily break the bones of any man or beast foolish enough to move too swiftly at any given point. Paul took his time when necessary and pushed the limit whenever he could. By late afternoon, the hungry dog lost its interest in him and Paul had caught sight of something that made his heart pump a little faster. In the direction of the next Comanche village, thin wisps of smoke rose to smear the sky. Most likely, they were traces of cooking fires.

Feeling as if he was becoming an expert at finding vantage points where the field glasses could best be put to use, Paul climbed down from his saddle and hiked to a spot that best suited his needs. Once there, he stretched out on his belly and dragged himself over a bed of cool dirt, gravel, and fallen leaves until he could get a look at the land below. Even before there was anything for him to see, Paul knew this place was different from the others. He could hear movement and the soft echo of voices. The wind was flavored by scents of burning wood and meaty stews. Every reflex that had been honed over the last few days all pointed him to one conclusion.

"This is the spot," he whispered excitedly under his breath. "This is it. I just know it!"

Settling into a place between the bases of two shrubs, Paul ignored the scrape of branches against the back of his neck and the occasional tickle of an insect skittering along his arm. His movements were more cautious now, as if he'd somehow known his previous scouting runs would turn up nothing of any value as he pressed his chest against the ground, emerged from behind the bushes, and brought the field glasses to his eyes. When he saw all of the activity bustling within the village, women carrying bales of wheat, children playing, men walking easily throughout the camp, Paul smiled widely. "Finally," he said to himself. "I got you!"

One step landed within inches of where Paul lay. Before he could do anything or even look in that direction, Paul felt the touch of iron against the back of his head.

"That's funny," a man said in a strained, rasping voice. "I thought it was my place to tell you that same thing."

CHAPTER 16

"Don't move," the man behind Paul said.

Reflexively, Paul lowered his arms and squirmed on the ground.

"I told you not to move," the gunman hissed. "You deaf or something?"

"No," Paul replied. "This is just the first time I've been held at gunpoint."

It was difficult for Paul to decide whether the sound he heard after that was a muffled cough or a scoffing laugh. Whichever it was, the sound was followed by a few more shuffling steps and the thump of a boot against Paul's side.

"Come back here before one of them savages sees you," the gunman ordered.

Paul scooted backward until the lowest branches closed in front of him. He could still hear and smell the village, but it suddenly felt a long ways away.

"Roll over," the gunman said. "Then sit up."

Once Paul was seated and facing the other direction, he got a good look at the man who'd crept up behind him. Since he was hunkered down low, it was difficult to tell how tall the man was. He was definitely a skinny fellow, dressed in filthy clothes that hung on a bony frame. His face was sunken and covered in thick stubble. The eyes set above those angular cheeks left no doubt that he would put the gun in his hand to use if he was even slightly provoked.

"Who are you?" Paul asked.

"I got the gun in my hand," the man said while waggling a .44-caliber Colt. "I'll ask the questions." After a pause and an uncomfortable shift of his weight, he asked, "Who are you?"

"The name's Paul Meakes. I own a store in a town not too far from here."

"Keystone Pass?"

"Yes," Paul said as his face brightened. "You know of it?"

"Course I do. It's the only town worth mentioning within a day's ride from here. You own a store?"

"That's right."

"No," the gunman snapped. "That's a load of dung is what that is. What would cause a shopkeeper to crawl around on his belly scouting Injun villages?"

"I want to have a word with one of the elders."

"Which one?"

"Doesn't matter," Paul replied. "But I'm here on business that must be resolved quickly. I assure you, whatever reason you're here, I'm no concern of yours."

"You got that right. Toss that pistol."

Paul's finger had barely grazed the grip of his holstered Schofield when the man in front of him tensed. "What's wrong?" Paul asked.

"Shut yer mouth."

Although the gunman's attention had been caught first, Paul could now also hear what had distracted him from his task. The steps were light, but too steady to be the wind and too heavy to be a wandering fox or wolf. The gunman's eyes darted in another direction less than a second before the next set of footprints reached Paul's untrained ears.

The gunman shifted his eyes back to Paul and scowled down at him. The muscles on either side of his jaw flexed before he snapped himself around to take aim with the .44 in his hand. Following the other man's line of sight, Paul spotted a dark-skinned figure closing in on them like a predator cat stalking a rabbit. Dressed in the scant amount of garb worn by Comanche hunters, the dark man moved erratically to make it even more difficult for the gunman to take proper aim.

Scrambling to his feet, Paul turned toward the sound of footsteps coming from the other direction and saw a smaller dark-skinned man rush toward the gunman's exposed back. The second Comanche's face was set in a mask of deadly resolve and a short knife was clenched in one fist. Before he could think otherwise, Paul leaped at the smaller Comanche and shouted, "No!"

If Paul had been thinking clearly, he would have had a better grasp of what happened immediately after he'd made his first move. Of course, if he'd been thinking clearly, he wouldn't have moved at all. The only things to truly register in his mind were the rush of movement, the burning of labored breaths filling his lungs, and the sharp jab of pain as one bone within his left arm ground against another. From there, Paul was tossed to one side as a gunshot blasted through the air.

Reaching out with his other arm, Paul kept himself from falling as his legs somehow got beneath him once more. Once he was mostly upright, he realized the smaller Comanche still had a solid grip on his gun arm. Gritting his teeth, the warrior twisted Paul's arm again in an attempt to force him to drop the pistol. Since he wasn't particularly handy with the firearm anyway, Paul was more than willing to comply. He flicked his hand toward the Comanche to make certain it was clear that he'd given up the Schofield. Not only did the pistol thump against the Comanche's shin, but it scraped skin from bone all the way down before smashing onto a moccasined foot.

The Comanche twitched and grunted in pain, which was enough of a distraction to loosen his grip. Thanks to sheer desperation on Paul's part, he pulled his arm free from where it had been trapped and bolted from the small clearing. A second later, the smaller Comanche ran after him.

The larger Comanche had dived to one side to avoid being shot by the man with the Colt. Not wanting to waste another bullet on a target he could no longer see, the gunman scuttled backward. The large Comanche had ducked into the foliage surrounding the clearing. As he watched for a sign of him, the gunman thumbed back his hammer and planted his feet.

"Come on out, boy," he said, sneering. " 'Less you'd rather run and hide behind —"

The insult wasn't even fully formed before it was answered. Charging with his head and upper body down low and his arms stretched slightly in front of him, the big Comanche emerged from behind a tree to the gunman's left. Even though he'd been hoping to spark an attack, the gunman was surprised at just how close the Comanche had gotten to flanking him. His finger clamped onto the Colt's trigger, sending another bullet through the air. Either the Comanche could tell by the angle of the barrel that the shot would miss or he simply didn't fear being hit, because his steps didn't falter as he rushed toward the gunman.

The skinny man's sunken features twisted first into an expression of surprise and then into panic once the Comanche had closed some more of the distance between them. Moving in a flicker of perfect timing and well-trained muscles, the gunman stepped to one side and then looped his left arm around the Comanche's right elbow. Using both of their momentum to his advantage, the gunman twisted his body and drove the Comanche's chest into the dirt. From there, he rolled to one side until a wet crunch announced the separation of the Comanche's shoulder from its socket.

"I'll take that," the gunman said as he scooped up the knife that had fallen from the Comanche's twitching hand. As soon as he'd picked up the weapon, the gunman snapped his arm out like a whip to send the blade spinning through the air toward another pair of Comanches that approached the clearing.

While the blade only slammed into the trunk of a tree a few inches away from one of those two approaching warriors, the gunman's Colt was much more accurate. It barked once and knocked the closer of the two approaching Comanches off his feet. The other Indian let out a sharp battle cry while sending a spear toward the gunman. Rather than stand still and be skewered, the gunman rolled over the back of the Comanche with the dislocated shoulder a split second before the spear sailed by.

The Comanche who'd thrown the spear wasted no time before plucking the knife from the nearby tree and rushing toward the gunman. He closed the distance between them in a few powerful strides and drew a knife from his own scabbard along the way. Now gripping a blade in each hand, the Comanche came at the gunman like a wild animal.

After firing one shot from the hip, the

skinny gunman didn't have time to aim and fire another before he had to dodge two Comanche blades. The sharpened stone weapons sliced through the air in a flurry of swings that came less than an inch from carving the gunman's face and neck like a Christmas goose. For a few seconds, it was all the gunman could do to keep bobbing and swaying to avoid attacks coming one after the other. When he spotted an opening, he thumped his left fist against the Comanche's side. The punch didn't do much in the way of damage but provided another opening that the gunman immediately put to use.

The Colt came up and around to point directly at the Comanche's chest. Before its trigger could be pulled, however, one of the Indian's knives slashed across the gunman's right wrist. Yelping more from surprise than pain as the pistol fell from his grasp, the gunman threw himself at the Comanche to rob him of the space needed to make another swipe with the blades. His gambit worked just long enough for him to deliver a few chopping uppercuts to the Comanche's stomach. Next, he dropped straight down to one knee to avoid being wrapped in a suffocating bear hug. From his lower vantage point, the gunman scooped up his pistol with one hand and grabbed hold of the Comanche's ankle with the other. One powerful tug was all it took to sweep the Comanche's leg out from under him. When the gunman jumped to his feet, he had no problem whatsoever in knocking the warrior down.

After taking a few steps away from both downed Comanches, the gunman took quick aim and fired. The Comanche had already started rolling to one side, allowing the Colt's bullet to dig a hole into the patch of ground he'd left behind. It only took a heartbeat for the gunman to shift his weight and adjust his aim. The Comanche had just planted the foot that he would have used to push off again and knew there wasn't enough time to do so.

Sighting down his barrel, the gunman spun around and ran into the nearby trees.

Comanche war cries could be heard from almost every direction. Every direction except for the one directly ahead of the gunman. He used his pistol to knock aside low-hanging branches while leaping over half-buried logs in his path. When he exploded through a row of bushes, he was confronted by the Indian that had taken off after Paul. The gunman's eyes widened as he attempted to stop. His feet skidded against rough ground but he was unable to avoid charging straight into the Comanche's waiting blade.

Crouching low and moving swiftly, the Indian slashed at the gunman's leg to send a spray of blood through the air. He then stepped aside to allow the gunman to stagger forward before dropping to one knee.

When the gunman brought his Colt around, his arm was immediately batted aside. He felt the sharpened stone blade slice along his forearm moments before a solid punch was delivered to his kidney from behind. The gunman clenched his eyes shut as the breath was violently forced from his lungs. When he tried to pull himself away, a second punch landed in the same spot as the first to drop him onto all fours.

The smaller Comanche paced in front of the gunman, snarling in his native tongue. Nobody had to be versed in his language to know the vicious intent being conveyed by those words.

Laughing through a series of coughs, the gunman looked up at him and spat back a short tirade of his own in the same dialect.

At first, the Comanche was surprised by the gunman's fluency in his language. Then the words themselves sank in and were quickly answered by a swift kick to the gunman's jaw.

CHAPTER 17

Paul wasn't sure how long the gunman had been knocked out. Mostly that was because he wasn't even sure how long he'd been knocked out himself. When his eyes finally opened, Paul found himself staring into the young rounded face of an Indian child. The child's features were soft, warm, and curious. As Paul started to move, the child jumped back in surprise.

"It's all right," Paul said reflexively. "I ain't gonna hurt you."

The child stood up straight and started to laugh. A thick mop of black hair hung slightly over his eyes as he covered his mouth and giggled even harder. Soon other children joined in the laughter. Paul was lying on his side, so he attempted to sit up. That's when he discovered he was tied up tighter than a calf at a rodeo. More than that, his ropes were attached to something that held them and him firmly in place. At least now he saw why the notion of him posing any sort of threat was so amusing to the children.

His vision was clouded, allowing him to see only what was right in front of him. Once the children were scattered by the scolding voice of an adult somewhere nearby, the only thing in his sight was the gunman lying on his side as well. With a bit of effort and a whole lot of squinting, Paul was able to make out the ropes binding the gunman's hands, feet, arms, and legs. Blood was dried on his face, and judging by the throbbing ache in his skull, Paul guessed he was similarly damaged.

"Hey," he hissed. When he didn't get a response, Paul spoke a little louder. "Hey! You there! Can you hear me?"

"Wh . . . wha?" the gunman moaned. "O . . . course I hear you," he said in a slurred voice. "Try'n t' sleep."

"Wake up!"

The gunman's eyes barely opened wide enough to form a pair of slits above his nose. Opening them farther took a great deal of strain and appeared to take quite a toll on the gunman before he could finally see more than a few shapes and shadows. "Where? Wh . . . what?"

"We've been captured," Paul told him.

Scowling over at Paul, the gunman replied, "Well . . . now, *there's* a revelation for ya! I thought we both just tripped into a pile of rope and rolled down a hill."

"Keep your smart mouth shut, then. This is your fault anyway."

"*My* fault? How do you figure?"

"You're the one that decided to start the fight in the first place. That's how. I was doing just fine before you came stomping along."

"Oh, were you?" the gunman snapped. "If I hadn't stopped you, there would've been even more Comanches to deal with. The way you were flopping around and flashing the sunlight off them expensive field glasses, you couldn't have attracted more attention with a bonfire."

"But you're the one who gave them a reason to fight," Paul said. "Why didn't you just try to get away before any more of them came along?"

"Because I thought you were clearing the way! You took off, and since you're obviously a scalp hunter, I guessed you would have brought down the little fella chasing you without a problem."

"I'm obviously a *what*?"

The gunman's brow furrowed and he looked around as best he could. "An Injun

174

hunter," he whispered.

Paul started to respond to that but found he didn't have the words. Instead he wound up shaking his head in disbelief before resting it on the ground.

"You ain't a hunter?" the gunman asked.

"Of course I'm not."

"But I followed you to two other camps before this one," the gunman said. "You snuck up to each one and strode right into them teepees like you aimed to clean them out. If those camps weren't already cleared out, I thought you meant to . . ."

"Meant to what?" Paul sighed.

Gritting his teeth, the gunman said, "Forget it. I was obviously mistaken. About you bein' a hunter and especially about you doin' much of anything during that fight other than running like a dog with your tail tucked between yer legs."

Paul tried to stretch his arms and legs slowly to get a feel for how securely they were bound. He could barely move them at all before the ropes drew taut. "For your information, the only reason I was captured was that I thought I might be able to lend you a hand."

While Paul had been testing the limits of his ropes, the gunman struggled against them as if they were living things that would eventually surrender to him. Thrashing as if he were having convulsions, he stopped and craned his neck to look at Paul when he asked, "And just how were you going to lend me a hand?"

"Well . . . I thought I'd lost the man who was chasing me and I didn't want to just leave you to be brought down by those others."

"You think I'll believe you were getting all sentimental after I'd gotten the drop on you before?"

"We could have talked things through," Paul replied. "I didn't want a man's death on my conscience. I'd like to think you or anyone else would have done the same in my position."

Throwing himself back into the war against his ropes, the gunman said, "Sure. Anyone would have done the same."

"That wasn't very convincing."

"Seeing as how you only managed to attract attention to us and then failed to gain any sort of advantage even after sneaking back around to face the Injuns that were trying to kill me, I'm not exactly feeling very charitable about you or anyone else around here."

"Are you hurt?" Paul asked. "Looks like you were cut on your arm and leg."

Still squirming, the gunman replied, "I've had a lot worse. Anyway, I think someone wrapped up the cuts before they bled too much. Looks like you got away in much better shape."

Paul let out a grunting laugh.

"What's funny?" the gunman asked.

"You still think I'm some sort of bounty killer?"

"I don't know what to make of you, mister. All I know is that I don't like what I've seen so far."

After a bit more struggling, Paul said, "You think I managed to lose the Comanche that was chasing me and then sneak back around to the spot where you were fighting?"

"All right, then. You were probably lying about wanting to lend me a hand with those murderous savages. I suppose that's fairly easy to believe."

"I was telling the truth about what happened," Paul explained. "And I did want to lend a hand. At least . . . to keep anyone from getting killed. When I started to come back and see what I might be able to do . . . that Comanche who was chasing me came at me from out of nowhere and knocked me cold. Next thing I know . . . I woke up here."

The gunman stopped struggling just long

enough to take a few gulping breaths. "Now, that . . . I can believe," he said.

"By the way . . . who are you?"

"You want introductions?" the gunman asked. "Now?"

"Since our escape plans don't seem to be going very well, it seems we don't have much else to do."

Unable to dispute that, the gunman said, "I'm Hank Adley."

"And I'm —"

"Paul Meakes," Hank said. "You mentioned that already. Right before we were jumped, knocked out cold, tied up, and dragged back to this here Injun camp."

"Oh," Paul said. "I suppose I did."

"You claimed to be a shopkeeper. Guess that makes a bit more sense now that I've seen you fight."

"And that'd make you a scalp hunter."

"What?" Hank replied as his eyes darted around and his mouth gaped open like that of a fish that had just been tossed onto shore by a grizzly bear. "I don't know what you mean!" In a harsh whisper, he added, "Keep yer voice down, you fool. Don't forget where we are! What makes you think I'm . . . someone like that?"

"Because you obviously knew where to look for those camps, you're fairly good at tracking someone, and can mostly handle yourself in a fight."

"Mostly?"

Before Hank could rise to his own defense, he caught sight of half a dozen Comanches walking straight toward them. They were armed with weapons ranging from spears and knives to a few rifles. "When the white man can't fight us," the lead Comanche said, "they fight each other. And they call us savages."

"You're the ones that attacked us!" Hank said defiantly.

Given what he'd already seen and pieced together about the other man, Paul couldn't help being impressed at how steadfast Hank was in defending his so-called honor.

The Comanche who'd made the observation wasn't the tallest of the group, but his manner and stance made it clear that he was the leader among them. Straight black hair hung to his wide shoulders, and the skins he wore hung over his muscular frame as if they'd been there for as long as bark had been wrapped around trees. "If you like," he said in a growling tone, "we can finish what was started outside the village."

"That won't be necessary," Paul quickly said.

One of the other Comanches stepped

forward holding his rifle by the barrel. Raising it up and pointing the stock down at Hank's jaw, he took a solid stance and was about to take his shot when the lead Comanche held him back with one arm.

"That won't be necessary either," the Comanche said. "Will it?"

Keeping his mouth shut, Hank shook his head.

CHAPTER 18

Paul's and Hank's ropes were secured to the ground by short stakes similar to what would be used to pitch a tent. They realized this only when they were hauled to their feet after the stakes had been pulled from the ground. From there, both men were unceremoniously shoved through the village while a growing group of children followed and laughed among themselves. The Comanche braves leading the prisoners to one of the larger teepees didn't find the process as amusing as the children did, but they did give the men an extra shove every now and then to give the kids something else to laugh at.

"This is degrading," Hank grumbled.

"I'd much rather be a little embarrassed," Paul said, "than left tied to the ground like a dog. Considering how we were brought here, things could have been a whole lot worse."

Hank didn't disagree with that, but he wasn't feeling charitable enough to agree either.

The village struck Paul as being too full for its own good. While it was the biggest of the three marked on his map, there seemed to be people stuck into every available teepee and just a few too many horses at each hitching post. Every so often, when he could get a look inside a teepee that wasn't full of occupants, he saw sacks of supplies piled almost to the top of the canvas structure. As for the people themselves, most of the adults looked tired and weary. The eyes that watched Paul and Hank were cautious and most heads hung low. The only exceptions to this were the younger men, who looked ready for a fight, and the children, who were simply keeping themselves busy any way they could.

When they arrived at a tall teepee near the middle of the village, Paul and Hank were stopped by strong hands slapped onto their shoulders. The Comanche at the head of the line stepped inside and spoke to a man with skin that was as smooth as the sand-blasted surface of a desert mesa and hair that flowed like white water almost down to his waist. Once the younger Comanche was done speaking to him, the old man nodded and motioned for the rest of the procession to step inside.

As the old man sat down, Paul and Hank were forced to follow suit by the same hands that had roughly stopped them in their tracks a few seconds before. Although Paul was more than willing to comply, Hank made a show of keeping his head up and back straight even if it meant fighting against the far superior strength of the Comanche warrior behind him.

"I am glad the two of you have been treated well," the old man said.

"Treated well?" Hank replied. "You call being trussed up and knocked in the jaw good treatment?"

"Considering how badly all of these young men wanted to kill you . . . yes."

"Point taken," Paul quickly replied. "Thank you."

The old man had yet to take his eyes off Hank. "A few of these braves had some very interesting ideas," he said in a deeply weathered voice. "Staking you to the ground with a dozen cuts in your flesh to let worms crawl under your skin was one of my favorites."

"All right, all right!" Hank said. "I understand."

Smiling, the old man looked up and nodded to several of the younger Comanches in turn. Although the nods seemed similar to Paul, some of the other men took theirs as an order to leave and a couple found a spot to sit near the wall of the teepee.

"I am Buffalo Horn," the old man said. "Chief to some of these people. Leader of all of them for the time being."

"Pleased to meet you, sir," Paul said. "I'm Paul Meakes."

Buffalo Horn gave him a nod that was a slow, courteous warning to keep minding his manners.

"And, loud one, you are?" the chief said as he looked toward Hank. When he was about to get the prisoner's answer, Buffalo Horn held up a finger and said, "Perhaps I do not need your name. Perhaps I have given you a new name. Loud One."

The Comanche who'd led the group to the tent let out a loud guffaw.

"Being named by the rest of the tribe is an honor," Buffalo Horn said. "For an outsider . . . even more so."

"I got my own name," Hank said. "Keep that other one and any other jokes you got to tell. How'd that be?"

Sitting with his back straight, the Comanche who'd just been laughing suddenly turned colder than a pond in the dead of winter. "Speak to our elder that way again and you will get another new name. Dead One."

Buffalo Horn smirked and said, "Perhaps you would rather tell us your true name?"

"Y . . . yeah. Hank Adley."

"That is more fitting. For now, at least." Turning his attention to Paul, Buffalo Horn said, "Now you can explain what you are doing in my people's village."

"Certainly. I was . . . um . . ." Although Paul had been hoping for an opportunity to get what his children needed, the moment itself was about to overwhelm him. Now that he was sitting among the Comanches, having a word with a chief, all he could think about was the fact that he was wedged smack in the middle of a group of armed warriors who'd already fired shots at him.

"Go on," Buffalo Horn prodded.

The Comanche chief had a formidable presence, but Paul didn't exactly fear him. Buffalo Horn had yet to make a single move that could be considered hostile. His men, however, were a different story. Then Paul reminded himself that he hadn't come this far just to back away now. "I'm . . . well . . . not exactly much of a spokesman," he said. "I'm not even certain coming here was such a smart idea."

Although Hank obviously agreed with that sentiment, he bit his tongue and rolled his eyes in a way that would have made Abigail proud.

"I can see you are not a soldier," Buffalo Horn said. "And you are not here to hunt my people. You don't even seem like a man who has carried a weapon into war. Whatever brings you here, it comes from your heart. That is why I am speaking to you now instead of leaving you to the younger men of this village. You are not soldiers and that is why some of our women cleaned your wounds while you were asleep."

"Much obliged for the courtesy, sir," Paul said with a slight bow. As soon as he lifted his head from the gesture, he felt foolish, so he continued along as though he hadn't even done it. "I own a store in Keystone Pass. Ever been there?"

Buffalo Horn nodded.

"Meakes Mercantile is the place."

"My granddaughter sold you some blankets," the chief said. "Many of our women sold such things to you."

"Yes! Those sell like hotcakes!" Paul said, eternally grateful to be talking about something so familiar. "Anyway, my children and I were at the trading post a few miles from here when . . . um . . . some of your . . .

186

well . . ."

Buffalo Horn's eyes narrowed, but he turned his disapproving gaze instead to the muscular warrior who'd brought the two prisoners into the teepee. "You were there when the trading post was attacked."

"Yes."

"I am sorry to hear that. Aren't you sorry as well, Red Feather?"

The muscular Comanche set his jaw into a firm line and didn't say a word.

Looking back and forth between the two men, Paul said, "My daughter was shot by an arrow in the raid. My son was hurt as well."

"Children were hunted?" Buffalo Horn asked in a voice that quickly rose to a snarl. "Are you sure of this?"

"Yes, sir. Arrow came through the window and caught my girl in the leg."

"What do you say to this, Red Feather?"

"I say he is a white man," the muscular Comanche replied. "That means he is full of lies."

"I do not think he is lying. He came all this way to seek vengeance, as any father would do after his children were harmed by a pack of wild animals!"

It was clear by the fire in Red Feather's eyes that if anyone else had spoken those words to him, a whole lot of blood would have been spilled soon afterward. "We hunted no children!" he said. "We killed no one."

"So . . . you were one of the men who rode in that raid?" Paul asked in a voice that grew as taut as a bowstring.

"I was."

Paul's heart thumped in his chest. His muscles tensed and his hands balled into fists. "Why?" he asked. "Why would you do such a thing?"

"Because your people must be taught they are not the ones who own this land. They have no right to push us off or try to keep us quiet like docile sheep by throwing a few dollars at us."

"I don't know what you're talking about," Paul said. "All I do know is that my little girl and boy are getting sicker every second we sit here flapping our gums."

"You say she was hit in the leg," Red Feather said. "I have pulled arrows from worse places than that without coming close to death. Even a child should be able to —"

"Quiet!" Buffalo Horn roared.

Not only did Red Feather stop talking, but every sound within the village seemed to cut itself short at that moment. The chief's eyes remained on the warrior until

Red Feather turned his head in deference to the Comanche elder. As Buffalo Horn shifted his gaze toward Paul, the change within him was like winter shifting into spring. "Your child was shot by one of my people's arrows?"

"Yes, sir," Paul replied, feeling as if he too was within the heat of the old man's fire.

"Your son, also?"

"No. You see, my girl was standing by a window when an arrow came through and my son cut himself while pulling it out."

"Cut himself?"

"That's right. Because of the poison on the arrowheads, both of them fell ill. That's why —"

"Poison?" Buffalo Horn said in a low rumble issuing from deep within his weathered body. Once again, he looked at Red Feather. "What kind of poison did you use? It is bad enough that you sent arrows flying where they could land in the flesh of children and women. . . ."

Red Feather sat up straight and moved as if he wanted to lunge but just didn't know which way to jump. "We rode to send a message! The only sort of message that the white man will understand. A message that will cost him money. Not the death of any child. Money!"

"Poison?" Buffalo Horn snarled.

"That is a lie spread by the army and scalp hunters. We need no poison to kill."

No matter how badly Paul might have wanted to wring the necks of the men who'd fired those arrows, he knew better than to insert himself into the confrontation playing out between the two Comanches. He hadn't known Hank for very long, but he doubted the other man would be foolish enough to make that mistake either.

"You were warned about this," Buffalo Horn said. "The last thing our people need to do is give any more reasons to hunt us."

"We never gave the first reason to hunt us," Red Feather shot back. "And none of our arrows were poisoned. That is just another in the string of lies used to chase us from our lands into —"

Cutting the warrior off with a slicing motion from one hand, Buffalo Horn looked to Paul and asked, "Do you know for certain the arrow was poisoned?"

"Actually," Paul replied, "that's why I came here. I wanted to find whoever fired those arrows so I can get a bit of whatever poison was used. The doctor tending to my daughter needs it so he can figure out some sort of antidote."

"I have never known my people to use

poison arrows," Buffalo Horn said in a voice that seemed incapable of lying. "And if we did, I would not hesitate to help a child in need. I have several of my own and they have children as well. My spirit could not bear the weight of doing harm to any lives such as theirs."

"I wanna know why that one there shot any arrows into a trading post," Hank said after his prolonged silence.

Glaring at him as though a mangy rodent had suddenly disgraced the human tongue by forming words, Red Feather said, "I do not have to explain myself to you."

"Maybe not, but it seems you still need to explain to someone."

Everyone else in the teepee turned to look at Buffalo Horn.

"It was a message," Red Feather eventually said. "Our people will not be subjected to the whims of strangers without a price being paid. Since those strangers will not listen to words, they will see what we do."

"I can understand that. What about the poison arrows?" Hank asked.

"I will say that if I did take the time to mix a batch of death, dip my arrows into it, and send it flying through your windows, I would want you and everyone else to know about it. I tell you for the last time that I did not do this."

Hank looked at him for a few seconds before giving a single, solid nod. "That's good enough for me."

"It is?" Paul asked in disbelief.

"Sure. Take a look at the man. Does he look like he cares whether or not we know the truth? And more important, doesn't what he said make perfect sense?"

"I guess so."

"Well, then," Hank declared while crossing his arms. "There you go."

Although he clearly wasn't as satisfied by Red Feather's explanation, Buffalo Horn shifted his gaze toward Hank. "I know why one of you is here. What about you?"

"Me?" Hank asked. "Oh. I'm with him."

"Are you?"

"I'm his guide. He wanted to find a Comanche to talk to about the raid on that trading post and I took him to the villages. Also, I was supposed to keep an eye on him in case any trouble sprang up."

"You hurt several of my hunters," Buffalo Horn said. "One is lucky to still draw breath after being shot."

"No offense, but they're the sort of trouble I meant."

"I see. Is that all you have to say?"

Hank nodded.

"What about you?" Buffalo Horn asked Paul.

Too flustered to come up with much of anything, Paul simply nodded as well.

"Good. I will have a word with Red Feather. Take them away."

Two of the Comanches who had brought them to the teepee grabbed Hank and Paul by their collars, dragged them outside, and hauled them to their feet. They were taken back to the spot where they'd awakened, their ropes were tightened once more, and they were staked back to the ground right where they'd started.

After their Comanche escorts left, Hank whispered, "That went better than I thought it would."

"You're crazy — you know that?" Paul hissed.

"Why?"

"Because you . . ." After looking around to see only a few curious children watching them from a safe distance, Paul said in an even softer voice, "You lied to them."

Matching and also mimicking Paul's tone, Hank said, "They don't know about that part."

"But I do. How did you know I wasn't going to tell them the truth as soon as those words left your mouth?"

"Because you're not that sort of fellow," Hank replied. "I could tell that much after talking to you for five seconds. Besides, being caught in a white lie would put me in less trouble than telling the truth."

"Which is?"

"Which is . . . something best left unsaid for the time being."

"You're an Indian hunter," Paul whispered.

"Then why do you keep askin' me about it if you already know? And *I'm* supposed to be the one that's crazy?"

"All I need to do is tell them the truth."

"Oh, and you think that'll get you out of this mess? You already told them your truth and here we are. What's my truth gonna do to help matters?" When he saw Paul start to trip over what he wanted to say next, Hank continued. "Telling them about me would only get me tossed into some cave or, more likely, killed. I'm more valuable to you alive. I can help you out with your problem."

"Why would you do that?"

"Because, in case you've already forgotten, you saved my hide by going along with me back there. The least I can do is return the favor. Besides, if what you said about them young'uns of yours is true —"

"Of course it's true," Paul snapped.

"Then I couldn't just let you fumble along on your own while they get sicker, could I? After all . . . I'm not some kind of animal."

"Maybe I don't want your help."

"Come, now, don't pout. Sounds to me like you need all the help you can get. Any idea where to look next?"

"First I need to worry about getting untied. Then I'll think about where to go from there."

"Let's ask them about that," Hank said as he nodded toward a small group of approaching men.

The Comanches who walked up to them stared down intently at the two prisoners. There were three men and one stood in front of Paul and Hank while the other two walked around behind them.

When he heard the sound of sharpened stone brushing against tanned leather, Paul closed his eyes and thought of his children. Although he was correct in guessing that sound was a knife being drawn from its scabbard, the blade was not meant for either his or Hank's back. Instead two swift cuts were made that didn't draw a single drop of blood.

"Stand," the Comanche in front of them said.

Hank was first to attempt to follow the

order and realized he was able to do so since the ropes tying him to the stakes had also been cut. Paul moved next, quickly discovering that he'd been freed as well. When they got to their feet, Paul turned around to see the Comanches were still behind them with knives drawn expectantly.

"Now," the lead Comanche said. "Start walking."

"Wh-where are we going?" Paul asked.

"Walk."

Without any other viable options in front of them, they started walking.

After less than a dozen steps, Paul knew they were being taken back to Buffalo Horn. Instead of being forced into the teepee, they were met outside it by the chief and Red Feather. Compared to the scowl worn by the younger warrior now, Red Feather had been positively jovial the last time they'd spoken.

"You are being released," Buffalo Horn announced.

"Thank you!" Paul said. Acting on reflex, he started rushing forward to shake the old man's hand. Before he'd taken more than one step in that direction, he was stopped by the two men behind him. Even being roughly pulled back to his starting spot wasn't enough to dampen his spirits. "I truly appreciate this. As far as the matter with the arrow goes, perhaps the poison came from one of the men riding with the raiding party. I've been thinking and . . . I know it's asking a lot, but perhaps if you spoke with them you might find out if one of them was particularly angry or wanted to do extra harm."

"We have already spoken to them," Red Feather said. "They know nothing of this poison."

"Then could you at least spare whatever poison you may use on some other occasions?"

"We use no poisons," Buffalo Horn said. "Not the way you speak of. But, poison or no poison, some of my people are responsible for your children being hurt. Because of that, it is only right that my people help set the matter straight."

"Oh, that won't be necessary," Paul insisted.

Much more vehemently, Hank added, "He's right. That won't be necessary. We know right where to go from here."

"Where will you go?" Buffalo Horn asked.

Hank looked over to Paul, who could only work his jaw as if chewing on potential responses like a cow gnawing on its cud.

The Comanche chief smirked and said,

"Another set of eyes can never hurt. And if you do find another group of hunters using poison arrows, they will most likely not want to help a pair of white men. Red Feather will go with you to deal with them and then he will speak to me about what he finds."

"Oh," Paul said. "Well . . . all right. I suppose."

"I am glad you agree," Buffalo Horn said. "Both of you will now have something to eat while your horses are being tended. Then you will move swiftly so that your children may once again breathe easy as children should."

"That's real kind of you, sir," Paul said.

"Yeah," Hank groaned less enthusiastically. "Mighty generous."

CHAPTER 19

The Comanches tending to the horses were wiry young men who did their jobs with swift and steady hands. As he rode away from the village, Paul rubbed his horse's neck and admired the smooth feel of her coat. "I don't think she's ever been in such good condition," he mused. "Probably won't be so well cared for again."

All three of them rode side by side with Red Feather on the farthest left end of the formation. Without looking over at him, the Comanche asked, "What is her name?"

"The horse?"

"Yes."

"I forgot," Paul replied. "Abigail . . . my daughter . . . I think she named her something or other, but I can't recall what it was."

"You do not care to know the names of your horses?"

"They pull the wagon and that's about it. I doubt they much care to learn my name,"

Paul added with a chuckle.

Red Feather didn't find the observation very amusing.

"So," Hank said. "Is it just you coming along with us on this ride?"

"Do you see anyone else?" the Comanche replied.

"You know just as well as I do that just because we don't see someone, that don't mean they ain't there."

Letting out a long breath, Red Feather said, "Our men are needed to watch our tribes."

"So it is the three villages all crammed together into that one camp, huh?" Hank asked.

"It is."

"Why might that be?"

"Surely you know already."

"Me and Paul here may both be white men, but we're not exactly in on the plans of every other paleface in Colorado."

For some reason, Red Feather cracked half a smile when he heard that. "I believe you two are not hired by the men who have made war with our three villages."

"You just figure that out?" Hank asked.

"Yes. Those men are rich. You smell like you have worn the same clothes for five seasons."

"Ho-*hooo*!" Hank bellowed as if he were performing in front of an adoring audience. "Listen to the savage calling me the filthy one! Least I can dress in something other than what you scraped off the side of a deer carcass."

"Stop it," Paul said. "We've got a job to do, so let's just keep at it until it's done."

"You've got the job to do. We're just along for the ride," Hank said in a huff.

"Where are we going?" Red Feather asked. "The sooner I can be rid of the both of you, the better."

Paul pulled back hard enough on his reins to bring his horse to a sudden stop. The other two quickly followed suit and looked to him for an explanation. Paul was all too ready to give them one. "You are supposed to be my guide, Hank. I tell you I'm looking for the raiding party that attacked that trading post, so tell me where else to look."

"Right there," Hank said while sweeping an arm over to Red Feather. "Didn't you hear him say so back at the village?"

Looking over to the Comanche, Paul said, "And you claim your men would never use poison on your arrows? I've heard tell that Indians poison their arrows when they want to be sure to make a kill, whether it's a clean kill or not."

"You have probably heard a lot of things about us," Red Feather replied. "Most likely, those stories are much like the ones we tell about the white man. Stories full of blood and evil spirits and monsters. I already told you my riders do not use poison on their arrows. There is no need for it."

"Then why are you here with us?" Paul asked.

"Because Buffalo Horn asked me to go."

"Did you intend on just riding alongside us and griping the whole way?"

"Neither of you knows where you are going," the Comanche said. "I will make sure you do no harm as you wander about like wild dogs with one good eye between you."

"Our one good eye brought us to your village," Hank pointed out.

"And now it seems you both are blind," Red Feather replied. "That does not seem better to me."

"He's right," Paul said. When he saw the smug grin taking root on Hank's face, he quickly added, "I mean Red Feather is right. If we don't come up with a plan, then we're just a pack of blind dogs wandering around hoping to stumble on a bone. My daughter doesn't have the time for that kind of nonsense."

"Are you certain your child was poisoned?" Red Feather asked.

"Yes. Would it help if you got a look at her?"

"I am not a medicine man," the Comanche replied. "One sick child looks the same as another to me."

"So if we're supposed to believe that none of them raiders were using poison —" Hank said.

"Believe whatever you like," Red Feather snapped. "I spoke the truth."

"Fine, fine," Hank continued. "All I meant to say was that if you know she was poisoned, then maybe you know someone else who uses a weapon like that. Or maybe you can think of someone else in your tribe who hates the white man enough to do more than break a few windows."

"Every member of every tribe has reason to break more than the white man's windows," Red Feather pointed out.

"Good Lord," Paul exclaimed. "How could I be so stupid?"

Both of the other two men forgot about their argument for the moment when they saw the startled expression on Paul's face. "What's got into you now?" Hank asked.

"If it was a snake, it would've bit me!"

Paul sat still for a moment, sifting through

everything he was thinking before saying another word. Just when the other two were getting impatient, he told them, "Doc Swenson was sure about one thing and that was that both of my children were poisoned."

"I thought you already knew that," Hank grunted.

"But if the Comanche didn't poison them," he continued without taking notice of Hank's comment, "then somebody else must have."

"You think someone else shot that arrow through a window?"

"No. I think both my daughter and son were treated by the same man after they were hurt!"

Scowling even deeper than usual, Red Feather asked, "You think your doctor poisoned them?"

"No," Paul said. "There was another kind of medicine man at the trading post that day. The kind that mixes his own tonics and sells them from the back of a wagon."

"Are you talking about Leandro Prescott?" Hank asked.

"Yes! You know him?"

"We ain't exactly close, but I buy laudanum from him all the time. I started drinking that stuff to relieve headaches. It does a whole lot more good for me than that, if you know what I'm saying."

Paul and Red Feather both knew what Hank was saying but ignored it.

"This man you both know," Red Feather said, "sells firewater and calls it medicine?"

"Well . . . yes."

"He is your enemy?"

"No," Paul replied. "We've been friends for some time."

"Then why would he want to harm your children?"

"I don't think he wasn't trying to harm them." Paul paused and his face darkened. "At least, he better not have meant to harm them."

"Weren't you there?" Hank asked. "Wouldn't you have seen him do anything that would hurt those young ones?"

"What I saw was him clean off their wounds using some of the tonic he mixed up in the back of his wagon," Paul said. "Far as I know, that stuff never hurt anyone, but maybe it was a bad batch or just wasn't supposed to be mixed into an open wound. Right about now, it's all I've got to go on."

"Are you speaking about the tonic that is the color of whiskey and has sand in the bottom?" Red Feather asked.

"I don't know if it was sand," Paul said to

him, "but there was some kind of grit at the bottom."

"And it tasted of rust?"

As he thought back to the taste he'd gotten, Paul reflexively winced. "Something like that. Sounds like you know of it."

"I do," Red Feather said. "Much of that swill was sold to tribes all through the mountains and along the river. Some of them acted as if they'd been given firewater, and many became sick."

"Firewater, huh?" Hank scoffed. "Sounds like Prescott, all right. He mixes a potent drink!"

"It is a kind of poison, to be sure," the Comanche told Paul. "Although I cannot say for certain if it is the same poison that was given to your children. Those of us that were sick got better in a few days."

"There's one way to find out if that's the stuff or not," Paul said. "We've got to find Prescott and see what he's got to say about it. Last time we spoke, he told me he was headed toward Leadville."

"If he's driving a wagon from that trading post into Leadville," Hank said, "there's only two trails that would suit him, and one of them was washed out in the last big rain."

"I know this trail," Red Feather announced. "We can get to it quickly, but it is a hard ride."

"Let's go," Paul said. "The horses are up for it." As he snapped his reins to follow the Comanche's lead, Paul hoped his horse was up to the ride. More than that, he prayed he was up to it.

CHAPTER 20

Paul was no stranger to hard rides. In his younger days, when his backside hadn't grown so accustomed to the feel of a wagon's seat beneath it, he'd ridden through country that didn't seem fit for a rodent to call home. He'd led horses through hip-deep Louisiana swamps. He'd crossed stretches of desert where the only thing to hear was the clap of iron horseshoes against arid rock. He'd even seen a good portion of the Rockies from several different angles. Even with all of that experience behind him, Paul hadn't been fully prepared for the Comanche's definition of what a hard ride truly was.

The worst part of the ride filled an entire day. In that time, the only words spoken between the three men were reports of bear sightings and requests to stop for a spell before someone fell from his saddle. Not a single one of those words came from Red

Feather. The number of times the Comanche had spoken that day could be counted on one hand. By the time they'd finally made camp, Paul couldn't remember what Red Feather had even said since he was too tired to recall his own name. He laid his head down on a rolled-up coat, closed his eyes, and slept so soundly that he barely felt as though he'd drifted off at all.

When his eyes snapped open again, Paul thought it was to a nightmare.

Something sharp scraped against his shoulder. A figure loomed over him, glaring down at Paul with sharp, predatory eyes. Paul wanted to reach for his gun but was too afraid to move.

"Time to go," Red Feather said.

Paul caught his breath and let it out. "You scared me," he said through a nervous chuckle.

Without taking a moment to share the awkward moment, Red Feather stepped over to where Hank was sleeping and slapped his shoulder with the side of his knife. Hank convulsed on the ground and fumbled for his pistol, which prompted Red Feather to pluck it from the holster strapped around Hank's waist.

"Good God!" Hank exclaimed. "You tryin' to scare me to death?"

Red Feather gave back Hank's Colt by tossing it so the gun landed heavily on his chest. "Time to go."

The trio ate a few scraps of bacon, drank some cool water, and resumed the treacherous course in front of them.

After seven grueling hours, Paul felt a strange warmth on his face. So far, he'd spent most of his time focused on the rump of the horse directly in front of him so he couldn't get lost amid a particularly thick patch of woods where they'd spent that afternoon. Looking up, he realized the warmth came from sunlight that had been blocked for too long. Even more shocking was the wide, mostly level terrain in front of him.

"What's this?" Hank asked as he also emerged from the dense trees. "Did we take a wrong turn?"

"No," Red Feather replied. "That is the trail to Leadville right in front of us."

"So we're done with that godforsaken shortcut?"

"Yes."

Both Hank and Paul let out deep, relieved sighs. When he took another breath and surveyed the land in front of them, Paul felt invigorated. "How much farther to Leadville?"

"Haven't you paid attention while we rode?" Red Feather asked.

"To be honest, I lost track of where we were after the twentieth cut I got from all those brambles and bare branches."

"Shouldn't be far," Hank said. "I'd guess less than a day's ride."

"For once, he is right," Red Feather said. "We'll join up with the main trail, take it all the way into Leadville, and we should be there before nightfall."

"Sounds good to me," Paul said. "Lead the way."

The Comanche and Hank galloped on ahead with Paul not too far behind. Already, the air was growing thinner from the increasing altitude of the ground beneath them. Although this was far from Paul's first time into the Rockies, being within the majesty of their towering embrace never ceased to amaze him. Throughout most of the journey after he'd left his children's bedside, the mountains always seemed to be on the horizon but just out of reach. Then, as soon as the woods had thinned out moments before, they appeared directly in front of them as if the mountains had been lurking in wait to pounce as soon as the riders had completed Red Feather's gantlet. Once they'd begun riding along the trail to Leadville itself, the Rockies closed in on them from all sides.

They arrived in Leadville on schedule, and as they rode through town, Paul felt as if he hadn't seen civilization for years. That wasn't due so much to the hardships of the last few days, but from the constant wringing of hands he went through in regards to his children. He was doing everything he could for them, but he had no way of knowing if they were getting better or had taken a tragic turn for the worse. Rather than put himself through the turmoil of those somber thoughts, he set himself back onto the path before him.

"There's Harrison Avenue," Hank said. "That'll take us downtown. Is that where we should be headed?"

After thinking for a moment, Paul replied, "I recall him saying something about visiting the Board of Trade. Downtown seems like a good place to start. Either that or city hall or possibly the business district."

Hank grinned and nodded. "I know the place. It ain't far." He then led the way to Harrison Avenue.

Leadville was a town that had its own distinct energy. Being a well-known spot on the gambling circuit, it was filled with saloons, gaming emporiums, and all the services that catered to patrons of such places. David had pestered his father several times to go there, and Paul had always insisted that they wait until he was older. Once he got a look at downtown Leadville, Paul knew his judgment in that regard had been perfectly sound.

The first thing he saw was a Western Union office on the corner of East Second and Harrison. Farther down the street were a clothing store and the offices of the *Leadville Chronicle.* From then on, saloons sprouted up like mushrooms around a dead tree stump. North of Third Street, several of them were lined up in a row. Every last one was filled with raucous sounds, men in varying stages of inebriation, and women in varying stages of undress.

"Looks like it's going to be a wild night," Paul mused.

Hank chuckled once. "Every night's pretty wild around here."

"Where are the offices for the Board of Trade?"

Hank reined his horse to a stop near a cross street that looked more like an alleyway. "Right over yonder," he said while nodding to the other side of Harrison. "Don't know if I'd call it much of an office, though."

The Board of Trade was actually a saloon. Although it was one of the quieter ones in sight, that was akin to calling one particular cloud in a roiling storm more tranquil than the rest. At the very least, there were no soiled doves in sight and no drunks collapsed anywhere on the street directly in front of the place.

"That ain't one of my favorite places to spend an evening," Hank said.

Draping a coat over his shoulders, Red Feather glanced up the street to where three more large saloons had been built in a row. "Those are more to your liking, I'd imagine."

Hank twisted in his saddle to get a look for himself. "Yeah," he said wistfully. "The Monarch's up that way. Great place. Cheap beer and cheaper women, if you know what I mean."

"It is never difficult to know what you mean," the Comanche replied.

"Great," Paul said. "If you'd like to go there and have a drink or two, be my guest."

"I thought you'd want some help," Hank said.

"Prescott is a friend of mine. I doubt I'll need any help."

"He may not be much of a friend once you accuse him of poisoning your

214

young'uns," Hank pointed out. "Fact is, most men tend to get downright nasty when accusations start to fly."

"I agree," Red Feather chimed in. "If this medicine man is able to harm children, he may be capable of many other things."

"Let me just get a feel for the situation," Paul told them both. "However things go, I've got to believe they'll go better if he's talking to me instead of me and two others wearing guns."

Anxious to make his way down to the rowdier section of the street, Hank shrugged and grunted, "Suit yourself. You know where to find me."

Red Feather stayed put after Hank rode away. "Are you sure you don't want someone to watch over you?" the Comanche asked. "I could stay behind and wait until there is trouble. If there is no trouble, then nobody needs to know about me."

"There are plenty of folks on this street," Paul said as he motioned toward the men and women flowing past them in every direction. "Surely someone's bound to have noticed you."

"And they will forget as soon as I leave their sight. Most people see only what they need to see."

"Why so much concern all of a sudden?"

"Buffalo Horn sent me to help and guide you. That is my job and I will do it. Also," Red Feather added grudgingly, "I am a father as well. If my little ones were sick, I hope someone would help and guide me."

"Much obliged." Paul was just about to send the Comanche to keep an eye on Hank but got a better idea instead. "Something that could be a big help is if we found Prescott's wagon. It's tall and has an awning on one side that can be folded out to give him a place to sell his wares."

Red Feather nodded. "I have seen many white men selling their oils and salts. Their wagons are hard to miss."

"Hopefully I won't be long in there," Paul said as he dismounted and cinched his reins around a wooden rail. "When I'm done, I suppose I'll join Hank at the Monarch."

"I will look for you there." Without another word, the Comanche pointed his horse toward the narrow side street and rode away.

A cold wind blew through town, carrying with it a biting chill from the highest peaks of the Rocky Mountains. Paul drew his jacket in tight around him and stepped up to the front door. Before opening it, he took a walk around the outside of the place to see if he might be able to spot Prescott's wagon on his own. When he found nothing but a few small carriages and a row of horses tied to a long rail beneath an awning behind the building, he made his way inside the Board of Trade Saloon. Upon first hearing the name of the place back in Keystone Pass, he'd expected to find clerks sitting at desks or tellers within bankers' cages to discuss matters of business and commerce. Instead he saw a short bar at the back of a large room, a row of faro tables on one side, and round poker tables scattered throughout most of the rest of the available floor space. Paul had done some gambling in his youth but not a lot of winning. Even after years of being away from the tables, he had no trouble recognizing the large amounts of money piled at some of those card games and the slick, professional look of the men making the bets.

As he approached the bar, Paul nearly walked straight past an attractive young woman wearing a simple dress that hugged a nicely rounded body. She stepped in front of him just enough to catch his eye and asked, "What would you like, mister?"

"Oh . . . um . . . I'm not interested," Paul replied.

"Are you sure? You seem like you could use something special."

"You're real pretty and all, but I . . ."

Her face became even prettier when it was adorned with a warm smile. She gave him a little giggle and put a hand gently on his elbow. "No need to be so nervous," she said. "I was asking if you wanted something to eat."

Paul looked around and saw that not every table was occupied by cardplayers. Some of the people sitting there were just folks having a conversation over a plate of food. And when he saw those plates of food, Paul was reminded of just how much dry jerky and cold beans he'd eaten in the last couple of days.

"You look hungry," the young woman said. "There's a nice hot batch of beef and vegetable stew in back. Would you like a bowl?"

"Oh, dear God, yes."

"How about some bread or biscuits to go along with it?"

Already taking a seat at one of the tables, Paul replied, "Biscuits, please," before he knew what he was doing. Even though he still had a job to do, his body wouldn't allow him to get up from that chair until he'd gotten something to eat. "How long will it take for the stew to get here?" he asked.

"You really are hungry! I'll go fetch you a

bowl right now and be back as quickly as I can."

True to her word, the server returned with a bowl of stew and a small plate of biscuits before Paul had a chance to rethink his decision to take the time to have lunch. The instant he drew some of the steam rising from that bowl in through his nostrils, he felt as if he hadn't eaten for a week. He attacked the meal with vigor and only paused so he could swallow without choking.

"You want something to drink?" the server asked.

"Water," Paul told her through a mouthful of stew.

"Be right back."

Once the edge had been taken off his hunger, Paul slowed down to savor each bite. The thick chunks of beef were tender from soaking up the broth and juices of the stew. The carrots were soft and the potatoes were hearty. After he'd stirred up some pepper that had settled at the bottom of the bowl, the entire dish became that much better. When the girl came back to set his water down, Paul's mind drifted back toward the business that had brought him there.

"Do you know many of the men who come through here?" he asked her.

She shrugged. "Some."

"What about someone named Leandro Prescott?"

After thinking for a moment, she shrugged again. "Doesn't sound familiar. Why don't you ask him?" she said while pointing toward the bar. "Everyone who comes along has to talk to him sooner or later."

"Much obliged."

"I'll leave you to your meal. Should I bring another bowl?"

As much as Paul wanted to take her up on the offer, he declined. There was still a job to do and he could no longer use starvation as an excuse for stepping away from it. He finished his stew, all the way down to the last savory drop of gravy at the bottom of the bowl, stuffed the final crumb of biscuit into his mouth, and approached the bar. Placing his hands flat on the freshly cleaned surface, he waited to catch the eye of the man working there before saying, "I'm looking for someone."

The bartender was a few years Paul's senior with a round, friendly face. Stepping up to him while drying a shot glass with a white towel, he said, "Most folks who come here are looking for something. Care to narrow the field down a bit?"

"His name's Leandro Prescott. He's a salesman who I believe comes through

Leadville every so often."

Still working the towel until his glass sparkled, the barkeep eventually shook his head. "Sounds familiar, but a whole lot of folks come through this town and just about every last one of them walks down Harrison to visit these saloons. If you'd like to give me a little time here so I can ask around a bit, I should be able to find something out in regards to your friend."

"I can come back later, if that would help," Paul offered.

"You can come back tonight if you like. I should have heard something by then."

Paul sighed. He'd been in business long enough to know when someone was fishing for business of their own. If the bartender wanted some of what was in Paul's pockets, he was welcome to it. He removed a bit of his money and placed it on the bar. "Will this help?"

"I'll take it, but it won't change the fact that I need to ask around. If you stayed here and kept busy for a spell, I can do my checking now. If you want to come back later, I'll check in later. I'm a busy man, mister."

"Do your checking now," Paul said. "I'll do a bit of gambling. Any games you can recommend?"

Without hesitation, the barkeep pointed to one end of the room. "Janie over there deals a fine game of faro. She's easy on the eyes as well."

And Paul figured she was also very talented at convincing men to drop more of their cash on a game with odds that were notoriously stacked in the house's favor. But if the barkeep was only willing to go the extra mile for a paying customer, Paul couldn't fault him for it. He took his money back, tucked it deep into his pocket, and walked over to the faro table with the attractive dealer.

She had long dark hair that flowed down to cover a good portion of what was exposed by her off-the-shoulder dress. Ample curves, creamy skin, and a seductive smile made Paul want to agree to just about anything she had to say before she'd even said it. Naturally the first words out of her mouth were "Care to place a bet?"

"I believe I would, although I'm fairly new to this game."

She smiled even wider while explaining the rules to faro to him in a soft, purring voice. Every time she referenced the table, she shifted her shoulders and extended an arm just a bit more than what was necessary to move her body in a slowly writhing display. By the time she was finished, she'd drawn two more players to the previously empty table. Paul knew more than enough about faro to play the game. He figured that listening to the rules and enjoying the show that accompanied the explanation were a good way to bide his time without losing a cent. Eventually, however, he had to place a bet. Once he saw the barkeep walking around to talk to a few other men while tossing the occasional nod in his direction, Paul was more than willing to gamble.

Faro was a simple game that flowed fairly quickly. Despite knowing the odds all too well, Paul couldn't help getting wrapped up in the process of bucking the tiger. He even won a hand or two, much to the admiration of the other players. Then again, those same men could very well have been appreciative of a fly landing on a wall just as long as their beautiful hostess saw fit to applaud. After a few more hands, the dealer leaned forward to have a word with Paul.

"Looks like you're wanted over at the bar," she whispered.

Paul looked over his shoulder to see the barkeep waving him over. "Much obliged," he said while setting a fraction of his winnings on the table. "That's for you."

"Come back soon," she told him while

pocketing the gratuity.

As soon as Paul stood up, another man hurried to take his spot since it was noticeably closer to the dealer than any of the available seats at either end of the table.

Approaching the bar, Paul asked, "What did you find out?"

"See them fellows over there playing poker?" the barkeep asked while discreetly pointing to one of many round tables nearby.

"Sure," Paul replied without truly knowing which men the barkeep was referring to.

"They know your friend," the barkeep said. "Salesman. Comes through here once or twice a month. Not a lot of hair up top."

"That's him. Any idea where I can find him?"

The barkeep winced, set down the glass he'd been working on, and picked up another. "Bad news for you in that regard. He's gone."

"Gone . . . as in out of town?"

"Gone . . . as in dead."

CHAPTER 21

A few minutes later, Paul stepped out of the Board of Trade and went to his horse. His eyes were glassy and he reached out to touch his horse's side as if he needed support to keep from falling over. Red Feather strode over to meet him from where he'd been standing near the Tabor Opera House.

"Did you have something to drink while you were in there?" the Comanche asked.

"Yes," Paul replied. "I needed it."

"Maybe you should have some cold water. Or stick your head into some. That always helps me."

"What? No. I'm not drunk. I'm just . . ."

"What's wrong?"

"Prescott," Paul replied. "The man we came here for. The bartender says he's dead."

Red Feather's only reaction to the news was the subtle upward movement of one eyebrow. "How did he die?"

"He was taken away by some armed men yesterday. They're real rough types who meant to kill him."

"And what you needed was in the salesman's wagon?"

Paul nodded. "Yeah. I guess so."

"Then we are in luck. I found his wagon." Quickly, Red Feather added, "I found a wagon that looks like it could be his. It is not far from here. Come and tell me if it is the right one."

Grateful to put the Board of Trade even farther behind him, Paul followed Red Feather down a narrow side street marked as St. Louis Avenue. Walking with buildings on either side, Paul felt almost as anxious as when he'd been trudging through the dense woods on the Comanche's shortcut.

"This man was a friend of yours?" Red Feather asked.

"Kind of. More of an acquaintance, really. We met every now and then to conduct business. Still . . . it's something of a blow to hear that he's gone."

Paul wasn't certain how much longer he walked before stopping. Thinking about Prescott's death made his head swim. When such grim notions eventually led him back to what might become of his children, he felt the ground tilt a few degrees to one side beneath his boots. The strong, steadying grip of a hand on his shoulder snapped him right back to the present.

"You had too much to drink," Red Feather said.

"No. I'm fine."

"Then look. Is that the wagon?"

Blinking away his last bit of queasiness, Paul spotted a lot that was about fifty yards ahead of them. The wagon parked there would have been impossible to miss, even through the daze that had nearly overtaken him. "That does look like the wagon," Paul said.

"We'll go to get a closer look."

"Someone is probably watching it."

"Distract them," Red Feather said. "If the owner is truly dead, then nobody should care too much if we see what's inside before the vultures come to strip away whatever they can carry."

Although it was a distasteful comparison, Paul knew the Comanche had made a good point. "All right, then," he said. "You keep watch and I'll get a look inside the wagon. I think I remember what the bottle looked like that he used to clean my daughter's wounds."

Both of them strode forward and Red Feather came to a stop several paces before reaching the wagon. Paul continued on, hopped the low fence surrounding the lot, and then took a quick walk around the wagon to see if any of the small doors on either side had been left open.

No such luck.

The door at the back of the wagon was sealed tighter than the others and didn't even rattle when Paul took hold of the handle and pulled.

There were no windows on the wagon, nor any other openings that he could see. Closing his eyes, he thought back to the times when he'd seen Prescott standing near the wagon to display whatever it was he'd been selling to the public or trading to him. Try as he might, Paul couldn't remember there being any other way into the wagon that he hadn't already checked. He was standing there, facing the rear door into the wagon, when he decided to go for broke. As a merchant, he'd quickly developed a seething hatred for thieves. As a father, and a desperate one at that, he was prepared to cross that line and several others beyond it if it meant seeing his children well again.

Paul took a step back, placed his hand on the grip of his holstered Schofield, and set his sights on the handle of the narrow door in front of him.

"What do you think you're doin' there?" a man shouted from the wide, squat building closest to the lot. He wore dark trousers held up by wide suspenders lying against the rumpled front of a white shirt that was yellowed beneath both arms. A bushy mustache covered his upper lip, and a mop of stringy dark hair fell to an even perimeter all the way around his head in the shape of an overturned bowl. "This here is private property," he said. "Tell me what you're doing!"

"Nothing," Paul said without taking his eyes from the wagon. "Just keep walking."

"If you mean to force your way into that wagon, you'd best think again, mister."

Paul turned toward St. Louis Avenue and saw Red Feather stepping into view. The Comanche silently plucked a dagger from one of the sheaths hanging from his belt. If push came to shove, Paul knew the dagger could be flicked through the air to find a spot just about anywhere within his target's anatomy.

As Paul tried to think of a threat that would be nasty enough to convince the other man to find somewhere else to be, he suddenly noticed the scattergun clutched in that man's hands. "The man who owns this wagon . . . is a friend of mine," was the best he could come up with.

"What friend?" the other man asked. "That dog lurking about right over there?"

Paul was ready to come to Red Feather's defense by scolding the guard for suspecting another man solely on the color of his skin or the look of his clothes. It would have been a show since the Comanche was preparing to throw a knife into that same guard, but it would have at least been a righteous show. When he turned to get a look down the narrow street as if he had no idea what the guard was talking about, he saw two men instead of just one. Red Feather had found a shadow to provide some bit of cover while Hank walked straight toward the lot, head held high.

"Hello again, Randy!" Hank called out.

The man with the bad haircut and shotgun guarding the lot must have been Randy, because he replied right away. "I already told you to get your sorry hide out of my sight unless you can prove you're supposed to be here!"

"I was just looking for my friend," Hank said. "And I see you've already found him."

"Any friend of that one . . . ," Randy growled through clenched teeth.

Paul raised both hands and backed away. "I understand. I'm leaving."

"Not fast enough."

Even if he was willing to concede to an angry man who already had a gun in his hands, Paul wasn't about to scurry off like a scolded child. After a good amount of distance was put between them, Randy proceeded to circle around the wagon to make certain Paul hadn't tampered with anything.

Paul headed back down St. Louis Avenue toward Harrison, where Hank and Red Feather fell into step on either side of him. "That's Prescott's wagon," Paul said.

"You are certain?" Red Feather asked.

"I've traded with Prescott plenty of times," Paul said. "Drove my own wagon right next to that one and hammered out plenty of trades. I was certain the second I laid eyes on it."

"I could've told you that was his wagon," Hank said.

"You've met him also?"

"No, but I asked a few questions over at the Monarch. Actually all I needed was one. Can't recall exactly what it was. . . ."

"It's no wonder," Red Feather snapped. "I can smell the firewater on your breath from here."

"All I had was one drink! Give or take."

Paul had been around enough drunks to

recognize one, and Hank wasn't too far gone just yet. "Is that why you went to that saloon?" he asked. "To ask about Prescott?"

"Actually I went there for the drink," Hank said. "While I was at the bar, I asked about something or other and dropped Prescott's name in the process. All I wanted to know was if the name struck a chord with the barkeep or anyone else who might be listening."

"And did it?"

"Oh yes! I barely got the words out when the barkeep and a pair of rough-looking idiots took notice. The barkeep knew where to find that wagon. Seems Prescott was spouting off any chance he got about a sale he was conducting of some sort of magnetic device that was supposed to help sniff out precious ores. When he didn't get a nibble on that, he mentioned other trinkets and such until the barkeep had him tossed out on his ear."

"And what of the other two?" Red Feather asked.

"Oh, they came along shortly after I was out here getting a look at that wagon. It's locked up real tight, by the way. Front to back, top to bottom. Don't even bother trying to bust in."

"Yeah," Paul sighed. "I found out that

much for myself."

They'd made it back to Harrison Avenue, where there were a lot more people about to swallow up the trio that seamlessly joined their ranks. Rather than head back to the row of nearby saloons, they worked their way toward the *Chronicle*'s offices. It was a bit quieter there and a pair of expensive black coaches was parked on the side of the street to put something of a barrier between that area and the rowdier section of town.

"I was walking back to the Monarch," Hank continued, "when them two ugly cusses from before pulled me aside to have a word with me. They said they knew where to find Prescott."

"I heard Prescott is dead," Paul said to him.

"Then someone forgot to spread the news, because these two seemed awfully certain he was still alive and well. Or . . . alive, at least. Dead's probably not too far away from him."

Red Feather scowled and let out a short, huffing breath.

Looking over at the Comanche, Hank asked, "What's wrong with you? Looks like you just ate a stinkbug."

"You were very busy in the short time we've been apart," Red Feather pointed out.

"I went to a saloon, tossed back a drink while having a word with the barkeep, and then took a short walk down this way," Hank said. "Unless you got yer feet covered in molasses, that shouldn't take too long. Besides, I thought we were here to find the salesman."

Before Red Feather could continue the argument he'd started, Paul said, "He's right. That is why we're here. What did those men tell you?"

Hank was still staring at the Comanche and didn't stop until Red Feather muttered something in his native tongue while walking away from them. "They told me they were looking for Prescott as well and knew right where to find him. Only problem was that they needed an extra gun hand or two to get ahold of him. Seems he ain't exactly traveling alone these days."

"I've never known him to have anyone else riding with him," Paul said.

"How well do you know this friend of yours?"

"Like I already told you. He's more of an acquaintance."

"Well, this acquaintance ran afoul of a few too many people the last time he was in Leadville and he soaked them for a whole lot of money."

"How much?" Paul asked.

"They didn't say, but it was supposed to be enough to make the job worthwhile even after it was split up."

Whoever those black wagons had been waiting for climbed into them and ordered the drivers to get moving. They pulled away and rolled down the street, leaving Paul with an unobstructed view of the saloons farther down Harrison Avenue. "I always warned Prescott about selling too many of those contraptions. You should let customers come to you for those and warn them properly. Talking them up too much and pushing them onto folks is asking for trouble."

"It don't seem as if he's too worried about practicing good business," Hank scoffed.

"These men who approached you. How many of them were there?"

"Two in the saloon. There was a third with them when they pulled me aside to have a word with me after I got a look at that wagon."

"And they think Prescott is alive?"

"Yep. Only, it seems fairly certain that he won't be that way for much longer. That's probably what that barkeep you spoke to meant when he said Prescott was dead. These men who spoke to me seemed pretty capable, and with them after some sales-man, I'd say the salesman doesn't stand much of a chance."

"Do you know where to find these gun-men again?" Paul asked.

"They'll be playing cards for a bit longer in one of the back rooms at the Monarch."

"Great. So go on over there and find out where Prescott is."

"They will not tell you," Red Feather said from a short distance.

Paul looked over to the Comanche. "Why not? Do you know who Hank's talking about?"

"I do not know these men, but I can recognize them as hunters. Any man hunt-ing another man . . . even if he is as clumsy and arrogant as most white hunters . . . will not be quick to give up their prey. They will be suspicious of anyone else trying to take it from them."

"I gotta agree with the Injun," Hank said.

Even though Red Feather didn't like be-ing called by that name, he let it pass for the moment.

Not knowing how close he'd come to get-ting swatted in the jaw by the irritated Comanche, Hank went right on talking. "Also, it seems these gun hands have some personal ax to grind with that salesman. It's probably just some bit of money they were swindled out of, but they seemed mighty interested in getting it back themselves."

"You don't think you can trick them into telling you what we need to know?" Paul asked.

Hank looked at him and said, "You're the businessman between the three of us. If anyone should know how to talk someone into parting with something they don't want to part with, it should be you! Surely you know a few good lies to run by those men to get them to slip up."

"I am a businessman. An *honest* business-man," Paul clarified. "There's a big differ-ence."

"Right," Hank grunted. "The difference is one's rich and the other's poor."

Red Feather chuckled at that.

Too focused to be offended by Hank's offhanded comment, Paul did his best to think things through from different angles. After a few seconds, he said, "All right, then. Since those men are going to go after Prescott soon, we can wait outside the Monarch and when they come out we'll fol-low them to wherever Prescott is."

"And then what?" Hank asked. "We just step up and ask for a quick word with the salesman before he's strung up by the gang that wants his head?"

"You don't think they'll agree to that?" Paul asked through a weak smile. Neither of the other two came close. Before he caught an earful from any of the other two, Paul said, "Then I suppose there's only one way we can find out what these men have against Prescott while also finding Leandro himself."

"Just so long as it's not something that'll get us killed in the process," Hank warned.

"I say we meet with them at the Monarch and join up with the gunmen."

Judging by the exasperated sigh that escaped Hank's lips, that wasn't a suggestion he liked very much.

CHAPTER 22

The Monarch was larger than the Board of Trade and had considerably less breathing room inside owing to the number of people milling about within the place. Situated at the hub of Leadville's saloon district, the Monarch was alive with drinking, gambling, fighting, and flirting as everyone from gamblers, brawlers, and soiled doves plied their trade. Hank knew exactly where he was going as he navigated through the sea of humanity. In fact, several people he encountered knew him as well. Paul simply kept his head down and walked in the other man's wake until they reached a row of doors along one wall near the bar.

"When we get in there," Hank said, "just let me do the talking."

"That's the plan."

"Yeah, but I just wanna make sure you don't jump ahead by getting overly concerned with finding this fella or helping your kids. The best thing for you to do is keep your head right here where it belongs."

"I'm not an idiot," Paul snapped. "Do your part and I'll do mine."

"I just don't wanna catch a bullet or a blade in the back."

"And I do?"

"That's the spirit." Taking a deep breath, Hank rested his hand on his holstered Colt and then reached under his jacket to tap the .38 that was strapped beneath his left arm as if he was going to go in shooting. Rather than do the very thing he'd warned Paul against, he simply knocked on the door and waited.

It was answered before Hank had to knock again. The man who opened the door was a Mexican with a clean-shaven face, dark eyes, and a tussled patch of black hair sprouting at odd angles from his scalp. He was several inches shorter than both of the men waiting to be let inside the room and glared up at them as if waiting for that fact to be brought up so it could be violently answered. When he didn't get an excuse to throw a punch, the Mexican asked, "What do you want?"

"You Hector?" Hank asked.

"*Sí.*"

"I was the one your partner met with a

little while ago."

"We met with a lot of men today." Looking to Paul, he asked, "Who's he?"

"He's with me. We're here to take the job that was offered."

Sighing as if he was put out by the notion of having to open the door any farther, Hector stepped aside and waited for the other two to come inside. Once Paul and Hank stepped past him, he shut the door and pointed over to a large round table in the middle of the room. Seated at that table were only two other men. One had an olive complexion, a bulbous nose, stringy black hair with strands of gray, and a full beard. He looked to be somewhere in his early fifties and was occupied by the solitaire layout spread in front of him. The second man sat reclining in his chair with one arm draped across the backrest of a neighboring chair. The only thing in front of him was a black hat that had been placed on the table. His wide shoulders and thick chest spoke of a man built up through years of hard labor, and his callused hands had a similar tale to tell. His hair had probably been dark brown, but all that remained of it was a layer of closely cropped bristle covering his scalp. Thick layers of whiskers sprouted from his upper lip and chin to hang down low like a goat's beard. Cold blue eyes stared over the table at the door as one hand drifted to his side to where a pistol was surely kept.

"Who's he?" the man with the blue eyes asked.

Slapping Paul's shoulder, Hank said, "This here is Georgie. He's with me."

"Georgie? Even he doesn't look like he believes that."

"Does it matter who we are?" Hank asked. "What's in a name, right?"

"I suppose so. Both of you want to take the job?"

"That's right."

The bald man stood up. "Looks like it'll just be the five of us, then." He walked around the table and stood close enough to Paul to make it clear that he was bigger than him in every way.

"My partner was just looking out for me. The name's Paul."

Nodding slowly, the bald man extended a hand. "I'm Starkweather. You already met Hector. That one there," he said while hooking a thumb toward the bearded man who was still playing solitaire, "is Bob."

Bob looked up from his game just long enough to nod.

Sizing up the men in front of him, Starkweather asked, "You two know how to use them pistols you're carrying?"

"Good enough to kill what I'm shooting at," Hank replied.

"Fine, then. Let's go."

And without any further delay, Paul Meakes found himself in yet another of many professions he would occupy in his lifetime: hired killer.

CHAPTER 23

The five of them walked north up Harrison Avenue, leaving the saloon district behind. Starkweather, Hector, and Bob knew exactly where they were headed and had enough purpose in their strides to pull ahead of their newly hired reinforcements. It wasn't until they passed the courthouse that Paul began to feel nervous enough to speak up. Even so, he made sure to keep his voice low so as not to be heard by the men who'd hired them.

"Do you think they truly mean to kill Prescott?"

Without hesitation, Hank replied, "Most definitely."

"Shouldn't we do something about it?"

"Yes, but now ain't exactly the time."

Paul might have been the one to bring them to this predicament, but some part of him hadn't truly believed they'd get this far. So many times throughout his life, all he'd needed was some sort of wild-eyed plan just to get him moving long enough to think of something better. Oftentimes, better opportunities would present themselves, plans would be altered, and things would work out. And then, usually when it was most inconvenient, a man would be forced to live with the original plan that he'd hoped so desperately to change in the first place. This was the spot that Paul found himself in as he continued to walk behind two other men who looked every bit as if they'd killed at least a dozen men between them.

Quickly noticing that one of the other men was no longer walking in front of them, Paul looked around for the third gunman. Hector walked a few paces behind them, watching Paul and Hank closely while keeping his hand on the pistol holstered at his side. The only thing that gave Paul any solace was that he could see someone else following even farther behind the group of five gunmen.

"He still back there?" Hank whispered.

Doing his best not to let on that he'd spotted Red Feather shadowing them from several yards back, Paul replied, "Yep."

"What about the Mexican?"

"He's back there too."

When they reached West Eighth Street, Starkweather rounded the corner and came to a stop. He waited until the rest of the group gathered around him before pointing up to the window of a building with two floors that was so skinny it looked as if it had been sliced off the side of another building. "The man we're after is in there," he said. "And he ain't alone. There's at least two or three others up there keeping an eye on him. We'll try to get as close as we can without drawing any notice, but once they get a notion that something ain't right, they'll start shooting."

"Will they know you on sight?" Paul asked.

"Yes," Starkweather replied. "That's why we brought you two along."

"You think we're just gonna stroll up there and draw someone's fire?" Hank asked.

Clapping his hand on Hank's shoulder as if they'd suddenly become old friends, Starkweather said, "It won't be anything like that. You two will go and scout out the place. See exactly how many of them are up there, if they're watching the door, that sort of thing."

"Sounds pretty serious," Paul said. "How much money does this man owe you anyway?"

"Don't worry about that. You two just do what you're being paid to do so we can do what we came to do. After all that's over, we all go away with more money in our pockets."

"What if we decide this is more than we signed up for?" Hank asked.

Bob wore a Smith & Wesson on each hip in a double-rig holster. He closed his hands around both firearms and took a step forward. In the space of that single step, he shifted from looking like a bearded man with a fondness for card games to someone who would fill another man with lead and not lose a wink of sleep over it. "See them ditches over there?"

Glancing over to a pair of ditches leading all the way back to a set of matching outhouses, Hank replied, "Yeah."

"You try to back out now and you'll bleed to death in one of them."

"No need for that, Bob," Starkweather said. "This is an easy job with a big payout at the end of it. These two will just run up to the second floor, go to room number six, and have a look-see."

"What happens after that?" Paul asked.

"You let us do our work and meet us back down here. Does that sound so hard?"

"Not as such."

"Good," Starkweather replied. "Now get a move on so we can be done with this." After saying that, he sent Paul and Hank on their way with a not so gentle shove toward the side door of the building they'd been watching.

Sensing the tension boiling within the man beside him, Paul whispered, "Keep calm and stick to our plan."

Hank grabbed the door's handle, pulled it open, and stomped inside. "This is a stupid idea," he said under his breath.

"Only if we do exactly as we were told."

"This was a bad idea. Why did I go along with this?"

"Because we don't have many options, that's why," Paul said. "And because it's obvious that Prescott has something valuable if these three men want him so badly. We needed to go after Prescott anyway. That's why we're here. Those men outside would have been coming after him no matter what. At least this way we know what we're dealing with so we have a chance of getting ahead of Starkweather before things get too far out of hand."

They'd entered a narrow room with coat hooks lining the wall on one side. Light from a few lanterns glowed in one of the other rooms farther inside, and the sounds of shuffling feet drew closer at a slow pace.

"They're treating us like we're idiots,"

Hank said.

"Good. That means they think they've already got us right where we need to be and won't be watching us as closely as they should. That's a big advantage."

"I suppose you're right about that. So, what do we do about the rest of this mess we're in?"

Paul grinned and gave Hank a pat on the back. "How about you come up with something and I'll follow your lead?"

Although that had been meant as a joke, there wasn't any time for a response or much of anything else to be added to it. Two men approached the small room and stood in the doorway. One held a lantern and the other had a shotgun. According to the small amount of light that was still casting wavering shadows behind them, there was at least one other person with a lantern that Paul couldn't see.

The closest man with the lantern took half a step back so the one with the shotgun could move forward. "Who are you?" the shotgunner asked. "What are you doing here?"

"We're friends of Leandro Prescott," Hank replied quickly.

"So what?"

"So . . . we're here to check on him. It's

been a while since he's been gone and we're concerned about his well-being."

"Are you, now? What are your names? I'll have a word with him and see if he's heard of you."

"I'm Paul Meakes. Go ahead and ask him about me. He knows who I am."

"And what about this one?" the man with the shotgun asked as he nodded toward Hank. "He a friend as well?"

"I'm George Wesley," Hank replied. "Me and Leo share a bottle of whiskey or two whenever he comes to Leadville."

The shotgunner's eyes narrowed. "Stay put." He then backed out and whispered a few words into the ear of the man holding the lantern. As soon as the shotgunner disappeared down a hall to tromp up some stairs, the man with the lantern drew a pistol from his holster and held it at hip level to point in Paul and Hank's general direction. The other dim lights Paul had spotted bobbed closer until another pair of men moved in to get a look into the coatroom.

"Howdy," Hank said.

None of the men responded. In fact, they looked in at him and Paul as if they were peering at a couple of mangy coyotes that had wandered in from the alley.

"Maybe . . . we should just leave," Paul said.

The man holding the lantern and pistol shook his head. "You'll stay right where you are, just like you were told."

"We can always —"

Before Paul could finish his statement, the sound of a solid impact followed by splintering wood exploded from the front portion of the building. One man's voice was raised to a shout, only to be quickly silenced by a gunshot. Two of the three men in Paul's line of sight turned in that direction while bringing their weapons up to fire. One of them managed to pull his trigger before both were cut down by incoming lead. Voices bellowed from the floor above as heavy steps pounded to the stairs that would bring them to the first floor. The man with the lantern dived into the coatroom with Paul and Hank as another volley of gunfire tore through the hallway a few inches away.

"They friends of yours?" the man asked as he set his lantern down and pointed his gun at Hank. "Answer me!"

On the floor just outside the coatroom, the second man who'd been carrying a lantern groaned and tried to prop himself up on one arm. Before he lifted his upper body halfway off the floor, another gunshot drilled through him and shattered the lantern. Two large figures rushed past the door in the same direction as the first man who'd left to go upstairs. When the gunman in the coatroom tried to lean out and take aim at them, he was knocked out by a clubbing blow from someone else out there.

As soon as the gunman fell face-first to the floor, Bob stepped into the doorway still holding the pistol he'd used to knock the other man unconscious. Looking into the coatroom, he said, "Well, now, it seems hiring you two was a real good idea."

CHAPTER 24

"What are you doing?" Paul asked.

Bob lowered himself to one knee so he could watch the hallway. Judging by the muffled voices and steps, there was a scuffle brewing upstairs that hadn't quite turned into another shoot-out just yet. "Doing what we came to do," Bob said. "And you two held up your end real good. Kept those men busy while me and the rest came straight in through the front."

"What now?"

"We're to hold things down here so Starkweather and Hector have a clear path outside when they're done upstairs."

"Why did you kill these men?" Paul asked.

Bob smirked. "I doubt they would've just lain down if we asked 'em to." Suddenly he spotted something farther down the hall that was well out of Paul and Hank's sight. Shoving past Hank, Bob stepped into the coatroom and held his pistol up near his head. When he slowly thumbed back the hammer, the metallic sound rattled ominously through Paul's ears.

"Joseph?" someone in the hallway said.

Bob placed a finger to his mouth to tell Paul and Hank to keep theirs shut.

"Joseph? Is that you? Can you hear me?" the voice asked from a little closer. As the noise upstairs died down to a rustle of tentative feet scraping against the floor, the man who'd been drawing closer to the coatroom stepped past the doorway without looking inside. He was too distracted by one of the bodies on the floor. Ignoring the little fire that was spreading near the broken lantern, he placed a hand on the dead man's face and said, "Joseph! Who did this to you? Aw, no." He was a man in his late teens or early twenties, clearly rattled by everything that had happened in the last minute.

In stark contrast to the young man's sorrow, Bob grinned and slowly extended his arm to aim his pistol at the target that had presented itself.

"No," Paul hissed.

Bob gnashed his teeth and shot an angry sideways glance at him. So far, the younger man just outside the door was still too overcome by grief and panic to have heard Paul's voice.

Seeing that he wasn't going to be able to talk Bob out of his deadly intentions, Paul grabbed hold of the older man's shoulder to try to pull him off balance. Bob was stronger than he looked and wasn't about to be distracted so easily. The commotion, however, was enough to catch the attention of the young man kneeling over his dead friend.

The instant that young man in the hallway started to turn toward the coatroom, Paul knew he was dead. Bob would pull his trigger, kill the young man, and then . . .

And then Paul fired the pistol that he barely remembered drawing in the first place. The Schofield roared and sent its round directly into Bob's chest at such close range that the older man's shirt caught fire. Paul fired again out of instinct before losing the strength needed to stay upright. Fortunately the walls around him were close enough inside that small room that he barely had to stagger backward half a step before one of them kept him from going any farther.

"Wh . . . who are you?" the young man in the hallway asked.

"Don't fret, kid," Hank said in a strained voice. "We just saved your life."

The young man nodded as if he barely

knew where he was. The gun in his hand trembled.

"Go on and get out of here," Hank said. "Things are about to get worse."

The young man straightened up to look down the hallway. Turning away from the stairs, he said, "I'll get reinforcements," and then took off running.

Hank looked over to Paul and said, "Take a breath and lower that pistol before you put one into me next."

When he heard that, Paul let out the breath that had caught in the back of his throat. Every one of his senses, which had been muddled a moment ago, now snapped into perfect clarity. When the mixed scents of blood and burned gunpowder reached his nose, he had to get out of that room. Joseph's body was still on the floor, so Paul turned away from it to see the stairs roughly where he'd guessed they would be. From the second floor, a few shots were fired and angry voices shouted back and forth.

"They're getting ready to really go at each other," Hank said. "Sounded like a lot of threatening back and forth until now, but I imagine the shots you just fired lit the fuse for the real powder keg to go off."

"I had to," Paul said. "Or he was going to —"

"I know. Just may not have been the smartest thing, is all." Now holding his .44 Colt in one hand and the .38 from his shoulder holster in the other, Hank added, "Let's see this thing through. You with me?"

Paul nodded once even though every ounce of good sense he had was telling him to follow the younger man's example and get out of that dark building as quickly as his feet could carry him.

By the time Paul and Hank had gotten halfway up the stairs, the shooting above them began in earnest. There were only a few lanterns scattered on the wall, casting just enough light to make the place feel like a shadowy nightmare filled with swearing voices and flashes from muzzles firing back and forth. Several steps shy of the top of the flight, Hank dropped down and motioned for Paul to do the same.

"Starkweather!" Hank shouted. "More of 'em are on the way!"

"Cover us!" Starkweather shouted from one of the open doors on the right side of a long hall.

Although it was still difficult to see much up there, Paul recognized the bulky shape of Starkweather leaning out from a nearby doorway. The moment he stuck his head out, gunshots erupted from the farthest end of the hall to punch holes into the walls and doorframe. Even with most of his body out of the line of fire, Paul still had to choke back the instinct to flee. There was so much gunfire coming from either end of the hallway that it seemed the world itself was cracking apart. Starkweather, on the other hand, embraced the chaos like an old friend.

He stepped out of the room where he'd sought refuge and shouted like a wild animal as he fired again and again. Walking at a slow, deliberate pace, he didn't even waver when one stray bullet tore his shirt and clipped his upper left arm like the talon of a diving hawk. Starkweather waited just long enough for the man who'd shot him to stick his head out to fire another round before squeezing his trigger again. The pistol in Starkweather's hand spat a round straight down the hall to snap the other man's head back and drop him to the floor.

Paul had seen more than he could stomach. He'd been too rattled to do much before, but that no longer mattered. Standing up, he shouted as loudly as he could while pulling his trigger.

Hearing Paul's voice and taking that as a cue to charge, Hector stepped out of the room nearby and swung the rifle in his hands toward the far end of the hall. When

Paul fired at him, the Mexican turned around to look for a target. He spotted Paul and Hank right away but didn't yet realize that they'd turned on him. Paul kept firing at Hector and Starkweather. Because he didn't settle on one target, he hit neither of them. Hector wasn't as cool under fire as his partner, especially when Hank joined in.

Starkweather fired a shot that forced one of the other men at the opposite end of the hall to duck back into cover. He pivoted on his heel and got a look at what was going on behind him. He and Paul locked eyes for less than a second, which was long enough for a chill to rake all the way down Paul's spine.

"Give it up!" hollered one of the men all the way down the hall. "It's over!"

Hector was the first to dive back into the room from which he'd come. As he rushed past Starkweather, he bumped the larger man just as he fired at Paul. That piece of lead whipped through the air a scant couple of inches from Paul's head, but he was too far into the fight to turn back now. When Paul kept firing, Hank did the same.

The shooting continued, only now the men at the other end of the hall barely had a target in sight. Starkweather only showed a sliver of himself as he calmly traded an empty pistol for a fresh one from his gun belt. Even with Hank filling the air with fiery lead beside him, Paul knew the fight wouldn't last long when Starkweather decided to go on the offensive once more.

"We have to get out of here," Paul said.

Hank dropped down and told him, "We do that now and this whole trip was a waste. We sure won't get a run at your salesman friend again."

Starkweather fired a shot that came dangerously close to the top of Paul's head.

"Besides," Hank added, "if we run, that maniac will just put a bullet into our backs!"

After pivoting around to fire a few shots down to the other end of the hall, Starkweather stepped out of the room where he'd been hiding and swung his aim back toward the stairs. Paul hadn't seen the small window behind him before, but he became aware of it when a single bullet shattered it and punched into the wall less than a foot away from where Starkweather was standing. While that shot didn't put a fright into Starkweather, the next one made him hop straight back into the room where Hector was still waiting.

At the opposite end of the hall, two men emerged from their own rooms and opened fire while marching straight toward Starkweather. Hank squeezed off another round, but it was the next rifle shot to come through the window that stopped Starkweather in his tracks. The round hissed dangerously close to its target, and what made it even more dangerous was the fact that Starkweather couldn't see who was pulling that trigger. As he backed into the room behind him, Starkweather fired down one end of the hall and then the other.

"He's retreating!" someone from the other end of the hall announced. "Close in on him!"

However many men were down that way, there wasn't one among them who was anxious to charge at Starkweather head-on. Only after the gunfire had stopped for several seconds did the first man from that end of the hall make his move.

"Cover me," Paul said as he climbed the rest of the stairs while hunched over as far as he could stoop.

Hank fired a few rounds into the ceiling as Paul hurried toward the room where Starkweather had gone. After a few seconds, Paul shouted, "They're gone! Must've jumped out the window."

A few more shots were fired, but all of them came from the rifle that had been shooting into the building's second-floor window to keep anyone else from getting too close to Hank or Paul.

Inside the room where Starkweather had been, Paul leaned out through an open window. He thought he saw some movement on the street below but had no way of knowing if he'd spotted Starkweather and Hector or anyone else who happened to be out and about that evening. Wheeling around, Paul holstered his Schofield and headed for the door. "Prescott?" he shouted. "You up here? Speak up. It's Paul . . . Paul Meakes!"

Feeling emboldened after having survived what he'd thought would surely be his last moments on earth, Paul strode into the hallway to look for Prescott. Gun smoke hung thick in the air, drifting like fog in front of the lanterns hanging on the wall. Bodies were strewn on the floor, but those were less of a concern than the bodies that stood facing him with guns in their hands.

"Drop your weapon!" one of the men demanded.

Hank stood at the top of the stairs near the doorway with his hands held high. "You might want to do what he says, Paul. Real slow."

Chapter 25

He was a dead man.

This wasn't the first time Paul had thought that, but it was the time when he surely thought it would come to pass. Three men stood in front of him, all with guns drawn and aiming at him and Hank. If they started pulling their triggers again, that entire hallway would become a slaughterhouse.

"You two," the man at the front of the group facing Paul said, "are under arrest."

"What?" Paul asked breathlessly.

Hank nudged him as if they were two boys sharing a dirty joke. "They're lawmen, Paul. Isn't that a relief?"

"I . . . guess so." Paul had been taking a look at the hallway as he set the Schofield on the floor and slid it away. Soon he spotted the face that had been the reason for him coming to Leadville in the first place. When he saw Prescott lying half in and half out of a room between him and the lawmen, Paul started hurrying toward the fallen salesman.

"Don't move!" one of the lawmen warned. "We'll shoot!"

"Paul?" Prescott croaked from where he was lying on the floor. "Is that really you?"

Seeing Prescott's reaction to him, the lawmen allowed Paul to get closer but were still ready to gun him down at a moment's notice.

Paul paid no attention to the lawmen, the guns in their hands, or the bodies he had to step over to get to Prescott's side. When he saw the salesman, every last one of his thoughts were brought straight back to the reason he'd come. And when it came to saving his children, there was nothing that could stand in his way.

"What happened to you?" Paul asked. One of the lawmen reached down to pick up his Schofield and roughly pat him in search of other weapons, but he didn't care much about that. "What's going on here?"

Lying on his back with his head in the hallway and his legs stretched over the threshold of the door into the next room, Prescott was eerily still. Some of the dim light in the hallway spilled onto him and reflected off a dark wet crimson pool spreading beneath his upper body. He reached up with one hand, swatted Paul's aside when he tried to comfort him, and waved at the men gathered nearby. "He's a friend," Prescott croaked. "A . . . friend."

The lawmen could have backed away or they could have been fashioning a noose for all Paul cared. He didn't take his eyes off the salesman stretched out on the floor. "Tell me what happened!"

"I been . . . shot. What do you think happened?"

"Who are these men?"

"Supposed to . . . protect me." Prescott smiled to display teeth smeared with blood. "Didn't do a very . . . good job, though."

"Protect you from what?"

"From getting shot!" Prescott coughed and grabbed the floor as if it were tilting beneath him. "They're from the . . ."

Seeing that Prescott was fading in and out, Paul looked at the men gathering around him and asked, "Is someone fetching a doctor?"

"He should be here soon," one of the men replied.

Paul turned back to Prescott. "What did you put in that tonic, Leo?"

"What tonic?"

"The tonic you used to clean my daughter's wounds at the trading post. She's sick and it looks like she's been poisoned."

"Maybe it was . . . the arrow."

"No," Paul snapped. "What was in that tonic?"

Prescott closed his eyes. "Is she . . . fever-ish? Weak? Dizzy?"

"Yes!"

"Oh no. Not her too."

"What can you tell me about what hap-pened?" Paul asked, doing his best not to lift the wounded man off the floor and start shaking him.

"That tonic . . . was mostly water," Pres-cott explained. He forced his eyes open wide and grabbed the front of Paul's shirt for support. "Others were getting sick too. From water. River water. From the lakes west of here. I got the water for that tonic from . . . bigger rivers . . . farther east. Thought they were safe."

"Something's wrong with the water?"

Prescott nodded and then winced in pain. "Territorial Mining Company. Tearing into the mountains . . . blasting away rock . . . dumping scrap ore. Don't know it all ex-actly. Could be chemicals . . . acid . . . something that got people sick."

"Why didn't you say anything?"

"I thought I was using clean water," Prescott insisted. "When I heard more people were sick . . . I did say something. I went to the law. That's why I'm here. That's why these men are guarding me."

Paul leaned down to try to hear more of what Prescott was saying. His arm brushed against the salesman's shirt and came away wet with blood. Feeling a hand on his shoulder, Paul turned around to get a look at the lawman who'd arrested him not too long ago.

"We should get him to the doctor," the lawman said.

Prescott shook his head and started to cough. "Leave me here. Please. Hurts too much. Don't move me."

"I'm sorry, Leo," Paul said. "I wish I could have helped you."

"I'm trying to help the . . . sick folks. I'm the one that should be sorry."

"I know a doctor who might be able to help with that. He just needs some of whatever poisoned my children."

"Not just . . . your girl?" Prescott asked. "Both children . . . sick?"

"Yeah. Afraid so."

Clenching his eyes shut, Prescott coughed up a short string of foul language cursing himself and the entire situation. The color was fading from his face quicker than water from a cracked bucket. "Vest pocket. Key.

Take it."

"Save your breath, Leo," Paul said. "We'll get you to a doctor and —"

"Ain't got much . . . breath left. Take the key. Open the wagon. Third cabinet up top. That's what you're after."

"Try to breathe, Leo. You're not looking good."

"I been shot, Paul," Prescott wheezed. "What do you exp . . ."

Grabbing both of Prescott's shoulders, Paul looked him in the eye and shouted, "Leo!"

Prescott didn't answer. Not only that, but there was nothing behind the salesman's eyes any longer. Not even the weakest spark to show there was any life left in him.

"Leo!"

Paul looked up to find Hank and one of the lawmen standing over him. The rest were checking on other fallen men. A few of those forms sprawled on the floor were moving or trying to speak. The rest were unnaturally still.

"He's gone, mister," the lawman said.

Prescott's eyes were still open, so Paul slid them shut. That same hand drifted down from Prescott's face to his vest. The pocket was over the salesman's heart and Paul couldn't help noticing how the other man's torso felt more like a lump of hardened clay instead of anything vaguely resembling a man. He took the key and stood up.

"You can arrest me later," Paul said. "I've got business to tend to."

"Now just wait a second," the lawman said.

As Paul headed for the stairs, Hank shoved past him to step in front of the lawman. "You saw what just happened," Hank said. "We stepped in to help turn the tide of this fight. We even saved the life of one of your young men downstairs, who I'm guessing is a deputy."

"We'll sort that out soon enough," the lawman said. "Right now I need to see exactly who you men are and why you're here."

Paul had reached the top of the stairs by now, and as he began his descent, he could hear the men behind him shuffling for position. He'd passed a young man on his way to the stairs but walked easily past him. That man wore a stunned expression on his face that reminded Paul of soldiers who'd barely survived their first walk across a battlefield during the War Between the States.

"You heard that man's last wishes," Hank said. "He wanted to give over that key, and that's what he did!"

The lawman said something in response to that, but Paul was at the bottom of the stairs by then and couldn't make out the exact words. Several sets of boots thumped toward the stairs behind him, but one more rifle shot through the window caused them to retreat. After that, nobody tried to stop Paul when he marched out of the building and headed straight down Harrison Avenue.

As he walked in the cool night air, Paul tried not to think about everything that had happened that night. Whenever echoes of gunshots crept into the back of his mind, he pulled in a deep breath or concentrated on the crunch of his boots against the ground as he continued to take one step after another. He must have been quite the sight himself, because the people he passed on his way to St. Louis Avenue looked at him as if they'd just discovered a specter haunting their town.

Whenever a door would slam or a shutter would be pushed by the wind to slap against its window, Paul was startled into reaching for the holster at his side. Nobody was out there trying to take a shot at him, so he quickened his pace toward the lot where Prescott's wagon was parked.

As soon as the wagon was in sight, Paul heard footsteps rushing to catch up with him. He spun around to see the young deputy who'd almost been shot in the back by Bob. Before that man could get within spitting distance of Paul, he was swept aside by a figure that moved so quickly it might as well have been a gust of wind. It wasn't until the young deputy was slammed against the wall of a building at the corner of St. Louis Avenue that either he or Paul could get a look at who'd so easily gotten the drop on him. Red Feather gripped the front of the young man's shirt with one hand and held a knife in the other.

"You're not going to stop me from getting into this wagon," Paul announced.

The young man was rattled but managed to keep his voice from wavering when he said, "I wasn't going to try. The sheriff just wants to make sure you didn't try to leave town before he had a chance to talk with you."

"I'll be right back. Just stay put." As he approached the wagon, Paul had no doubt the young deputy would be rooted to his spot like a butterfly pinned to a specimen board.

The key in Paul's hand fit into the lock in the wagon's rear door. After opening that, he kicked a set of steps that folded down to allow him to climb inside. The wagon was dark apart from a bit of light from the moon that allowed him to see blocky cabinets built into the walls on either side. Running his hand along them, Paul counted over to the correct cabinet and opened it. When he reached inside, something sharp and cold bit his hand. After all he'd been through thus far, Paul wouldn't have been deterred from his task if every cabinet in that wagon was filled with rattlesnakes. He kept feeling around in there, only to be cut some more.

Ignoring the pain, he moved his hand enough to realize there were no bottles or vials inside. Paul worked his way through all the cabinets, most of which were empty. He then went back to where he'd started, grabbed one of the small things that were in there, and climbed down from the wagon. Once outside, he could see well enough to confirm what he already knew.

"Did you find what you needed?" Red Feather asked.

"Broken," Paul said as he tossed a jagged shard of glass to the dirt at his feet. "They're all broken."

CHAPTER 26

The cuts on Paul's hands weren't much more than scrapes. One or two sliced deep enough to cause some biting pain, but that was nowhere near enough to distract him from the despair that closed in on him from all sides. Heavier than any sadness was the frustration of thinking he was so close to returning victoriously to his children only to be turned away yet again. He sat in an uncomfortable chair in the sheriff's office, looking down at his bloodied hands, thinking what he should do or where he should go next. Unfortunately the more he thought about it, the murkier everything became.

Paul was shaken from his daze when Hank sat down in the chair beside him as if he'd been dropped into it from the sky. Leaning all the way back while stretching out his legs, Hank let out a heavy sigh and pressed his palms flat against his eyes. "Law dog wants to have a word with you."

"Tell him to get stuffed," Paul grunted.

"I did. Several times. He doesn't like it too much. He also doesn't stop asking questions. It's your turn to be raked over the coals for a while."

Paul leaned his head back and then looked over to Hank. "I want to thank you for what you've done."

"I already told you, I owe you."

"And you repaid me by walking into that gunfight. Not only that but you helped keep us both alive to walk out again."

Hank shrugged. "Just doing what's right. Besides," he added with a smirk, "if that Comanche finds out I lied to his chief about being your partner from the start, I'll probably get skinned alive. Leaving you before this matter is settled might tip my hand."

"But you can leave any time you want," Paul insisted. "I'll cover for you if Red Feather has any questions."

"Only questions you need to worry about right now come from that man right over there," Hank said while pointing to a desk on the other side of the room. "By the way, if it comes up, we've known each other for three years."

"Got it."

Paul stood up and walked across the room. There were only two other men in there with him and Hank. Any other deputies were cleaning up the mess from the shoot-out or checking on the men who'd been taken to see a doctor. When he got to the desk, Paul sat down in the chair that Hank had been using.

The man who sat across from him was the fellow who'd done most of the talking back at the shoot-out. His thick black hair was in need of a trim, as was the mustache that was less than an inch away from taking over the lower portion of his face. Small, sharp eyes watched Paul's every move from beneath iron eyebrows. "You want something to drink?" he asked.

"Some water might be nice," Paul replied.

Reaching into a drawer, the man pulled out a half-full bottle and two glasses. "I was thinking of something a bit stronger. Looks like you could use it."

"Hey!" Hank shouted from his spot on the other side of the room. "You didn't offer me any whiskey!"

"That's right," said the man with the bottle in his hand. "Now shut your mouth and keep it that way!"

Hank did as he was told but clearly wasn't happy about it.

"We never got a proper introduction," said the man with the bottle as he poured a splash of whiskey into each glass. "I'm Sheriff Teller."

At first, Paul was going to refuse the drink. Then he realized the sheriff was correct and that he could use it after all. "Paul Meakes," he said while picking up the glass. He took a long drink and closed his eyes as the firewater worked its way through him. He hadn't been much of a drinker over the last few years, but the last few years hadn't been quite as taxing as the last few days. The liquor he drank from that bottle calmed him better than an old friend by loosening knots that had been tied in his muscles and nerves. After another swallow, he was able to take an easy breath.

"Care for another?" the sheriff asked.

"Better not. Thank you."

"According to what Hudson said, I should be the one to thank you."

"Hudson?"

"He's the deputy that nearly got bushwhacked by that man you shot," the sheriff explained. "If you hadn't stepped up when you did, there'd be one more coffin to bury. There's too many already after tonight."

"What happened back there anyway?" Paul asked.

"I was gonna ask the same thing from you. I suppose I can start, though. The short of it is that a few days ago, Leandro Prescott came to me asking for protection. His life was threatened and he was convinced the men that approached him weren't just full of smoke. I had one of my men keep an eye on him and he was there when one of those killers walked right up and took a shot at Prescott."

"Why would someone want to shoot Prescott?"

"He told us it had something to do with Territorial Mining," the sheriff replied. "That sound familiar?"

"Only from what Leo said to me before he died. I'm guessing you heard it?"

"I did. What are you and your friend doing in Leadville?"

"I'm here to have a word with Prescott on a pressing matter," Paul said. "I thought he'd poisoned my children. He told me it was the water used in his tonic."

Sheriff Teller nodded. "I also heard you say your children were running fevers, sweating, shaky on their feet, and such?"

"That's right."

"Lots of other folks as far away as Denver have been having the same symptoms. With a good amount of doctoring, most of them feel better in a week or two."

"Perhaps if they drank it, it's not as bad,"

Paul said. "My children had the poison spilled directly into their blood."

"Good Lord. How'd that happen?"

"It's a long story, Sheriff. To be quite blunt, I'm sick of telling it. All I know is that their lives are in danger. You said most of those people who were sick got better. Not all?"

"That's right. Some of them . . . well . . . didn't fare too well."

"You mean they died."

Now it was the sheriff's turn to take a drink. "Yeah. They died."

Recognizing something in the other man's haunted expression, Paul asked, "Did you lose someone in particular?"

"Almost. My sister damn near died, but she pulled through. Just barely, though. Thought I was gonna lose her for sure."

"That's where my children are," Paul said as he leaned forward. "Right on the verge of being lost. I came all this way because a doctor back home said if he got a look at whatever made them sick, he could work out some sort of cure or antidote or something."

"A few other doctors tried something like that," Teller said. "Doctors in Denver and Colorado Springs, I believe. They never found much of anything."

"Well, the doctor tending to my young ones seemed real certain he could mix something up that could help. Since that's all I've got to hang my hat on at the moment, I'm doing my level best to get him what he needs."

"Hudson told me you took a gander inside Prescott's wagon."

"Yeah," Paul said. "Someone had already gotten in there and broken every last bottle of what I was after."

"Must have been those same killers who stormed that lawyer's office where we were keeping Prescott hid away. How'd you come to be there at just the right time to keep Hudson from meeting his maker anyhow?"

Paul told the sheriff how he and Hank had wound up throwing in with Starkweather. "I just wanted to find Prescott," he said. "If he was in trouble, I thought I could help, and if he was just conducting business with those men, I thought I could at least get a word with him about that tonic."

"After all that thinking you say you did," Sheriff Teller said, "you should have thought some more before joining up with the likes of Starkweather."

"I didn't really join him," Paul explained.

Teller chuckled. "That's right. You pretended to join him and then shot one of his men. Trust me, that ain't a real good thing in his eyes."

"I didn't guess it would be."

"Do you know who Starkweather is?"

"Beyond what I've seen in the last few hours?" Paul said. "No. But I suppose you're going to tell me."

"I only wish I could have told you before. Starkweather is wanted for at least twelve killings in nearly as many states. Anyone who knows him will be quick to add that there's probably plenty of other killings he's taken part in that just ain't common knowledge."

"Sounds like the sort of man who'd charge into a building and shoot it full of holes."

"More like he's the sort of man who's good enough with a gun in his hand that he charged into a building outnumbered three to one, kept me and my men cornered, and managed to put down his target without a whole lot of trouble. I'm not exactly proud to admit it, but if you hadn't been there, Starkweather or his men might not have had a casualty among them."

"I'd wager he's gone now," Paul said.

Teller nodded. "You'd be right about that. He got what he was after."

"Do you know why he wanted to kill Prescott?"

"To keep him quiet. Your friend the sales- man was blamed when some of the folks who drank his tonic got sick. Once word started coming in from Denver that it had to do with the water instead of his so-called medicines, Prescott was mostly off the hook. Of course, there was still the matter of him swindling some folks with that cheap tonic of his, but that's something for another time. In the end, Prescott decided to do the right thing and testify to a judge about what he saw when he was gathering his water and the offers made by Territorial Mining for him to keep his mouth shut about what they were doing."

"Prescott was a good man," Paul said. "He would have done the right thing no matter what."

Sheriff Teller nodded solemnly. "I believe that's true. We did our best to keep him alive. It's a shame it wasn't enough."

"So it's chemicals from that mining com- pany that are poisoning the water?"

"That's what Prescott said. I've seen a few big mining operations do their work and it's never a pretty sight. They blast holes in the ground, use currents of water to rip into the sides of mountains. All that machinery kicks up smoke and spits out all manner of grease or oil. They've got chemists testing the purity of what they find, and when they're done, Lord only knows where they dump their leftovers. It's not a lot, but it's potent."

"Acid's like that," Paul grumbled. "Doesn't take much of it to do a good amount of damage."

"Well, there's nothing good about what Prescott saw."

"Can't you do something to Territorial Mining for having him killed?"

"Sure," Teller said, "if I had proof it was them. Proof that'd stand up in court, that is. All I've got is the body of that man you killed, and though he's also wanted for murder, there's nothing that proves he was here to kill on the order of Territorial Mining."

"Where is Territorial Mining anyway?" Paul asked.

"Just about anywhere there's ore to be dug. The company was founded in Virginia or somewhere out in the Appalachians, I believe. They've got interests all across the country and some in Mexico."

"If they were spread out so far, wouldn't the entire country be getting sick by now?"

"Could be this is just the start of it," the lawman said. "Could be their operations in the Rockies are just messier than the rest. Only ones who know for certain why this mess is here instead of anywhere else is that mining company and they don't seem overly fond of sharing their motives with the likes of us."

"I suppose not."

Sheriff Teller drummed his fingers on his desk. At first, it seemed he was studying the label on the bottle of whiskey he'd produced from his bottom drawer. Then he said, "Who else have you got with you? Apart from that scalper over there, I mean."

"Scalper?"

"Don't tell me you don't know who your friend is. Hank's not just some affable fellow who decided to go along with you to visit Mr. Prescott. He hunts Indians for a living. Hasn't been at it very long, though."

"You know him?"

"Any lawman who shares territory with the tribes had better know what scalpers are in the area," Teller said. "Even if they get paid by the army, they're still killers."

"So are bounty hunters," Paul said.

"And good lawmen should keep track of them as well. But men like Hank over there are different from bounty hunters. They stick to certain areas. The dangerous lands. Men like him stir things up even worse than they already are."

"Why are you asking me this?"

"Because Hudson told me he was jumped by an Indian while he was following you to Prescott's wagon. He says the Indian seemed to be taking orders from you."

From the moment he'd stepped foot into the sheriff's office, Paul had been waiting for someone to mention Red Feather. He thought it would have happened right away, but since the Comanche had practically vanished after releasing the young deputy, he figured there was always a chance that Hudson was neglecting to bring up the matter to salvage some of his reputation. Now that the subject had been broached, Paul was somewhat relieved. When Sheriff Teller spoke of the Comanche, he displayed more curiosity than hatred or disgust.

"He wasn't taking orders from me," Paul said. "But he was helping me."

"Obviously," Teller said. "Was he the one shooting through the window back at the lawyer's office?"

"Yes."

"I guessed as much."

"How did you know?" Paul asked. "Did one of your men see him?"

"Quite the opposite. None of my deputies saw him and they were looking for any riflemen posted on a rooftop or such. The fact that he went unseen and also managed to pick off his targets from a distance at such a difficult angle all point to a Comanche. Damn fine hunters, whether they're carrying a bow or a rifle. From my experience, they're no good with pistols. What do you say to that?"

"I say it's never a good idea to judge any large group of people in such a sweeping manner."

"Very true," the sheriff replied. "Now comes the question that's really stuck in my craw. How'd you get an Injun to work with you when you're also riding with a scalper at your side?"

"That's another long story."

"But I imagine it's an interesting one."

"Hey!" Hank said from his seat. "Are you two talkin' about me?"

"Why?" the sheriff hollered back. "Were your ears burning?"

"Hank's just trying to help me," Paul said. "And so is . . . so is the Indian." He'd almost called Red Feather by name. But the sheriff was correct about these being dangerous lands. The tribes already had plenty of trouble, and having killers like Starkweather after them for some measure of retribution was no way to repay someone who was fighting for his children's lives.

"If that's the case," Teller said, "then I'll

buy him a drink. Hudson, bring this over to Mr. Adley over there."

The young deputy approached the desk. Having nearly been shot in the back and then held at the point of Red Feather's blade, Hudson was justifiably shaky. His hands didn't tremble as he carried the glass of whiskey that the sheriff had poured, but the sheen of sweat on his brow reflected his nervousness well enough.

"That's more like it!" Hank said once he got the whiskey in his hand.

"Now I've got a question I've been meaning to ask," Paul said. "Are we still under arrest?"

"That didn't seem to keep you from doing what you pleased a little while ago after the shooting stopped," Teller pointed out.

"I wasn't going far," Paul said. "As I already mentioned, I've still got business to conduct away from this town."

"Well, you did step in on my deputy's behalf, so you'll be free to leave in the morning. In the meantime, I've got a secure place for you and your friend to spend the night, seeing as how those killers could still be out there somewhere." Teller hooked a thumb toward the next room. The door was open, so the jail cells within could be seen.

"Are you serious?" Paul asked.

"Call it protective custody."

"I call it a heap of bull dung!" Hank shouted.

"You can call it that too," the sheriff said, "but them cots are still where you'll be laying your heads this evening."

CHAPTER 27

Strangely enough, Paul slept better on that cot than he had in a while. There was something restful about being in a spot where there was only one thing to do while he was in it. His thoughts were still troubled and lingered on his children, but that couldn't be helped. For that short stretch of hours while all his choices were taken away, he could allow himself to just stop and take a breath. He dreamed he was lying on a raft being swept down a long stretch of white water. When he opened his eyes again, he could still hear the rushing sound that had filled his head.

Wind blew through the back room of the sheriff's office and went all the way out one of the front windows to create a hollow roar. Paul sat up amid the grating creak of his cot and looked through the bars into the next cell. Lying there curled in a tight ball was Hank, snoring loudly and adding another part of the churning rush of wind that had filled his hectic dream. Walking to the cell door, Paul touched one of the bars, which was enough to cause them to swing an inch outward. With a harder push, the door swung all the way open and filled the back room with the screech of rusty hinges.

"What's that?" Hank groaned as he flopped over and reached for the empty holster at his side. "Where . . . oh. That's right." He got up, scratched, and cleared his throat. "You couldn't sleep either, huh?"

"I slept fine and so did you."

"I did?"

"Yeah," Paul said. "If not, you were just snoring to make noise and even you're not that inhospitable."

"Guess I did nod off for a spell. You think we're free to go?"

"You're free to go now," someone shouted from the next room.

Paul walked out there to find one of the deputies sitting at the sheriff's desk. He was one of the older of the bunch and even had five or six years on Teller himself. Looking up at Paul from behind the newspaper he was reading, he said, "That's what the sheriff told me. So long as you didn't try to leave before sunup, you could go and it's well past that."

"What about our guns?" Paul asked.

"Collect 'em on your way out," the deputy said. "Sheriff Teller couldn't have armed men sleeping in his jail. Wouldn't look right."

"Yeah," Hank said while stretching in the next room. "Wouldn't want to give the drunks and vagrants the wrong impression."

The deputy flipped the page of his *Chronicle.* "Exactly. You won't be able to take that dead salesman's wagon with you, though. Speaking of which, Sheriff Teller would like you to leave that key here."

"Fine with me," Paul replied while digging the key from his pocket. "Before I go, I'd like to take one last look inside since I'll be able to see what's in there much better than I could last night."

"Suit yourself," the deputy said. "You can walk over there and have your look. Your guns and horses will be waiting here when you get back."

Hank stomped forward while hitching up his pants. "We'll take them now because they're our property! Just because you're the law around here don't mean you can steal from us whenever you like."

The deputy didn't have anything to say to that. He simply stared at his paper until it was time to once again flip the page.

"I don't mind going," Paul told Hank. "I'll be right back and I won't need my gun just to look inside a wagon. The walk will do me some good. Could do you some good as well."

"I should probably stay here to make certain our things aren't trifled with," Hank said while glaring at the deputy.

"Now I really think you should come with me. Let's go." Before Hank could protest again, Paul grabbed him by the collar and dragged him along much as he'd dragged David to church on several sleepy Sundays.

As soon as they were outside, Paul let him go and asked, "What's the matter with you? Those lawmen showed us a courtesy by putting us up for the night and turning us loose."

"Not like they're a bunch of saints. You saved one of their lives last night and the Injun saved some more of them by covering all of us with his rifle."

"They still could have kept us locked up for any number of reasons. The least of which was that we happened to throw in on the wrong side of that fight."

"Wasn't that the plan?" Hank asked. "It's not like we were going to step out of line once things went sour."

"I know. Even if I was the one to come up

with the idea, it still never sat right. I've carried a gun before but never had to use it so much as I have over the last few days. More and more, I'm being reminded that I'm still a businessman that's been away from his store for too long."

"Could've fooled me," Hank said as he slapped Paul on the back. "You handled yourself like a real man when the lead started to fly. I've got to admit I was also pleasantly surprised by how well that Comanche held up his end. Speaking of the redskin, where did he get to anyway?"

"Probably watching over us right now. You might want to watch what you say when you're calling him anything but his name."

"Eh, he's used to it. If he was so offended, he would've stuck a knife in me already."

They'd made it to Harrison Avenue and could see St. Louis Avenue a bit farther down. The saloons might not have been as crowded as they were the night before, but even in the morning hours they were still seeing a good amount of patronage. The more he walked, the more cheerful Hank became. When they got close enough to the Monarch, he sniffed the air like a dog following the scent of fresh meat. "They serve a good breakfast in there," he said. "And some of the finest coffee in the Rockies."

"What about griddle cakes?" Paul asked. "It's been too long since I've had griddle cakes."

"Of course they serve griddle cakes! At least, I think they do. If not, the ladies that'll bring you your coffee will make you forget all about 'em."

"First I need to get a look inside that wagon. After that, if there's time, we can stop for some breakfast."

"Still trying to do right by those law dogs?" Hank groused. "Forget about them. They're probably sleeping the day away like usual. No need to make nice with them and no need to fret so much about the Injun."

"What do you have against lawmen?" Paul asked.

"In my line of work, me and them don't tend to see eye to eye. Even when we do, they take it upon themselves to run me out of town after I did their jobs for them."

"I don't think lawmen's jobs include killing Indians."

Judging by the smug grin and humorless grunt of a chuckle that came from the back of Hank's throat, he didn't quite agree with that statement. Even so, he wasn't about to argue the point any further. "Guess I gotta admit the lawmen here have been friendlier than the last time I came through this town."

Paul was about to ask what had happened on that last visit to Leadville but decided against it. He doubted he truly wanted to know all the details, and the lot containing Prescott's wagon wasn't much farther ahead.

From a distance, the man sitting in one corner of the lot looked more like a giant sack of something that had been left to rot in the sun. When he got to his feet and stomped toward the fence, Randy was already sputtering and angrily shaking his fist at the two approaching men. "I'm glad you came back! Saves me the trouble of calling the sheriff to collect you from wherever you been hiding."

"We've been hiding in the sheriff's office, you idiot," Hank replied. "Better than the pigsty that you obviously slept in."

Too riled up to continue fighting with Hank, the caretaker shifted his focus to Paul and said, "You're the one that trespassed on my property and busted into that wagon!"

"I may have trespassed," Paul replied, "but I didn't break into anything. I had a key and I still do." He extended his hand to show Prescott's key to Randy while making certain not to get it close enough for it to be snatched away.

"That don't prove nothin'!" Randy snarled.

"Then tell it to the sheriff," Hank said as he put himself between the wagon and the angry caretaker. "Right now this man's the closest thing to that wagon's rightful owner, so you can step aside and let him pass."

There was plenty more back and forth between those two, but Paul ignored it as he walked through the gate, approached the wagon, and fit the key into the rear door. Now that there was sunlight flooding inside the wagon, Paul could see nearly everything within the cramped confines. It was even worse than he'd guessed when he was fumbling in the shadows the night before.

The floor was littered with paper labels and pages torn from ledgers. He checked the cabinet Prescott had mentioned to find it littered with broken glass and soaked with the liquid that had been spilled. Just to be thorough, Paul continued looking through the rest of the cabinets. Not everything was broken. He found several jars of various powders, a few jugs of syrup, several dry goods including sugar, wheat, and oats, and plenty of dyes. There were also many different samples of all the contraptions that had captured Prescott's imagination. When he came upon those items, Paul stopped what he was doing.

Seeing those devices, many of which didn't come close to performing the functions for which they'd been built, reminded him of his friend. Prescott had been an accomplished salesman, but when he described those contraptions, he did so with a flair and spark in his eye that could only be genuine enthusiasm. He loved those cockamamie devices, and even if they worked halfway, he saw it as a small miracle. On more than one occasion, he and David had stood outside that wagon, watching one of those contraptions sputter and rattle, laughing joyously at the loud display. They would laugh even harder at the machines that shook themselves apart or exploded in a cloud of black smoke. All the while, Paul and Abigail had looked on while shaking their heads.

Now Prescott was dead.

And Paul's children . . .

"Stop!" Randy shouted from outside the wagon. "I said stop! I'll get my shotgun!"

"Go ahead and get it, you ape," Hank shouted back as he approached the open door at the back of the wagon. "Threaten me with your shotgun and see what happens. I guarantee you won't like it!"

Paul drew a quick breath and swiped at his eyes with the back of one hand before Hank stuck his head inside.

"This one's getting uncooperative," Hank said. "You find what you need?"

"There's nothing here," Paul said. "Let's go."

They left the wagon and its angry caretaker behind them.

On their way back to the sheriff's office, Paul and Hank stopped in for breakfast. The griddle cakes were almost good enough to bring Paul's spirits back out of the shadows.

CHAPTER 28

When Paul and Hank arrived back at the sheriff's office, Teller himself was there to greet them. "Took you long enough," the lawman said as he walked around his desk and toward a tall cabinet in one corner of the room. "I thought maybe you'd left town before I had a chance to wish you well."

"Not without our horses," Hank said.

"Very true. Did you find anything worth seeing in that wagon?"

"No," Paul replied. "And I won't be needing to see anything else. What will happen to that wagon from here?"

"It'll be kept safe until we can find the salesman's next of kin. Would you be able to help in that regard?"

"He used to mention a sister every now and then. I believe she lives in Wyoming. I can check on it and send word back to you, but that will have to wait until I'm through with my business in Colorado."

Teller unlocked the cabinet and opened it. Inside, there were several rifles and shotguns held within a wooden rack as well as an array of pistols hanging from pegs and resting at the bottom of the wooden container. Among the pistols were Paul's Schofield and Hank's Colt. The sheriff took one of those pistols in each hand, spun them so the grips were facing outward, and offered them to their owners.

"Here you go," Teller said. "As promised."

Paul placed the wagon key on the sheriff's desk and then took his pistol. When Hank reclaimed his weapon, he immediately asked, "What about the .38?"

"I have only two hands, Mr. Adley." The sheriff turned and picked up Hank's second pistol so he could hand it over.

When Hank took the gun without another word, Paul asked, "Don't you have something to say to the sheriff?"

Glaring at him, Hank said, "I ain't one of your kids."

"Then stop acting like one."

Hank sighed, faced the sheriff, and said, "Much obliged."

"There, now," Paul said to complete the illusion that he was having a conversation he'd been through countless times before with David and Abigail. "Was that so hard?"

Muttering curses under his breath that the Meakes children hopefully wouldn't learn for some time, Hank left the sheriff's office.

"Your horses are out back," Teller said.

Paul nodded. "Your deputy already told us. I'd like to thank you for putting a roof over our heads for the night."

"Well, I couldn't exactly let you charge out after those gunmen in your state of mind. You only would have gotten yourself killed. Also, I owed you for your help in the middle of all that shooting. Still do."

"I'm sure you've saved a person or two in your day. Consider this some small amount of repayment."

Sheriff Teller didn't seem to quite know what to do with that. Obviously he wasn't accustomed to receiving compliments and waited for a few seconds for some barbed words to go along with this one. When they didn't come, he nodded and gave Paul a simple thank-you.

"I don't suppose you'd have more detailed instructions on how to get to that Territorial Mining site?" Paul asked.

After locking up the gun cabinet, Teller went to his desk and picked up a folded piece of paper. "Already drew you a map. These are two of the biggest sites that came to mind. There's bound to be plenty more throughout the Rockies, but this should give you a fairly good start. From what I hear, that mining company hasn't heeded any requests to stop what they were doing, and when fines come along, they just pay them. Because of that, I'd guess any one of their sites should suit your purposes just as well as another."

Paul took the map from the sheriff and gave it a quick look. "Am I reading this right? The closest site is only about five miles from here?"

"That's right. And if you don't like those I showed you, just pick a direction and ride for a while. Follow your nose, listen for the noise, and you should find another Territorial claim real quick."

"Think you could spare four or five gun hands to go along with me?"

"You don't know how close I am to taking you up on that," Teller said with a smile. "Truth of the matter is, and I'm ashamed to say, a man in my position needs to tread lightly around rich men and big companies who have the pull to make a lot of bad things happen through official channels. That probably don't make a lot of sense, but it's a roundabout way of saying . . ."

"I've dealt with plenty of businesses and

have seen enough to know how the world works," Paul said. "What you said makes perfect sense. I was only joking about you lending me some of your deputies. I know you've got plenty to worry about in just doing your job here and keeping it. Thanks for all you've done on my behalf."

Teller's eyes narrowed and he lowered his voice a bit when he asked, "You ever work in a factory?"

Taken aback by the abrupt subject change, Paul said, "One or two."

"Territorial Mining is just like any other machine. The bigger it gets, the easier it is for something small to break loose and bring the whole thing crashing down. You can whack away at it all day long with a hammer, but toss a little stone into the wrong gears or take out the right spring and . . ." He held out one fist and then opened it like a blossoming explosion. He then closed that fist again to keep one finger pointed toward Paul. "You can do a hell of a lot more damage on your own than you could with me and all of my deputies riding alongside you. Just do me a favor and make sure to be far enough away when the machine starts to smoke."

"I'll sure try." With that, Paul tipped his hat and left the office.

Outside, Hank was waiting with all three of their horses. "He give you any more grief?"

"No. He gave me a map."

"I know where we're headed."

"Do you?" Paul asked. "And now you're an expert in where to find Territorial Mining sites?"

"I do plenty of traveling in my line of work, and lots of that traveling takes me through these mountains. All I needed was some time to think things over so I could recall some good spots to check."

Holding out the map, Paul asked, "Are these any of the spots you were thinking about?"

Hank leaned over to study the map. After taking just a bit too long to do so, he climbed into his saddle and said, "Yep. I can tell you exactly which one to go to first."

Paul mounted his horse and got himself situated before flicking his reins to head down Harrison Avenue. The reins to Red Feather's horse were looped around his saddle horn, and that animal followed along without a lick of protest. "Is this just a way for you to seem more useful than a lawman?" Paul asked.

"You think I would want to do something like that?"

"I haven't known you for very long and I'm already certain you would want to do something like that."

As they rode past the Monarch, a single figure stepped out of one of the small bunches of people gathered outside Mannie Hyman's saloon next door. Having been stooped over just enough to blend in, Red Feather strode into the street and swung onto his horse's back without breaking stride. "We are leaving?" he asked.

"That's right," Hank said. "By the way . . . that was some nice shooting back there."

Red Feather twisted around in his saddle to look behind him. "Back where?"

"Back at that lawyer's office the other night."

Growing more confused by the second, the Comanche gave up on Hank altogether and looked over at Paul.

"That building where Prescott was being held," Paul explained. "It was a lawyer's office."

"Were any lawyers killed?" Red Feather asked.

"Not that I know of."

"Too bad."

For several seconds, neither of the other two men knew how to respond to that. Paul was the first to break out laughing and

Hank quickly joined in. "I didn't think you redskins had a sense of humor," Hank said.

"Call me that one more time and you'll be laughing from a fresh hole in your face."

"All right, all right. Last time I use that phrase. What do you prefer instead? Injun or savage?"

Now it was Red Feather's turn to scowl before giving in to a chuckle that caused his shoulders to rumble slightly. "You are funny," he said. "Or brave. Possibly foolish. Either way, you're amusing to me."

"Oh, good," Hank sighed. "That's all I ever wanted."

"Where are we going now?" Red Feather asked. "Since you spent the night in jail, I will guess that it is far away from this place."

"It's not too far," Paul replied.

"And when we get there?"

"We'll be tossing cogs into a real big machine."

CHAPTER 29

It would have been a short ride if the three men could have gone as the crow flies. Since Paul, Hank, and Red Feather had not one set of wings between them, they needed to follow twisting mountain paths and trails that led to crumbled passes or washed-out ravines. Still, where their lack of wings failed them, sheer tenacity saw them through and they made a good amount of progress over the course of a grueling day. By late afternoon, they'd caught a taste of what they were after.

Hank rode in the middle of the group with Red Feather up front and Paul bringing up the rear. The order changed throughout the day, depending on who needed to rest his eyes and who was so anxious that he couldn't bear to be anywhere but at the tip of the spear. Grimacing and smacking his lips, Hank started shifting uncomfortably in his saddle. "What in blazes is that?" he groaned.

"What are you talking about?" Paul asked.

"You don't smell that? Ugh, for that matter, you don't *taste* it?"

Paul pulled in a deep breath and quickly regretted it. The foul stench of burning metal mingled with sulfur, and when enough of it filled his nose, it seeped to the back of his throat to become a taste that quickly brought a sneer to his face. "Now I know what you're talking about. Tastes like I licked the inside of a steam engine."

"Hey up there," Hank said. "Don't you smell it?"

"Of course I do," Red Feather replied. "I just do not bleat about it like a crying child."

"Or maybe you're just more accustomed to horrible stenches than the rest of us."

"That could be," the Comanche said. "After riding with you for this long, I have had to learn to live with many bad smells."

"And he just keeps getting funnier by the day."

"Stop, both of you," Paul said.

Hank groaned while tying a bandanna over his nose and mouth. "We were just having a bit of fun."

"No. I mean . . . stop!"

Instead of stopping what they were saying, the other two pulled back on their reins to stop moving down the path that was about to lead them between two large boulders forming a natural gateway in front of them. Paul unfolded the map he'd been given so he could see every mark the sheriff had made. It wasn't a detailed diagram, to be certain, but there was enough scrawled onto the paper to convince Paul of one thing.

"The mining camp," Paul announced. "It's got to be right past those rocks."

"That is what we are smelling," Red Feather said. "It is the blood of this land being spilled by men and their machines."

"It's either that," Hank said, "or the chemicals used to maintain those machines and test whatever ore that's collected."

"I can scout ahead," Red Feather offered.

Paul folded the map up and stuck it into his pocket. "I'll go as well," he said. "After coming this far, I want to get a look at this place."

Red Feather nodded once and flicked his reins.

After Paul had ridden past him, Hank said, "Yeah, well, I suppose I'll just stay put right here."

As they rode between the boulders, the clatter of horses' hooves became a loud banging of iron against stone. The echo rolled between Paul's ears like a locomotive that scraped its stacks against every inch of a low tunnel. They emerged on the other side of the rocks, ready for a hostile reception. Instead Paul and Red Feather got a good look at a large mining operation stretched out below their position.

There were half a dozen wooden shacks and plenty of tents scattered along the bottom of a mostly flat basin. Several covered wagons were lined up on opposite ends of the camp, enclosing it like a pair of half-moons curving toward each other. Two conveyor belts carried broken rock out of a large cave at the eleven o'clock position relative to where Paul and Red Feather were observing. At the three o'clock position was a tall crevice in a wall of rock that seemed to be a focal point for much of the activity within the camp.

After dismounting, Paul grabbed his field glasses and made his way to the edge of the trail marking a sharp descent into the basin. Red Feather led the horses farther back along the path between the boulders where they could remain without being spotted from below. When he returned to Paul's side, the Comanche moved in a low crouch that made him look like a predatory cat.

"There's something strange about that crevice," Paul said while squinting through the field glasses.

"It looks more like a wound."

"You're right. The sides are too straight. I'm guessing it wasn't there before this bunch showed up. Doesn't exactly look like it was blasted out, though."

"Could have been stripped away by water," Red Feather said. "Other mining companies use it to tear into the mountains and sift through what is left behind. It makes a rain that is filled with gravel that pelts all those below when it falls."

"Sounds delightful."

"It is not."

Slowly shifting his gaze through the camp, Paul eventually spotted a series of connected pipes. There were larger ones leading into the camp from one side, and the diameter of the connected pipes gradually decreased until they stretched into the straight crevice.

"I think you're right," Paul said. "There must be a river just out of sight. I can see the pipes they're using to bring water in and blast at that rock. Seems a bit close to the rest of the camp to be doing that sort of work, though."

"That camp is designed to be moved

quickly. Much like ones used by my people when we are moving to richer hunting grounds."

Looking away from the crevice, Paul studied the perimeter of the camp. "Looks like there's at least two paths big enough for wagons to come and go from there. Could be another somewhere below us."

"I will go and see. Stay here." Without waiting for Paul to give his thoughts on the matter, Red Feather crept away. When Paul looked back to try to find him, all he saw was the Comanche scaling one of the boulders that formed the passage they'd used to get there like a giant lizard finding a good spot to sun its back. Paul could make out some of the hand- and footholds that Red Feather was using, but he didn't fool himself for an instant into thinking he could follow in the Comanche's steps.

Settling into his spot near the edge of the drop-off, Paul studied more of the camp. Instead of looking through the field glasses, he took in the wider scope of things with his naked eyes. The mining camp wasn't very busy at the moment. There were people walking in and out of the shacks and various tents that had been set up in the basin, but there didn't seem to be nearly enough to justify a camp of that size. While the smell that had caught their attention earlier was stronger, Paul's senses were slowly acclimating to it. His first guess as to the source of the stench was the three shacks on the outskirts of camp that spewed dark gray smoke through black pipe chimneys in the center of their roofs.

Paul watched those shacks for a few minutes until he saw one of the doors open. Quickly bringing the field glasses to his eyes, he was able to get a good look at the spindly fellow who emerged wearing what looked like a butcher's apron and heavy gloves stretching halfway up to his elbows. He wore a bandanna around his face, which he tugged down as soon as he took a few steps out of the shack. From this distance, it was impossible for Paul to tell how much of the discoloration on the spindly man's face was filth from whatever smoke was being belched into the mountain air or how much had grown there from lack of a straight razor. The man took a few moments to stretch his back and rub his hands together before being approached by someone else.

In the space of a few seconds, Paul could tell this other man was higher up the chain of command than anyone else he'd seen thus far. Although he wasn't much bigger than the burly workers going about their assigned tasks, he carried himself with undeniable authority. The clothes he wore were just a bit cleaner and the cut of his jacket was that of a more expensive garment than those worn by the rest of the men. When this man got closer to the fellow in the butcher's smock, he only needed to say a few words to get him to stand up straighter as if coming to attention.

The man in the fine jacket spoke easily enough and wore a smile beneath a perfectly trimmed beard of thick black whiskers. His rounded face even seemed friendly at first glance, but the smaller man in the smock was obviously on his guard while near him. When the man in the jacket turned and walked away, the fellow in the smock waited a short while before exhaling and allowing his posture to return to the tired slouch it had been prior to the other man's arrival.

Paul was about to lower the field glasses again when he noticed the man in the jacket quickly stop and change course. Instead of walking back to the tent from which he'd emerged, he strode toward a wooden rack laden with lengths of pipe of various diameters. Glancing ahead to see what had caught the man's eye, Paul saw a familiar face among the strangers.

If Starkweather hadn't been wearing a hat, his shaved head might have been easier to spot from a distance. As it was, the coldness of his stare and the vulturelike angle of his head were more than enough to catch Paul's eye. While the man in the jacket didn't defer to Starkweather, there was a noticeable change in his demeanor in comparison to how he'd been around the man in the smock. Both men exchanged a few words and when the conversation was over, Starkweather started walking toward the crevice.

Suddenly Starkweather stopped and wheeled around to look toward the ridge overlooking the camp. Paul reflexively angled the field glasses downward and pressed himself flat against the rock. The cold seeping into his flesh from the stone was nothing compared to the frightened chill that ran down Paul's spine as he waited for the killer to raise an alarm or fire a shot up at him.

Paul worried that he'd been spotted.

Then he worried that Red Feather had been spotted.

If neither of those things had happened, there was always the chance that Hank had gotten tired of waiting, wandered somewhere to see the camp for himself, and skylined himself so he could be spotted.

After a few moments, Paul shifted so he could once again see what was going on in the basin below. Starkweather was still in the same spot, staring up at the ridge. Every so often, Paul swore he could feel a ghostly presence sweep over him as if the killer's gaze actually had a weight of its own.

Paul even felt as if looking at Starkweather for too long was a mistake in itself. Every man had felt the sensation of being watched, and a man like that must have honed those instincts to a much sharper degree. Then again, if Paul moved too much, there was just as big a possibility that that would be enough to give him away.

Finally Starkweather looked away from the ridge and continued walking toward the crevice.

"Thank God," Paul sighed.

Less than a second after giving his heartfelt praise, Paul heard movement coming from the rocks above. Since it was the opposite direction that Red Feather had climbed, he drew his Schofield and prepared himself to fight for his life. Instead of a gunman, he saw the Comanche peering down at him. Red Feather must have been even fleeter of foot than Paul had thought and crossed from one side of the ridge to the other. As soon as Paul looked up at him, the Comanche pointed down to the side of the camp with the smoke-spewing shacks. Paul looked down there to see the man in the smock speaking to a small group of similarly dressed partners.

The men who'd come to join the first were carrying large wooden trays that were roughly the size of a house's windowpane. Through the field glasses, Paul saw rocks on the trays. He also saw the first man in the smock remove a vial from a pocket and pour a small amount of something onto one of the rocks. Smoke curled up from the rock, which was fanned aside so as not to obscure any of the men's vision. Whatever the first man saw, it made him happy enough to hurry into the shack and motion for the others to follow.

Paul looked up to Red Feather and was immediately shown three spots where men were posted at the camp's perimeter. He didn't need the field glasses to know those men were guards and most likely armed. Nodding up to the Comanche, Paul scooted back until it was safe to get to his feet and hurry back to his horse. By the time he'd climbed into his saddle, Red Feather had scaled down from the top of the boulder and jumped onto the back of his horse as well. The two of them rode out the way they'd come and found Hank waiting right where they'd left him.

"You're back!" Hank said.

Paul slipped the field glasses back into his saddlebag while saying, "You sound surprised."

"I am. Considering how well things have been going lately, I thought one or both of you would have been killed or captured in the amount of time you were gone. Does that mean there's no mining operation over there?"

"Not at all. There's a mining operation all right," Paul replied. "A good-sized one, at that."

"Great. So, when do we head down there and get . . . whatever it is that you're here for?"

"It's not going to be that easy."

"Right. We'll wait until nightfall." Now that all three of them were close enough, Paul could speak so he didn't feel that his voice was echoing back through the boulders and down into the basin. "It's guarded," he said. "By at least three armed men."

"Six," Red Feather said. "There were more behind some of the tents and within the crevice."

"How big is this camp?" Hank asked.

"Wait. Don't tell me. I'll see it for myself. No need to get all worked up until it's absolutely necessary."

"We'll backtrack a ways and find a spot to make a camp for ourselves," Paul said.

"Right," Hank added. "Keep the fire down low to keep from sending up too much smoke or making too much light. After we've got some good shadows to maneuver in, we can slip into that basin and slip right back out again. Six guards really ain't too much, especially since they don't even know we're coming."

"There's more than six guards," Paul said.

"Oh? Seven?"

"Starkweather is there too. I didn't see the Mexican, but it would be safe to assume he's around there somewhere also."

Suddenly Hank didn't seem so anxious to proceed with the plan.

CHAPTER 30

The fire they built was barely large enough to take the chill off when Paul was sitting less than an inch away from it. Of course, part of that was due to the extraordinary cold that had swept in as soon as the sun went down. Having given up on warming his hands, Paul went to the spot where the small campsite they'd found met up with the trail that led back to the ridge. He tapped Red Feather on the shoulder and sent the Comanche back to the fire to eat his share of lukewarm beans that was their supper.

When he heard footsteps behind him, Paul said, "Go on and eat. I'm fine right where I'm at."

"Already ate," Hank said. "And I'd rather forget the experience."

Paul nodded. "Thought you were Red Feather."

"He's already packing away the rest of

them beans. Probably better than the mess he usually eats."

"One of these times, he's going to split your lip when you say something like that."

"And I'll deserve whatever I get," Hank chuckled.

"You're either a real brave man or a real stupid one."

"The great ones usually are a little of both, ain't they?"

After a few moments of consideration, Paul had to admit, "Yeah. I suppose they are. It just seems strange to see you two talking instead of trying to kill each other. I thought for sure one of you would have gone your own way by now."

"But that would mean the other had won and we can't have that. You mind if I make an observation?"

"I suppose not."

"You seem . . . nervous."

Paul laughed under his breath. "I think I'd be stupid if I wasn't."

"But you seem to have lost a bit of that fire you had in you before. For one thing, you haven't mentioned your young'uns for a little while. Why is that?"

"Because I figure anyone in their right mind would have been sick of hearing about them by now."

"Every man's got to stay close to what drives him on," Hank pointed out. "Otherwise he just tends to drift. I've been in plenty of situations where I had no business making it out alive and the only thing that saw me through was whatever kept pushing me forward when everyone else took a moment to catch their breath. You had that before."

"And now?" Paul asked tentatively.

"Now . . . I'm concerned. If you've lost your steam, then I sure as hell don't have any reason to be here."

"Why *are* you here? You should know I appreciate any help I can get, but this isn't exactly your fight."

"I'm here because I'm selfish," Hank replied. "Always have been. Then again, everyone is. They do what they'll do for as long as they can get away with it. You know what I was doing when our paths first crossed?"

"Looking for Indians?"

"That's right. Men like me have killed a number of them and they've killed plenty of us. The reason why it all started don't matter anymore. Not to the ones doing most of the shooting. I stayed in it because I'm good at it and when you're good at killing, you got to be real careful how you ply your trade. There's a fine line between getting paid for providing that service and getting hanged for it."

Paul was taken aback. It wasn't so much that he was surprised by any sort of revelation, but he hadn't expected Hank or any other man to own up to something like that so readily.

"You want to know why I'm here?" Hank continued. "Probably for the same reason that anyone else has been helping you get this far. There's been a fire in your eyes and a justness in your cause that's pretty damn rare. Some men go their whole lives without finding something so pure. Love, hate, rage, whatever it is, it can drive a man to the ends of the earth so long as it's pure. I'll be honest and say I stuck with you at first because it was the quickest way to get out of a sticky situation with them Comanche. After a while, though, I liked being on the good side of a fight for a change. Let's face it; even the men that pay someone to weed out a bunch of Indians don't respect the man that does the weeding. But someone helping a man with a pure cause? That's something else, my friend."

"I'm in a line of work where you have to be a good judge of character," Paul said, "and I never would have pegged you as someone who likes to talk so much."

"Just trying to see if there's any of that fire left in you, is all. Because if you lost it and we're a short ride away from a camp full of men who'd like to gun us down, then I will point my horse in any other direction and start riding."

"What do you want me to do?" Paul asked. "Beg you to stay?"

"I want to make certain you've got what it takes to make it through this alive. Being in on a just cause is one thing, but I'm in no rush to die in a blaze of gunfire."

Paul clenched his fists until his fingernails dug deep into his palms. "I'm not a killer. I can barely fire a gun with any proficiency. I got no business whatsoever being out here and stepping up to those men in that camp."

"You're not a doctor either," Hank said. "But you insist you know what's best to get your kids healthy again."

"That's different."

"Nah. I don't think it is. You handled yourself well enough when a fight was thrust upon you, but this here is different. This is us sitting and waiting and thinking about the fight before walking straight into it. I've done this a few times myself and it ain't ever easy. The first time for me was when I was still riding with the cavalry in the

Dakota territories."

"You wore an army uniform?" Paul asked.

"And made it look damn good too! Is that so hard to believe?"

Not wanting to open that particular can of worms, Paul kept his mouth shut and motioned for the other man to continue.

"One of the older riflemen, not the commanding officer but some grizzled old dog who looked like he'd been chewed up and spit out a few times over, had some advice for me that helped. He looked me in the eye and told me without a flinch that we were all dead men."

"That . . . doesn't seem very helpful," Paul said.

"Not at first, but it puts things into perspective. If we charge into that camp or if we sit here and stare at the stars, we'll eventually die of something. Those kids of yours are in the same boat. They're dead too."

"Don't say that."

"It's nothing new, Paul. It's the oldest truth there is. And as soon as you really take it in for what it is, that's when you yank the teeth straight out of its head. Do you fret about falling asleep? Gettin' hungry? Bumping your head? No! Because that sort of thing is just gonna happen. Live with it and move on."

"I should live with the fact that I'm already dead?" Paul asked. "That's about the dumbest thing I've ever heard."

"Isn't it, though? But knowing that makes the rest easier to bear, right?"

Paul's first reaction was to disagree. Then he simply realized that he couldn't.

"Your young'uns," Hank said. "Tell me about 'em."

"What?"

"You heard me."

"Why do you want to know about them?" Paul asked.

Hank let out a short snort of a laugh. "After coming all this way to help bring them back into good health, don't I have a right to know a little something about the folks I'm putting my neck on the block for?"

"I suppose so. Abigail is my daughter and she's becoming more willful every day. More beautiful too."

"I bet," Hank said with a toothy grin. When he saw the warning glare from Paul, he quickly added, "Not in that sense! I just mean in the way that every daughter can charm her papa. Lord knows my sister had that knack."

Paul nodded. "She's smart too. Well . . . she could stand to do better in school. It's more like she's wise. Wiser than she should be."

"What about your boy?"

Without wanting to, Paul hung his head slightly and pressed his lips together into a tight line.

"Ahhh," Hank said. "Looks like there's a bit of friction between you two."

"Sometimes."

Hank leaned back and made a dismissing wave with one hand. "Ain't nothing new with that. I don't know any man who didn't lock horns with his father on a regular basis."

"It's not like that. We don't really fight. Of course, he's still young."

"Then what's making you turn sour just by thinking about him?"

"It shouldn't be anything," Paul sighed. "He's a good boy. Does well in his studies. Reads every book he can get his hands on. It's just that . . . he's afraid."

"I'd imagine he is!" Hank said. "Sounds to me like the boy's real sick. Anyone would be afraid when them fever dreams start to come."

"It's not that. He's always afraid. He's afraid of the dark, afraid of animals, afraid of the wind blowing outside."

"When I was a boy, I used to be afraid of

the scarecrow in the field next to our barn," Hank said wistfully. "Used to always think the damn thing would yank itself out from the ground and take a run at the house."

Looking over at Hank, Paul said, "David's afraid to go to the outhouse alone, and when he gets there, he wants the door open. He's afraid of every other noise he hears. He's afraid of moths."

"Hmm," Hank grunted as he scratched behind one ear. "Can't say as I ever knew of anyone who was afraid of moths."

"Now you do. He's just so . . . timid. I try to tell him there's nothing to get so worked up about, but it never helps. Every time I see him cringe the way he does or cower on account of absolutely nothing, I just want to . . ."

"Smack him in the face?"

"No!" Paul snapped.

"That's what my papa used to do to me when he didn't like something I was doing."

"And look how good you turned out."

Hank looked down and scratched a shape into the dirt. "Yeah. Good point."

"Sorry. I didn't mean that. I just don't like folks speaking ill of my boy . . . not even me . . . and I'm afraid that that's just what they'll do if he grows up to be a weak little man who flinches at every shadow, including his own."

"He lost his mama, ain't that right?"

"Yes."

"Did he know her very well?"

Smiling at even the slightest memory of his Joanna, Paul said, "Well enough to miss her."

"Well, you told me he's a smart boy. He probably knows a lot about a lot of things. This is a harsh world, and after it took his mama away from him, he knows just how harsh it can get. There's a lot of things to be scared of, especially when most everything is bigger than you."

"Except for moths," Paul chuckled.

"Right. Do you honestly think your boy will be just like he is now when he grows to be a man?"

"I hope not."

"Of course he won't," Hank said. "If that's how it worked, this would be a mighty strange place we live in."

Paul laughed and nodded.

"It don't take a professor to figure what has been eating at you," Hank went on to say. "You're worried your young ones won't be there when you get back home. That right?"

Reluctantly Paul said, "Part of me wants

to get on my horse and ride back home as fast as I can. The other part doesn't ever want to see Keystone Pass again because of all the pain it already holds . . . and all that is probably waiting for me when I go back."

"Answer one question," Red Feather called out in a voice that drifted on the wind like so much smoke. "When the loud one told you your children were already dead, did you think he was right?"

"No," Paul said almost immediately. "I . . . I thought it wasn't true."

"Then you have your answer," the Comanche said. "There is work to be done. Soon . . . we do it."

"That's what I was going to say," Hank grumbled. "Eventually."

"The loud one speaks in many circles," Red Feather said. "Sooner or later, every patch of land will be covered."

"Right!" Hank scowled in the direction of the Comanche. "Wait a second. Was that an insult?"

"I don't think so," Paul said in a voice that wasn't nearly as heavy as it had been a few moments before. "Let's get a bit of rest and then head out again. Hopefully we can get this whole thing settled before much longer."

"Sounds good to me," Hank replied.

"Long as that Injun over there keeps quiet long enough for us to rest."

The only sound Red Feather made was a rough exhale that could just as easily have been a laugh as a discontented grunt.

Once Hank had left him alone, Paul sat and drew shapes in the dirt at his feet. His thoughts were no longer darkened by fearful images of what horrors may await him back home. He didn't think about the many ways his life could end right there in those mountains. The shapes he drew were rough sketches of what he could remember in regard to the layout of the nearby mining camp. He planned ways to get around the armed men and how best to approach those shacks with the chimneys.

He listened for anyone coming for them and watched for any sign that he or the other two men had been discovered. It was a busy way to spend a couple of hours, but it sharpened Paul's mind better than a blade against a whetstone.

CHAPTER 31

It was well past midnight when Paul and Red Feather crept away from their camp and climbed the boulders framing the path they'd ridden earlier that day. Paul was chilled down to the bone, and scurrying along rocks that seemed to have soaked up every last bit of that cold didn't help him warm up. Even with the luminescent glow drifting down from the stars and moon above, he had to concentrate just to make out the slightest detail of the route in front of him.

"Maybe we should wait until daybreak," he whispered. "At least at first light, we'll be able to see something."

"And the men in that camp will be able to see us as well," Red Feather replied. "If we move slowly, we can cover much ground. It is not much farther until we can get a look at what is happening in that basin."

"Easy for you to say. I feel like I'm gonna

slip and fall to my death at any second."

"Then just watch me instead of trying to watch everything else. Step where I step. Do what I do."

"Yeah," Paul grunted as his foot skidded on a loose patch of gravel. "That's really gonna help." When he got a scolding backward glance from Red Feather, he hunkered down to mimic the Comanche's stance and moved onward as best he could.

Actually watching Red Feather did help. It not only showed him how to move and where to step, but it kept his mind too busy to dwell on all the worries that had plagued him before. It wasn't a complete solution to his woes, but it served well enough to get him across the tops of the boulders and down to a narrow ledge that led into the basin.

"Guards," Red Feather whispered. He then pointed to his right and left.

Following the Comanche's gestures, Paul spotted two figures standing several paces away. One was close to the shacks that were still spewing smoke from their chimneys and the other was posted near a pen where several horses were tethered. The man near the horses was shivering and stomping his feet. Judging by the other one's lack of movement and steady current of steam that issued from his mouth, he was either dozing off or getting real close to it.

"I want to get a look inside one of those shacks," Paul said. "I should be able to slip by that guard, so you can take a look around here and see what we're up against."

"No," Red Feather replied. "I am coming with you."

"There are only two of us. We need to split up and cover more ground."

"Yes. There are only two of us. If something happens to one, the other is vulnerable. I have raided many bluecoat camps. I know how to do it."

"Fine. Come along with me. I shouldn't take long anyway."

Red Feather nodded once and continued moving onward. They reached the basin floor in good time. Thanks to a howling wind, they were able to move faster without worrying about making too much noise. In fact, the sound of the wind was even louder at the bottom of the basin. Before he knew it, Paul found himself approaching one of the shacks from behind.

By now, his eyes were as used to the dark as they were likely to get. When he took a few steps closer to the row of shacks, the smell of burning chemicals washed over him. Fortunately the swirling winds changed direction and took the stench away from his nose before he started hacking. As Paul approached the closest shack, that same wind tugged at his hat and loosened it from his head. Paul reflexively slapped his hand down on top of it to keep it from rolling into open ground like tumbleweed. After being in the cold for so long, his hat was stiff as a board and the impact of his hand against it made a sound like a piece of wood being dropped onto the ground.

Although Red Feather made no noise at all, Paul could see the Comanche's face twist into a stern expression as he extended an arm toward him that became rigid as a spear. Paul obeyed the silent command and froze where he was. After having circled around to another side of the shacks, he couldn't see what Red Feather was seeing, but could hear a change in the nearby guard's breathing.

Slowly, Red Feather bent his knees to bring his entire body even closer to the ground. The arm he'd stretched toward Paul was now brought in to his belt so his hand could find one of the knives kept there.

The guard grumbled something about the cold, stomped his feet, and cleared his throat.

Red Feather had become motionless,

standing at the edge of the guard's field of vision. The only thing that kept the unknowing gunman alive was his apparent reluctance to look in the Comanche's direction.

Paul heard a long sigh, followed by what he guessed was the sound of the guard's hands slapping against his forearms or chest. There was a crunch of a set of shoulders resting against the side of one of the shacks, followed by a somewhat contented grunt. Red Feather was still crouching low in preparation to end the tired guard's life. Without taking his eyes from his prey, the Comanche made a subtle movement with his hand that was akin to him shooing Paul away. Even after getting the signal, Paul was reluctant to move. His first couple of steps were agonizingly slow and when he got no reaction from either the guard or Red Feather, he took his next few at a quicker pace.

Each one of Paul's nerves had risen to the surface of his skin. He could feel every imperfection of the ground beneath his boots and the touch of every bit of cold dust blown across his cheeks. When he reached the shack he'd set his sights upon, Paul swore he'd already been spotted by some other guard that he and Red Feather had missed. When he grabbed the handle of the back door, he would have bet anything that it was going to be locked. And when he pulled the door open, he found himself less than two yards away from a surprised young man wearing a butcher's smock and a bandanna wrapped around his nose and mouth.

Without taking time to appreciate all the good luck that had brought him this far, Paul rushed into the cabin. He flung the door shut behind him with one hand while drawing the Schofield with the other. When he spoke, it was as though an animal had crawled into his skull and taken over his mouth. "Make one move I don't like," he snarled, "and I'll burn you down."

The man in the smock was taller than Paul, but lanky. Even with a good portion of his face covered, it was obvious he was much younger as well. His eyes were wide as saucers and his hands shook as he held them in front of his body without knowing what to do with them from there.

Since the young man looked to be on the verge of panic, Paul asked, "What's your name?"

"B . . . Braden."

"Step away from that table, Braden."

The young man did as he was told, granting Paul a few moments to get a look at the interior of the shack. A single aisle went from the back door to the front door, covering a space that was roughly the size of a modest bedroom. Crates were stacked along one wall, many of which were soaked through with a dark fluid. Several narrow tables were lined up on the other side of the aisle, half of which were occupied by racks of glass vials and a few small burners. In the corner closest to where Paul was standing, a stove gave a small amount of heat and spewed most of the smoke it created out through a flimsy series of tin cylinders connected to a hole in the roof.

"What are you doing here, Braden?" Paul asked.

"Please . . . don't shoot."

"I won't just as long as you do what you're told. First, tell me what you're doing here."

"Just working. I'm here late because I'm new on the job."

"You work for Territorial Mining?"

"That's right," Braden replied.

"And what's going on in here?" Paul asked. "What is all this equipment?"

"This is where ore is tested to see how pure it is, what it is, even how much more of it there might be."

"How can you tell all of that with a few pans and vials?"

Braden became nervous as he shook his head. "I'm still new to this. Mr. Quincy tells me what to do and I do it. When we find gold, I make sure it's the real thing. There are different tests to do for silver and zinc and such. When it comes to the other tests, I just do what Quincy tells me to do."

"And what's the stench I smell?"

"There are some things cooking on the stove over there. Mr. Quincy makes some of his own compounds for tests and to mix up his own products."

"What products?"

Braden shrugged. "He's made soap for the men, solutions for the machines, even something to add to the water used for strip mining."

"And what happens to what's left over?" Paul asked as his grip tightened around the Schofield. "Waste and whatnot?"

"It — it's tossed out. Dumped, I guess."

"You . . . guess?" Paul snarled. He glared at the younger man with all of the anger that had been building inside him since he'd first seen his daughter lying in her sickbed. "You're gonna have to do a lot better than that."

As Braden sputtered to try to figure out what to say, a set of knuckles cracked roughly against the shack's front door. Both men stood still and, as surely as he could read the intentions of his children before they acted up, Paul knew something was racing through young Braden's mind. Before those troublesome thoughts could get very far, Paul held the Schofield up to the younger man's eye level and thumbed back the hammer. "Don't be stupid," he whispered, "and you won't get hurt."

Braden nodded fiercely.

Although he only moved with a fraction of the grace he'd picked up from Red Feather, Paul managed to get close to the front door and even closer to Braden without making more than a few subtle squeaks in the floorboards. "See who's out there," Paul said quietly. "And then send him away."

Braden approached the door, steeled himself, and then cautiously opened it. Before the door could swing too far inward, Paul stopped it with the edge of his boot.

"How much longer you got in there?" asked the man who'd knocked on the door.

"I'm almost done," Braden replied.

"When you're finished, bring some of Quincy's powder over to the tents on the far west side. Some more men have taken ill and they need to be well enough to work tomorrow."

"I'll be over as fast as I can. If not," Braden quickly added, "come on back and remind me."

"Will do."

Paul knew what signal the young man was trying to send, and judging by the lack of interest in the voice of the man outside, it wasn't clearly received. Either way, Paul didn't intend to be around if the man outside did come back after all. He couldn't see much through the crack between the door and the frame, but Paul could hear the crunch of boots against cold ground as the man outside turned and walked away. Braden stood at the open door for a few seconds too long, so Paul gave him a gentle nudge with the barrel of the Schofield. His message was received much better than Braden's, and the door was quickly shut.

"What was he talking about?" Paul asked.

"What do you mean?"

"You want to drag out this conversation or would you rather I leave as soon as possible? Tell me what that man was talking about just now."

"You mean about the workers who got sick?"

"That's right."

"It's . . . just what he said," Braden explained. "Happens all the time."

"What's making them sick?"

Stepping away from the door thanks to a shove from Paul, Braden eyed the pistol in his hand. He might have been contemplating making a grab for it, but Paul kept the firearm back just far enough to make it a difficult proposition at best. When his heel bumped against the crates stacked along one wall of the shack, Braden spoke as if his words were spilling out of him.

"Workers get sick all the time," he said. "Sometimes from the cold. Sometimes from exposure."

"What else?"

"Sometimes they just get too many chemicals in their water."

Paul smiled. "Chemicals like the ones used in strip mining?"

"Or any of the others that are used around here," Braden said while sweeping an arm to encompass the entire setup from the tables to the little stove. "Territorial Mining prides itself on using every advantage they can to be a better operation than anyone else. We dump the chemicals that are left over and the men carry it away in barrels. Every now and then the workers get some on their hands or skin and clean off in one of the troughs or washbasins around here. Some other fella might come along and drink that water or get it in his mouth or who knows what else."

"When they get sick, what are the symptoms?"

Although Braden seemed grateful for not being shoved or threatened, he was mighty confused about this line of questioning. He still did his best to answer while edging his way closer to one stack of boxes. "They vomit. They get dizzy. They fall over."

"What about a fever?" Paul asked. "Do they get a fever?"

"Sure they do. They get a fever if they're forced to work in the mines or out in the elements for too long. Everybody knows that."

"I'm talking about the men who get those chemicals in them. Do they get a fever as well?"

"Yeah. Why are you so concerned about all this? Are you sick?"

"What if I was? Would I need some of that powder the man who knocked on the door a moment ago was talking about?"

"Yes."

"Where is it?"

Braden was nearly overcome by a series of confused blinks. "Th . . . there's some in that top crate over there."

And then Paul did something he immediately regretted. He turned to look at the crates, giving Braden an opening to lunge at him.

CHAPTER 32

Paul's first instinct was to twist his body away from the incoming attacker to prevent Braden from getting the Schofield away from him. If there was more room in that shack, he might have been able to dodge the younger man completely. Braden might have had youth on his side, but he was frightened and not much of a fighter. Even so, the momentum of his body colliding into Paul's was enough to take Paul off balance and send him staggering into the narrow table behind him.

Whatever Braden had been working on before Paul came along was now splattered on the wall and floor amid the clatter of pans and tin cups. Glass vials on the table next to that one rattled together, but before they could be sent to the floor, Paul shoved Braden backward into a stack of crates. Those boxes splintered on impact, exposing a load of dirty rocks that had yet to be cleaned and tested. Braden reached out to grab one of the rocks and swing it at Paul's head. Before the blow could land, Paul snapped his head forward to thump it into the other man's face.

Reeling from the head butt, Braden closed his eyes as pain spiked through his face and blood dripped from a freshly opened cut above one eye. Even though he was feeling almost as much pain from the knock as the younger man, Paul steeled his expression and hoped he wasn't bleeding even more than his opponent.

"Stand still," Paul said.

Those words were intended to calm Braden down but had the complete opposite effect. Braden tried to pull away from Paul while reaching with both hands toward a small gap between two stacks of boxes. Paul shoved the younger man against the boxes one more time and then reached past him to grab the ax that had been hidden there.

"Is this what you wanted?" Paul asked in the same tone of voice he'd used when scolding his children. He could only wish someday that tone would elicit the same response in David or Abigail as it did in the man standing before him now.

Braden's face turned whiter than the caps of the Rockies outside and his entire body shook. "No! Please!"

"Keep your voice down."

"Y-yes, sir," Braden said as he slid down to one knee. "Please . . . just don't kill me."

Paul had only been concerned with ending the fight before it got out of hand without bringing any guards in from the rest of the camp. Now he realized that he was looming over Braden with a pistol in one hand and an ax in the other. He no longer wondered why the younger man seemed ready to either soil himself or grovel on the floor like a whipped dog.

Paul took a step back and holstered the Schofield. "I don't want to kill you," he said.

Although the words were sinking in a bit, Braden's eyes were still drawn to the ax.

Easing the ax down, Paul set it on the table behind him. "There," he said. "Better?"

Reluctantly Braden nodded.

Seeing a hint of returning bravery in the young man's eyes, Paul erased it by placing his hand on the Schofield's grip. "I didn't come in here to harm anyone, but I will if you force me to. Understand?"

"Yes."

"Now tell me about this powder that's used to help cure the sick men."

"It's a medicine mixed up by Mr. Quincy,"

Braden explained. "He stirs it into some sort of tea or something that's boiled in water and he gives it to men suffering from drinking or breathing in too many of the chemicals around here. Depending on what the men drank or breathed in, different amounts of the powder are used. It doesn't do anything for the men suffering from the elements, though."

"Can you tell me how to mix it up?" Paul asked.

"I suppose, but it depends on the symptoms. That man that was knocking on the door came to me because I need to get a look at the sick men to mix up a batch of the medicine. Even then, I may have to wake Mr. Quincy so he can get it right. Otherwise it'll just make them sicker."

"What about for someone who's had those symptoms you already told me about? The dizziness, fever, and all of that. What would you do for them?"

"I'd ask Mr. Quincy about it," Braden replied.

"Is he a doctor?"

"I think so. He sure knows a lot about those chemicals and such."

Paul could feel his time for talking without being interrupted again was growing short. He was concerned about that, but there were a couple of things that concerned him a great deal more. "What would you do in that situation if this Quincy fellow wasn't around?"

"Do you know someone who's sick? I can go talk to him about it if you like. I could say it's on behalf of one of the men."

"Just tell me," Paul said without putting enough of an edge to his tone to force the younger man back into his shell. "You've obviously treated these men on your own more than once. What would you do in that situation?"

"I'd just mix up an extra-large dose of the remedy and hope for the best. If it's not spit up right away or if there aren't any convulsions, they should be on the right track."

"All right. Now I want you to get me some of that powder and I won't tolerate any more tricks. You understand?"

"Yes. How much do you need?"

Just to be on the safe side, Paul told him, "Enough for four men. You'll also tell me exactly how to prepare it."

"I need to go over to that crate at the front of the row. Okay?"

"That's fine," Paul said without taking his eyes off Braden.

The young man cautiously approached

the crate he'd pointed to and opened it. Paul was just able to get a look inside as soon as the top came off. All he saw were burlap sacks the size of what were used to hold portions of sugar to be sold in stores like his back in Keystone Pass. Braden took one of the pouches and said, "There's enough in here to make a good-sized portion for half this camp."

"I'll take that and another sack."

"Fine." Braden removed the second sack and set both on the table. He then proceeded to tell Paul how to prepare the solution.

"I thought you said Quincy added something else as well," Paul reminded him.

"Not every time," Braden said. "Just in the worst cases."

"What does he add?"

"Some kind of syrup or something. It's a dark, thick liquid he keeps in small vials in his tent. You want me to go and get some?"

Paul did want Braden to get whatever might be needed to help his children. If he let the young man go, however, Paul would most likely call down the rest of the camp to attack him and Red Feather as well. After weighing his options, he said, "Just tell me where Quincy's tent is."

"I can show you."

"You'll tell me," Paul said with enough ferocity to make Braden worry again.

"Please, mister. I don't know who you are and won't tell anyone you were here. Just take that medicine . . . take it all if you like . . . and I swear I won't lift a finger to stop you."

Paul tucked one small sack of powder into his jacket pocket and brought the other to his nose. He didn't know exactly what the bitter scent was, but he knew it wasn't sugar, flour, or anything else that was very common. "Sit down in between those stacks of crates," he said while pocketing the second sack and waving the Schofield toward a narrow gap between the supplies piled against one wall.

Panic crept in around the edges of Braden's face. After all the time he'd spent raising his son, Paul recognized it well enough.

"Wh-what are you gonna do?" Braden asked.

"You are going to sit where I told you and then I am going to walk out of here."

Braden moved cautiously over to the gap while Paul moved even more cautiously to keep some space between them. Once he felt the two stacks of crates against his shoulders, Braden shifted sideways to get between them and then slowly lowered himself to a seated position. After his rump hit the floor, Braden's head continued to fall until he wilted as far down as he could go.

Even though he knew he couldn't just leave him sitting there, Paul wasn't certain what he should do about the young man. If he was better at such things, he'd knock Braden out with a blow to the head using the grip of his pistol. There wasn't any rope to be found, and before he could ask if there was some nearby, shouts rolled through the air from elsewhere within the camp.

"What's that?" Paul asked.

Braden squirmed uncomfortably in his spot. "I don't know. I don't know, I swear!"

A second later, more angry voices arose from the camp outside. When a few gunshots cracked through the air, Paul jabbed a finger at Braden and said, "Stay here and don't move!"

The tone in Paul's voice was enough to keep Braden still, so he pulled open the rear door and looked outside to find Red Feather in the same spot he'd been in before. Not only that, but the Comanche was crouching as if he'd been turned into a stone statue during Paul's conversation with the young man in the shack. Hunkering down, Paul hurried over to him and was stopped by a swiftly raised hand. Once Red Feather lowered that hand, Paul rushed over to his side and whispered, "What's going on out here?"

"Nothing," Red Feather replied, "until a few seconds ago."

"Is that guard still here?"

"He just left."

As soon as the noise died down, a pair of shots was fired that stirred everything up again.

"Sounds like the whole camp is waking up," Paul said.

"Pulled from their beds in a cloud of smoke." Red Feather smirked. "This might just work in our favor."

As more voices filled the night, a few more shots were fired from various spots within the camp. Soon the rumble of horses' hooves joined the discord.

Red Feather cocked his head to one side like a wolf that could hear much more than a man. Something amid the rest of the noise must have struck his fancy, because he started moving quickly toward the perimeter of the camp and signaled for Paul to follow. As soon as they moved clear of the shacks, Paul saw a small group of men carrying rifles run directly in front of him about twenty yards away. Thanks to the darkness and plentiful distractions happening all over the place, the men didn't even cast a glance in his direction. Accustomed to moving without being seen, Red Feather calmly proceeded as soon as the way was clear.

"Did you get what you needed?" the Comanche asked.

"I think so. It's not exactly what I was expecting, but it should do the trick."

"Is it enough for you to be willing to leave this place?"

"Perhaps I could take a look down that way," he said while looking in the direction of the crevice. "I should be able to get a canteen full of the poison I was after."

"That might have to wait," Red Feather said. "Whatever has stirred this hive has done a very good job of it."

They'd made it to the edge of the basin, where the shadows were thicker and a scattered number of scrub bushes provided some much-needed cover. Paul couldn't get there fast enough, and when he finally got behind a barrier of half-bare branches, he felt as if he'd put a brick wall between himself and the mining camp.

After hunkering down in the shadows for a minute or so, Paul whispered, "The shooting's stopped."

Red Feather responded with a low grunt.

"What are they doing now?" Paul asked.

"I might know if you would let me listen," the Comanche said.

Squinting into the distance, Paul spotted a small group of men: one leading two others. As he watched, more men streamed out from the tents and wagons to gather around them. Some men hollered and others laughed.

"What are they doing?" Paul asked. "Where is that man leading those others?"

"That man is not leading them," Red Feather told him. "He is being pushed into one of the tents."

"Why?"

"It's Hank. He's been captured."

CHAPTER 33

When Paul made it back to the little spot they'd staked out for their camp, he felt no comfort. He paced so much that he could have walked back and forth from both camps at least twice. Red Feather, on the other hand, remained perfectly still.

"How can you just sit there?" Paul hissed. "Hank's . . . well, there's no telling where he is now or what's happening to him."

"Those are miners," Red Feather said. "Not soldiers. Not monsters."

"Then why are there armed men guarding this place? Why would they capture someone at all if they're just innocent miners?"

"Perhaps they are uneasy after someone broke into one of their buildings and questioned one of their workers."

"There was shooting!" Paul said. "What could they have been shooting at? You think Hank was hurt?"

"Why does he concern you so?"

"Because he wouldn't be here if it wasn't for me!"

"He may not be here in this spot, but he would have gotten what he deserved while he was in another spot."

"You think he deserves this?" Paul snapped. "Those men may have killed him already."

"They are miners."

"Not all of them. Remember, Starkweather is down there too. He's one of the gunmen from Leadville."

Red Feather drew a long breath and held on to it. His eyes narrowed into slits that seemed to be focused on a point a thousand miles away. "That man is indeed a killer. Hank is a killer too. If either one of them was going to bury the other, they would have done it by now.

"If there is anything else you needed from that basin," Red Feather continued, "now is the time to go and get it."

Paul looked around at the dark, swaying shadows surrounding the campsite as a cold breeze raked across his face and neck. The chaos that had filled the mining camp not so long ago had faded, leaving the mountain pass feeling barren and abandoned. Even the jangling nerves along his back that made him worry about a man wandering up from the basin to stumble upon him were silent. A few days ago, he would have welcomed calmness like that. Now it was unnerving.

"And what about Hank? We just leave him to whatever is going to happen to him down there?"

"Yes."

"It can't be that easy for you. I may have only known you for a short stretch of time, but that's long enough to see that you're a good man. Leaving another man to die like that . . ."

"Do you know what that man is?" Red Feather snarled as he looked over at Paul sharply enough to cause the ends of his dark hair to snap like whips. "You may think he is your friend, but he is a killer. He takes money for killing *my* people. If he can do that, then he can kill your people just as easily."

Paul met the Comanche's stare. Like putting his nose within an inch of a fire and looking for the embers within, the longer he tried to keep it up, the harder it was. "When I think about any man making money from killing another, it turns my stomach. To be honest, I'm amazed you haven't put Hank down like a dog just for being what he is. After a while, I figured that's the best way to change what he is. You'd have to be blind to not see how he's already changed. He doesn't look at you the way he did at first," Paul said.

"And I should be thankful for that?" Red Feather spat. "I should be happy a killer no longer sees me as someone he wants to kill?"

"A killer wouldn't go this far just to help a couple of children he doesn't even know."

"There is something in it for him. Otherwise he would not be here."

"So that means we should just leave him to whatever awaits him at the hands of men we know are capable of murdering him? What does that say about us?" Paul asked. "Think what you want about everyone else, what matters is how we act ourselves."

Red Feather's voice became colder than his eyes when he said, "You act for you and your family. That is not such a difficult decision to make."

"If that was true, I could take this medicine I got and start riding home. Odds are, it's the best I can do to helping my little ones get well. Or I could take your advice without question and loot that basin for anything else that might help me and mine while those miners are distracted. Instead I'm still here trying to think of what can be done to get Hank out of this jam he's in."

"Then perhaps you are a good man. That

doesn't mean he is."

Knowing that he was running out of options, Paul said, "You're still here as well. That makes you a good man too. Right?"

"I agreed to help you. Not help a murderer."

"It's more than that. There's something else."

"Like what?" Red Feather asked.

"Like the same something that made you lead a raid on a trading post where someone could have gotten killed just so a few windows could be broken."

"No one would have gotten killed," Red Feather said in a solemn tone.

"If the arrow that hit my daughter had been aimed a little higher, it would have done her in for sure."

If Paul ever had doubts that Red Feather truly did have children, they would have been wiped away when he saw the look in the Comanche's eyes as he contemplated the death of a little girl.

"Why were those arrows fired at a store?" Paul asked.

"You already know why. The mining companies want to take what is not theirs and are willing to push my people away from their homes to get it. The men in suits would not hear our words, so they must see what we do."

"Injustices will make any man want to fight back. Even though my girl was in the way of that fight, I understand how it started. Accidents happen. Ugly ones. It's part of living and so is working to set things right again."

"That is why I ride with you," Red Feather said.

"Maybe, but this ride also gives you a chance to take another stab at this mining company. You get to come here and stir up a little more trouble."

"Would you rather I hadn't?"

"What I'd rather is that you stop acting like you're doing everything for honor and righteousness and the rest of us are out for ourselves," Paul said. "Everyone's got to look out for themselves and their kin because hardly anyone else out there will do it for them. If those interests happen to line up with what's honorable and righteous . . . then so be it. Folks make mistakes. They do bad things. They should also be given a chance to make up for those things. Every now and then, those same folks also do good things. If you just keep your eyes open for those times, it makes this world seem a lot less harsh."

Although Red Feather didn't do much

more than blink, a change came about him that could be felt more than seen.

"I've got no way of keeping you here, but your help would be appreciated," Paul continued. "Just don't look down your nose at us while you're doing it."

The Comanche stood up and grabbed his rifle.

"What are you doing?" Paul asked nervously.

"We're going to get that savage away from those hired killers."

CHAPTER 34

Some of the tents in the camp were supported by wooden frames to become even larger than the shacks on the opposite side. One of the largest of those tents was away from the smaller tents on one side of the camp where it had a good view of the angular crevice cut into the nearby rock wall. Hank was dragged into that tent and thrown up against one of the wooden beams supporting the roof. Whenever he tried to give them any lip, he was punched or otherwise beaten until he shut up. Hank being Hank, he quickly wound up with a face covered in welts.

The group of men who brought him into the tent dispersed once Hank was tied securely. One man remained behind: Hector, who still had a shotgun in his hands and a mean scowl on his face. There was plenty of movement outside the tent along with hushed voices speaking excitedly back and forth. Hank couldn't help smirking when he heard mention of some young chemist who'd been knocked around and left shaking in his boots earlier that night. At least Paul and Red Feather had been busy while he'd been getting dragged through the mountains.

"So, what now?" Hank asked.

Hector tightened his grip on the shotgun and said, "Now you shut your damn mouth."

"Then what?"

Instead of playing Hank's game, Hector followed his own advice and kept quiet. He only had to stay that way for another minute or two before another small group of men entered the tent. Two of them were the guards who'd brought Hank in. The other was a bearded fellow with high cheekbones, bright eyes, and dark hair. Everything from the boots on his feet to the hat on his head looked to be of higher quality than anything worn by any of the other men in camp.

"Hello there," the well-dressed man said in a cordial tone. "Do you know who I am?"

"Why would I?" Hank shot back.

"You and your partners have gone through a lot of trouble to find me and disrupt my men's sleep, so I figured you might already know my name."

"Nope. Me and my partners were just passing through. I was just trying to warm my hands when I was rudely interrupted by a gang of armed men with ropes."

Narrowing his eyes a bit, the man replied, "I believe the second part of that but not the first. I'm Jonas Frakes, by the way. Have you heard of me?"

"Yeah. I suppose it's important to you that I have."

"It saves me a bit of time," Frakes said. "Since you already know the resources and money at my disposal, you shouldn't have any trouble believing that I can follow up on any promises I make. When it comes to the more . . . unsavory promises . . . the Territorial Mining Company has already hired someone to follow through on my behalf."

Those words were obviously meant as a threat in themselves. Maintaining his coarse exterior, Hank said, "That don't explain why you had your boys here drag me in when I was just sitting by a fire."

"Don't treat me like a fool, sir. You were here for a reason and you weren't alone. Since some of my men have recently had unpleasant encounters with cowards who've been attacking from the shadows, I can only guess the reason for you being here isn't something I would approve of."

"Tell me one thing," Hank said through a leering smile. "How unpleasant, exactly, were those encounters?"

Frakes looked over to Hector and nodded. After setting his shotgun down, Hector stepped forward to deliver a punch that had all of his considerable weight behind it. Beefy knuckles pounded against Hank's face, snapping his head around and sending a spray of bloody spit from his mouth.

"You want to give him another reason to strike you?" Frakes asked.

"I didn't want to give the first one," Hank replied.

"Then tell me why you're here, how many of you there are, and what the others are doing."

"After what happened to me," Hank said, "my guess is that they're rushing right on over to introduce themselves."

Hector didn't wait for a nod before giving Hank another thump to the head.

Frakes stepped in a bit closer and hunkered down as if he were addressing a small child when he said, "Trust me. From here on, things get a lot worse for you than taking a few knocks. What are you men doing here?"

"Camping," Hank said. Hector gave Hank

one punch that dropped him to his knees and then gave him a solid kick to the ribs that sent a wave of pain thundering throughout his entire body. When Hank tried to draw a breath, the gunman's boot slammed straight down onto his leg.

"Tell me," Frakes said, "while you still have the ability to form words."

Hank was curled up into a ball. When he uncurled a bit so he could look up at Frakes, every fiber inside him let him know just how strongly it objected to the idea. "We're here . . . on account of the poison you're dumping into the water," he grunted.

What Frakes did wasn't exactly a flinch. It was just a subtle shift in his facial muscles as he ingested what he'd heard. There was no surprise and no feigned disgust with the accusation. "I wouldn't call it poison, exactly," he said. "That would imply an intention to harm people. Mining is a messy business, and when enough of that mess runs away from a camp, it might find its way into a stream. The same could be said for animal dung or mud and yet nobody accuses those things of poisoning the water. They simply find cleaner streams and get on with their lives."

"And what happens to the folks who find out about the list of things Territorial Mining is dumping?" Hank asked. "What happens to someone who gets angry or concerned enough to do something about it?"

"Something tells me you already know what happens to them. Isn't that right?"

Hank didn't answer that, which was just as well since the question wasn't meant for him. One of the other guards who'd come in was like so many others in the camp who had a good portion of his face covered by a bandanna. This one pulled the bandanna down to reveal the cruel mouth and brushy goatee of a killer who'd already made Hank's acquaintance.

"Yeah," Starkweather said. "He knows."

Frakes nodded slowly and brought himself up to his normal height. He stood ramrod straight as he fished into one of the pockets of an expensive leather jacket for a cigarette case. The polished metal container flipped open so he could take a cigarette rolled in light brown paper and place it in the corner of his mouth. Snapping the case shut and putting it back where he'd found it, he said, "That explains part of it. You were in Leadville."

"Yep," Hank replied.

"Were you a friend of that salesman with the big mouth?"

"Not as such."

"So you were hired by a friend of his?" Plucking the unlit cigarette from his mouth and holding it as though it were already burning, Frakes squinted in thought. "No. You don't strike me as a hired gun. I suppose it's possible you're just not a very good one."

"You know what else is possible?" Hank snarled through the blood that had welled up in his mouth.

"That you'll die here in this tent for no good reason?" Frakes asked. "Yes. That is very possible."

"Actually I was thinking more along the lines of me busting out of here."

Cocking his head to one side while putting the cigarette back in place between his lips, Frakes said, "Possible, but not very likely."

One of the guards had remained in the entrance flap as if his only job was to act like a door with a pulse. That door was ripped off its hinges by a dark-skinned arm that snaked around the guard's throat to pull him backward into the shadows. The rest of the men inside the tent turned toward the door as soon as they heard the guard's muffled yelp. Frakes moved off to one side, allowing his men to raise their guns and fire. Starkweather was first to pull his trigger, and the report from his gun filled the tent with thunder.

Most of the shots that were fired were done as knee-jerk responses to the swift departure of their partner. As such, the shots ripped fresh holes through the front wall of the tent and blasted jagged chunks from the doorframe. Hank simply tried to keep his head down as low as possible.

The first wave of gunfire came to an abrupt halt, leaving the guards standing in a gritty haze of black smoke.

Something scraped against the dirt outside. When the scraping drew closer and someone crept into the tent, every gun in there was pointed in that direction. The guard that had been plucked from the tent now crawled back inside, much to the displeasure of the man who'd posted him there in the first place.

"What happened to you?" Frakes snapped. "Who's out there?"

"Don't know," the flustered guard replied. He was shaking like a leaf and clawing at the ground with desperate hands. "Didn't get a look at him."

"Just one or more than that?"

"I don't know!"

Before Frakes could chew the guard out any more, Hector fired a shot through the front door. After his shotgun tore a gaping hole in the tent, a knife hissed through the air to land solidly in Hector's shin. He dropped to one knee and grabbed for the knife. When he felt the sharpened stone blade, he didn't have the strength to remove it.

"Pull it out!" Hector wailed. "Pull it out!"

While the other men in the tent all hurried to do something or other, not one of them made a move to give the wounded Mexican a hand. Hank almost felt some pity for the guy. Almost, but not quite.

"Go and find who's out there," Frakes said. All of the guards still on their feet except for Starkweather inched toward the front of the tent. Hank could hear the slightest rustle somewhere in the night, which caused those guards to hurry outside with guns blazing.

Starkweather approached Hank and jammed the barrel of his pistol beneath Hank's chin. "Who's out there?" he snarled.

"The same one who covered my back in Leadville," Hank replied. "If I was you, I'd pack it in and call it a day."

"That's not going to happen," Frakes said. "I'm through making deals with the likes of you. Either make yourself useful or I cut my losses right here and now."

370

"I got nothing for ya," Hank told him.

"Well, that makes my decision real easy." Without batting an eye, Frakes looked to Starkweather and said, "Kill him."

When Hank heard the explosion, he guessed the next thing he'd see was the face of his maker.

CHAPTER 35

A wave of heat surged through Hank's upper body as he was knocked flat onto the floor. Even with his ears ringing and head spinning, he found it odd that he wound up facedown instead of -up with the gun being fired directly in front of him. Hank opened his eyes and saw Starkweather staggering backward.

"What was that?" Frakes asked as he pulled himself up to his feet.

Shaking his head in hopes that something would fall back into place between his ears, Hank instinctively reached for his temple. Surprisingly enough, he was able to wipe his brow. Looking at his wrists, he saw the ropes that had been binding him were still there. The rope that had connected his hands behind the post, however, had been messily severed.

"Answer me!" Frakes roared. "What was that?"

Judging by the way Starkweather blinked and rubbed his ear with his free hand, he had a few bolts loose in his head as well. Right about then, Hank noticed the section of the tent's back wall that had been torn. The edges of shredded canvas were still smoldering, and when he pulled himself to his feet, Hank saw the curved section of metal that was now wedged in the tent's support post. Most likely, that metal had once been a barrel hoop and was somehow turned into the piece of debris that had set Hank free. A similar chunk of iron still connected to a jagged piece of wood was lodged in Hector's chest, putting him down for good.

Although he was still unsteady on his feet, Hank headed for the hole in the back of the tent as quickly as he could stagger. Starkweather didn't need to be able to hear and he certainly didn't need to speak in order for him to raise his gun and fire a shot at him. Whether it was due to Hank's wavering steps or some lingering bit of disorientation within Starkweather's head, the killer's first shot was well off its mark. The second was fired at nothing but shadows since Hank had already made it outside the tent.

As he fled into the night, Hank heard Frakes shouting behind him. Since he was

more interested in escaping than responding to any threats or commands, Hank
didn't bother stopping to listen to what the
businessman had to say. All around him,
the camp was enveloped in chaos. Men
rushed in every direction, most of them clad
in nothing more than long underwear or
nightshirts after having been roused from
their sleep. The ones that spotted Hank
weren't overly concerned with him since
there were still gunshots and a fire to
capture their attention.

The shots were cracking through the air
from several different spots. The fire, however, was much easier to pinpoint. One of
the shacks situated away from the others
had been reduced to a smoking ruin. Several
tents between it and Hank were on fire as
well. As flustered men tried to stomp out
the flames, Hank rushed past them to approach one of the few figures who didn't
seem to be surprised by everything that had
just happened. As Hank got closer, the
figure he'd spotted retreated into a small
section of the camp that wasn't alive with
commotion. He followed it behind a tall
wooden rack of pipes near a cart resting on
a set of temporary tracks that led into the
nearby crevice.

"Get over here before you bring everyone

straight to us," the figure scolded while furiously waving Hank over.

Hank rushed over to the figure's side and was immediately handed a pistol. The weight of the .44 was the best thing he'd felt in quite a while.

"I took that from one of the tents after the explosion," Paul said. "I hope it's loaded."

After checking for himself, Hank said, "It is."

"Red Feather should be around here somewhere."

"He took out one of the guards in the tent where I was being held. You mind telling me what caused that ball of fire a few moments ago?"

"One of the shacks was being used to store dynamite," Paul explained. "All it took was something to pry one of the crates open and a lit match to heat things up. I was making my way to try to free you when I saw you run out on your own."

"Part of a barrel came flying through the tent and provided an escape route instead of taking my head off. Much obliged."

Paul took a quick look around. Since most of the men in camp were still running about in a frenzy, he asked, "How did they get ahold of you anyway?"

"Scouts must have seen me," Hank told him. "Or someone happened to catch sight of the fire. All I know is that I nodded off for a minute or two and was woken up by a swift kick to my gut. Two men with guns pulled me to my feet and were joined by a few more. They walked me back into camp so the man in charge could start asking questions."

"Man in charge?"

"Someone by the name of Frakes. Sound familiar?"

Paul didn't have to think for long before shaking his head. "Never heard of him, but I wouldn't know anyone connected to Territorial Mining. What did he want from you?"

"Just to know who we are and why we're causing him so much trouble."

"Did you mention anything about the poisoning?" Paul asked.

Before Hank could respond, a feral war cry rose above the other sounds filling the basin. Several men shouted in confusion while more shots were fired.

"Sounds like our mutual friend," Hank said. "To answer your question, I did mention something about the poisonings just to see how he'd react."

"And?"

"And he didn't seem to care much about it. His only concern was that his hired guns take care of anyone who might make it a bigger problem for him. I can tell you firsthand that he's got no qualms with putting a man into the ground to keep his operation here running smoothly."

"It won't be running smoothly after tonight," Paul said as he twitched from the sound of more gunfire. "Not this mine anyway. Before I lit the fuse to that barrel of dynamite, Red Feather took a few sticks to —"

A smaller explosion ripped through the far side of the camp, followed by the sound of flames roaring to life.

"I think I just figured out what he intends on doing with his share of the dynamite," Hank said through a wide grin. "After getting knocked around by some of those men, I'm ready to raise a little Cain myself."

"Go right ahead," Paul told him. "With everyone distracted, I'm going to get a look inside that crevice to see if I can find a sample of what's being dumped into the water."

"What makes you sure you'll find it there?"

"Because I've already checked the other spots in this camp where chemicals were being stored, and that crevice is the last place where I might find some of the runoff water that's actually making its way into the streams. Once I get a sample of that, I will have done every last thing I could do within the amount of time I've got to work."

"Then we can head back?" Hank asked.

"Yes. Then we can head back."

Hank held the .44 so it was ready to fire. "So now's my last chance for a bit of revelry. Once I draw them away, you head for that crevice. Got it?"

Paul might not have been completely ready for what was coming next, but he was as ready as he would ever be. Nodding that he understood what Hank was telling him, he placed his hand on the holstered Schofield and set his sights on the crevice. There was at least sixty to seventy yards between him and the opening that had been blasted into the rock wall. Most of that space was empty, but there were more than enough startled workers and armed men wandering nearby to make him uneasy. Before Paul could worry himself into a useless heap, Hank bolted away from the rack of pipes.

His first several steps were as swift as they were silent. Once he found his stride, Hank hollered like a madman and rushed one of the guards who was carrying a shotgun. The shotgunner was taken so completely by surprise that he only had time to let out half a grunt before Hank's knee was driven into his stomach with all of his momentum behind it. When the shotgunner doubled over, his weapon fell from his hands and was caught by Hank before it hit the ground. Now carrying a firearm in each hand, Hank ran between two rows of smaller tents that were being used as sleeping quarters for the miners.

Following Hank's example, Paul stuffed his fears down deep, kept his eyes on his destination, and made a run for it.

CHAPTER 36

More than once as he was running, Paul was certain he would be discovered. Every time he had that thought, he expected that he would be shot. Fortunately Hank was extremely proficient at making a spectacle of himself. Whenever a guard saw past the commotion and started moving too close to the path that Paul had chosen, he was distracted by something from the shadows that Paul could only assume was Red Feather. The Comanche was a perfect complement to Hank's efforts. He was a creeping predator moving on the periphery of Hank's roiling storm. When Paul made it to the rock wall, he did so without being accosted in the slightest.

Towering rocks on either side of him were ridged in a linear, symmetrical pattern. The air hanging between them was thick with humidity and stank of stagnant water. Paul could smell the chemicals, but either he was getting used to their odor or they weren't as prevalent in that spot compared to the shacks where the purity testing and other work was being done. After he walked for only a few more feet, the noise from the camp seemed to be miles away. It was only when he had a moment to think in what felt like relative solitude that Paul realized he didn't know exactly what he was looking for.

Moonlight trickled in from above through a narrow fissure in the rock. Starlight came through a wider angle, and the combined illumination was just enough to reflect on portions of the wall that were more than simple stone. Whether he was looking at embedded mineral deposits or a vein of silver, Paul couldn't tell. He didn't even feel a reaction to any of it until he saw a few rivulets of water running down the surface of the wall. Paul's eyes followed the water down to little pools that had collected along either side of the path. Smiling victoriously, he reached into the pocket of his jacket for a flask he'd brought along for that very purpose. When he dropped to one knee so he could dip the flask into the largest pool of water he could find, Paul felt richer than if he'd pulled a nugget of solid gold from the ground.

"Whatever you're looking for," someone said in a voice that rolled down the narrow path and bounced off the walls, "you won't find it down there."

Paul turned to look at who was speaking, afraid of what he might find. Those fears were realized when he found Starkweather looking back at him.

The gunman slowly walked down the path and stopped within a dozen paces of the spot Paul had chosen. "Mr. Frakes is real particular about scooping up anything valuable that might be taken from these mountains."

"I don't care about whatever you're mining for," Paul said while collecting every drop of water he could. "All I care about is what's left behind."

"You one of them folks with a sad story about people getting sick from the water?" Starkweather scoffed.

Paul shook his head and returned to his task. "I'm almost done here. I'll be on my way and you men can get back to your business."

"I think we both know it won't happen that way."

"Why not? I'm not after anything of value." He held up the flask, flipped the lid shut, and said, "This is it. I'm finished."

"Yes. You are."

Paul wanted to stand but felt his nerves jangle if he so much as blinked. Every move he might consider making from that point forward could be his last, which froze him in his tracks.

Starkweather grinned in a way that made a sun-bleached skull seem downright friendly. "It's real easy to come in the dead of night and set a few fires, especially when you got a savage working for you."

"You killed Leandro Prescott."

After thinking for a moment, Starkweather said, "That salesman? What's he got to do with anything?"

"You've killed men on orders from other men."

"That's how it works."

"Do you even know what I've got in this flask?" Paul asked. "Or why I want it?"

"Don't care."

"Exactly. What I've done . . . what I'm here to do . . . it's nothing compared to the damage you've done. And as far as the damage done by the men who hired you is concerned . . . I don't even want to think about it. All I wanted was to look out for my young ones and get on with my life."

Starkweather slowly shook his head. "Too late for that, mister."

"Right," Paul sighed. "I suppose it is."

When Paul put the flask away, his trembling hand caused the dented metal container to rattle against one of the buttons on his jacket. As he moved his hand closer to his holster, he opened and closed his fist, flexing his fingers to keep them from trembling too much to be of any use.

The morbid smile returned to Starkweather's face. "You're afraid." He sneered. "Just a sniveling little mutt with a yellow streak running a mile wide down his back. Pathetic."

Paul's eyes narrowed and his mouth formed a determined line.

"Oh, you don't like hearing that, do ya?" Starkweather chided. "That might mean something if it came from a man. But from a dog . . . it's kinda funny."

Paul knew what the gunman was trying to do. Even though he fought to keep himself from getting sloppy because of the anger boiling inside him, the struggle was difficult to control. Starkweather's was such a simple strategy, which made it even more maddening that it had such a good chance of working.

"You're a coward, mister," Starkweather said. "And I imagine them young ones you want to protect so badly are cut from the same cloth as you."

Paul lowered his head as those words sank in. When he heard the slightest rustle of Starkweather's sleeve, Paul snapped his head up, pulled the Schofield from its holster, and pulled the trigger.

Somehow, probably owing to the close range, Paul's bullet managed to hit the man in front of him. It was a grazing shot at best, nicking Starkweather's left thigh. His second, third, and fourth rounds, however, traced a deadly path up along Starkweather's hip, stomach, and chest respectively.

For the next few moments, Starkweather was still.

In those moments, Paul was certain he would join the other man in his pain thanks to the bullet that was sure to come his way. Those moments dragged on for far too long, and when they passed, they did so the same way that Starkweather passed. Quietly.

The gunman looked down at the bloody wounds in his torso, strained to exhale, but didn't even have the strength to keep his arms raised. The gun in his hand weighed him down, dragging him all the way to the ground. When he hit the rocky dirt, he kicked once and was gone.

Paul stood up with the smoking Schofield in a solid grip. He blinked at the sight of the body on the ground, waiting for it to get up again and bring him to an end. Surely that had to be the next event to pass, considering one shopkeeper's stand against an experienced killer. But Starkweather had been done in by his own arrogance just as much as by Paul's bullets. It was a lesson learned one time only.

Another explosion rocked the nearby camp. This time, however, Paul didn't flinch. He reloaded the Schofield, checked that the flask was still in his pocket, and made his way back down the path that led out of the crevice.

The men that had scattered after the first explosion were scattered even farther by the most recent one, leaving the camp all but abandoned. Paul could hear them nearby. Some were still hollering to each other, and others were riding their horses down the passes that took them anywhere but where they'd started. Paul had barely taken three steps out of the crevice when he saw someone standing near the rock wall. Even as he pivoted around and fumbled for his Schofield, Paul knew he wouldn't be able to draw quickly enough to get a shot off. That bit of luck had been used up already.

Frakes took one step forward. He held his pistol at hip level. His eyes were pointed in

Paul's general direction but didn't seem to focus on much of anything at all. Leaning over to one side, Frakes bumped his shoulder against the rock wall before sliding down to one knee. Now that the crooked businessman was down, Paul spotted Red Feather directly behind him. Frakes flopped forward onto his chest with both of the Comanche's knives protruding from his back.

"He was a murderous dog," Red Feather said as he walked up to pluck his knives from where they'd been lodged. "He did not deserve a warrior's death."

"He probably didn't even think I'd come out of there alive," Paul said.

Red Feather shrugged. The explanation he'd given was enough and he didn't need any more.

"What was that other explosion?" Paul asked.

"Hank beating a dead horse," Red Feather said. "He found another barrel of dynamite and couldn't help himself."

"Where is he now?"

"Just follow the sound of the loud one's voice." Before long, Hank could be heard howling like a madman amid a flurry of gunshots. "I think he wants to die here," Red Feather said.

"Well, I don't. Let's find a way out of this basin and head home."

Red Feather nodded once and led the way back into camp. He and Paul circled around to the spot where the shacks had been. Two of the flimsy structures were reduced to cinders and the rest were shrouded in foul-smelling smoke. There were more miners in the camp than Paul had originally guessed, most of whom were now working to douse the flames that had spread to the smaller tents. As he passed them by, Paul did his best to assess the damage that had been done that night. Most of it had been done to property. There were a few casualties to be found, but they seemed limited to minor burns and a few bumps taken during the ensuing commotion. The only men that had been hurt worse than that were gunmen who'd been shot or stabbed. Paul didn't feel too sorry for any of them.

It wasn't until they'd reached the slope that led back up to his campsite that Paul caught sight of a slender older fellow with a scraggly beard. He was the same man whom Paul had spotted in the butcher's apron the first time he scouted the camp from high ground. Without anyone else to turn to, the remaining miners seemed to be coming to him for instruction. After hearing the name

Quincy tossed around, Paul guessed that was the doctor that Braden had mentioned during his earlier questioning. All Paul had to do was watch for a few more seconds to see which of the larger tents was the one Quincy was most concerned about. In fact, the older fellow was even more frantic to move his supplies out of that tent than anyone else still in the basin.

Although only a small section of the mining camp had been destroyed, the company's interests in that basin had been unraveled like a poorly made sweater. Miners were gathering their possessions and finding their way to one of the three paths leading out of the basin. Even the few armed men left standing were collecting their horses instead of carrying out whatever demands Quincy was making of them.

Wheeling around as if to address the entire range of Rocky Mountains, Quincy shouted, "The saboteurs who did this must still be close! Somebody find them and shoot them!" When nobody lifted a finger to obey that command, he added, "Territorial Mining will pay handsomely for anyone who brings in the murdering cowards who set fire to this camp!"

A few men hollered back, emphasizing their sentiments with dismissive gestures tossed back to the frustrated doctor.

"Get on out of here," Paul said to Red Feather. "There's supposed to be some vials of medicine that may also be a help to my young ones, and I think I just figured out where to find it."

"Should I try to bring Hank with me?" Red Feather asked.

"Nah," Paul replied. "He'll catch up. Let him have his fun."

CHAPTER 37

For Paul, the ride home wasn't much more than a rush of wind in his face and a steady flow of uneven terrain beneath his horse's hooves. After that horse had dealt so well with all the strain Paul put her through, he finally decided to give her a proper name. Sophie was easy on the ears and she seemed to like it, so Sophie it was.

Hank did catch up with them, but not until the day after their visit to the Territorial Mining camp. His face was flushed and the smile he wore was etched so deep that it had most likely been there since that second shack had gone up in fiery smoke. "Where did you two get off to?" he asked breathlessly when he'd reined his horse in to trot alongside Paul's and Red Feather's.

"We agreed on the route we'd take if we got separated," Paul replied.

"I know, but you missed all the fireworks."

"Not all," Red Feather said.

"Well, it was quite a show!"

"What was left when you finally decided to move on?" Paul asked.

"Not much. The miners uprooted most of their tents in their haste to leave. The more that Quincy fellow kept yelling at them, the more of the camp those men decided to knock over out of spite. Quincy ordered some men to open fire on the rowdiest workers, but they refused and cleared out with the rest of 'em. After watching that old man kick and fret like a spoiled child for a spell, I took one of the horses that was left behind and rode away. Serves 'em right," Hank added. "Seeing as how they took my horse and I don't know where it went."

"Stealing a horse is the least of your worries," Red Feather said. "That mining company will be after all of us to answer for what happened. They will hire more gunmen and give them orders to kill."

"I been thinking about that," Hank said. "Maybe we should stick with Quincy and whatever is left of those gun hands to . . . discourage any further misbehavior."

Red Feather smirked. "That might be wise."

"And a hoot! Too bad Paul can't come along. I'm sure he needs to get back to his young ones."

"I do," Paul sighed. "I just hope they'll be there for me."

Red Feather closed his eyes and pulled in a slow breath. When he exhaled, he opened his eyes and said, "They will be."

Hank let out a grunt. "I don't put much faith in mystical mumbo jumbo, but I think he's right. If them children were so bad off, you would've known it and never would have left." He winced. "You know what I mean."

"I do," Paul replied. "Thanks. Both of you."

Turning to Red Feather, Hank asked, "So, do I have to worry about you stabbing me in my sleep when we're riding after Quincy and whatever killers might be hired on to protect him?"

"You are offering to do so as a way to make up for my people that you killed?" the Comanche asked.

"Partly," Hank admitted. "Truth be told, I really didn't kill any Injuns. I took a job hunting them down about a month ago. The only scalps I ever cashed in were collected by a man wanted for killing his wife and her sister. I was trying my hand at bounty hunting, and after dragging a few pieces of human trash across a few counties, I decided to see if hunting Injuns was any better. It wasn't. I got a knack for hunting, though."

Red Feather nodded. "I believe you. Perhaps that is why I did not stab you in your sleep."

"Whatever the reason," Hank said while extending a hand to Red Feather, "I'm mighty grateful."

Red Feather shook his hand and then sat so he looked straight ahead.

"What happens if this Quincy fellow just scampers back to the Territorial Mining offices and lies low?" Paul asked.

"He will," Hank replied with absolute certainty. "When he gets there, another greedy pig like that Frakes fella will want to find us or maybe some of them miners that ran into the mountains to shut them up the way Starkweather shut up that salesman in Leadville. I imagine hunting down any of Starkweather's other associates might be a good way to do some real damage to Territorial Mining."

From what Paul had seen since leaving Keystone Pass, he agreed that Hank was onto something there. He didn't quite understand one thing, however. "Why go through so much trouble where that mining company is concerned?" he asked.

"Because it seems like sniffing out a bunch of greedy businessmen who hire killers to murder salesmen is a good way to put my hunting talents to work."

"What about you, Red Feather?" Paul asked.

"That mining company has desecrated my people's lands as well as the lands of other tribes," the Comanche said. "It is best to cause them misery instead of blindly striking at anyone in my sight. While I am not the one who fired the arrow through that window, I am sorry for what happened to your daughter and son. I cannot make them well, but what I do to those rich white men who poisoned the waters, I do in their names."

"You've already done plenty," Paul said. "I'd hate for you to be in harm's way any longer on my account."

Hank shrugged. "Eh, it's what we do."

"For now," Red Feather said, "yes. It is the path we ride."

They didn't speak much after that. There was a good amount of land to cover and precious little time in which to cover it. Red Feather scouted ahead to make sure there were no dangerous surprises lurking over a ridge or around the next bend. When they reached a long stretch of trail leading to Keystone Pass, the Comanche told him about a shortcut that would shave a mile or two off the journey home. Paul expressed his gratitude one last time and was on his way.

He made it into town by early evening. Paul didn't bother himself with details like how quickly he'd ridden or how far he'd come. All that mattered was that he was back where he most needed to be. When he stormed into Doc Swenson's office, he barely even noticed the surprised expression on the face of a young woman lying in one of the other rooms who didn't know if he was some wayward outlaw looking to rob the place.

"Oh my!" Swenson said from his chair at Abigail's bedside. "It's you!"

"How is she, Doc?" Paul asked breathlessly.

"Doing a little better. I've been applying remedies for various different ailments and some of them have taken hold."

"What about David?"

"He's in the next room. His fever isn't nearly as bad as his sister's and he's been responding much better to my treatments. Still . . . he hasn't been in good spirits."

Paul reached into his jacket pocket for the small sacks of powder and the vial of thick liquid he'd taken from the mining camp. "Try these on them," he said.

"What are they?" Swenson asked as he opened one of the sacks and took a tentative sniff of its contents.

"There were other folks suffering from the same ailment. This is supposed to be the antidote." Paul then quickly explained the process of making the tea as the doctor nodded and tested the powder by pinching some between his fingers and even dabbing some on the tip of his tongue.

"I suppose I can try a small amount as a test," the doctor said hesitantly.

"You do whatever you need to do. Here you go," Paul added as he set his flask down on a nearby table. "This is the water that poisoned those folks, and it should be mostly the same as what got Abigail sick."

The doctor picked it up and sniffed it just as he did with the powder.

"Isn't that what you needed?" Paul asked.

"Sure it is," Swenson replied. "I just didn't really think you'd get it."

"Well, I did," Paul snapped. "Do your part or you'll have to answer to me."

When the doctor looked up at him, there was a touch of fear in his eyes as he said, "Of course I will. Don't worry. I'll work as fast as I can. I won't even sleep."

Paul guessed that kind of fearful respect was shown to plenty of other ranting men who wore guns on their hips. There was some part of him that he wasn't very proud of that enjoyed getting that kind of response. Rather than push it any further, Paul kneeled at his daughter's side and brushed the hair from her eyes. She'd always been a heavy sleeper, so he wasn't surprised that she didn't wake up during his conversation with Swenson. When he kissed her cheek, she shifted slightly just as she always did, which went a long way to soothing Paul's troubled mind. He then left the doctor to his work so he could step into the next room, where David was resting.

The boy was lying on his side facing the door. When he saw Paul enter the room, David curled up into a tighter ball.

"You feeling all right?" Paul asked as he came over to sit on the side of the cot.

"No."

"The doctor says your fever broke. What hurts?"

"Nothing."

"Must be something," Paul said as he felt David's forehead. "Otherwise you'd feel better."

"I'm sorry."

"What for?"

"For being too afraid to go along with you," David said in a meek little voice. "For being afraid of everything."

Paul ran his fingers through his son's hair. "Have you been lying here thinking about that the whole time I was gone?"

"No." After seeing the stern glare from his father, the boy added, "Yes."

"Well, you should set your mind at ease. More than once over the last couple of days, I've been pretty scared myself."

"Really?" David asked as he sat up straight. "Why?"

"That doesn't matter. What matters is that everyone gets frightened. It's what keeps someone from charging into danger like a fool. You've got it where it counts, son. And that's right here," Paul said while tapping a finger against the boy's chest. "You're not a coward. You're just cautious. Just promise me that you won't be so cautious that you don't get around to living every day to its fullest."

David smiled warmly and wrapped his arms around his father's neck. "I promise."

Paul hugged his boy for a good, long while. Everything that had come before that moment just didn't seem to matter anymore.

CHAPTER 38

Nearly a month later, Paul still didn't feel back to normal. He'd covered a lot of dangerous land, which had a way of sticking to a man's bones. He simply wasn't the same man as the one who had ridden out of Keystone Pass to trade with Prescott for what would be the final time.

After spending several hours stocking shelves in his store, Paul sat down on a stool behind the counter and let out a contented sigh. There was nobody helping him that day, but Abigail came in to grab something to eat before heading out again.

"How are you, Dumplin'?" he asked.

"I told you not to call me that!" she groaned as if he'd committed a cardinal sin.

"Sorry. Feeling all right, though?"

"Yes, Daddy," she replied while coming around the counter to give him a quick peck on the cheek. "Love you."

"Love you too, Dumplin'."

She moaned again and was on her way through the door.

For once, Paul didn't know exactly where David was. Ever since he'd left Dr. Swenson's care, his son had reintroduced himself to some friends from school and spent most of his days getting into bits of trouble here and there with the rest of the boys. On stormy nights or every so often at random times, David would still become nervous or fidgety. That seemed so unimportant anymore that Paul hardly ever noticed. The world was full of dangerous lands, and a man who didn't have some healthy amount of fear in him wouldn't survive them for long.

Paul wasn't the same man he'd once been and would never get back to normal.

He was a better man who was content in the life he'd made. What he'd used to consider normal was a long ways behind him and he wasn't about to look back.

ABOUT THE AUTHOR

Ralph Compton stood six foot eight without his boots. He worked as a musician, a radio announcer, a songwriter, and a newspaper columnist. His first novel, *The Goodnight Trail,* was a finalist for the Western Writers of America Medicine Pipe Bearer Award for Best Debut Novel. He was also the author of the Sundown Raiders series and the Border Empire series.